She was his woman, his property, to do with as he pleased.

Who cared what *she* felt? What did it matter?

Einar tossed his drinking horn into the corner and stood up.

The Saxon woman paused, the wine bottle halfway to her mouth.

"Put it down," he said slowly, staring at her luscious full lips stained red with wine.

She did not move.

"I said, put it down!" He used the tone of voice in which he gave orders aboard ship—the tone of voice that made battle-hardened warriors jump to do his bidding.

She still did not move.

He strode toward her and yanked the bottle from her hand, throwing it against the wall and shattering it. "When I tell you to do something, *anything,* you will do it!"

He hauled her to her feet. And then his mouth crushed hers in a fierce kiss.

Dear Reader,

The holidays are upon us and Harlequin Historicals is celebrating with a quartet of keepers!

First, *New York Times* bestselling author Elizabeth Lowell brings us *Reckless Love*. Janna Wayland is as untamed as the wild horses she trains. But when Ty Mackenzie comes into her life, her unbridled passion forces her to make a painful choice.

Margaret Moore, author of the Warrior series, takes us back to the age of Norsemen in her latest release. *The Viking* is Einar, a warrior whose decision to take Saxon woman Meradyce hostage changes his life forever. Filled with adventure and romance, this is a *must* read.

In *Providence,* Ananiah Snow—a woman with a scandalous past—risks everything when she hires handsome sea captain Sam Colburn to find her missing father. Yet losing her heart to Sam proves the greatest risk of all. Another swashbuckling, romantic tale on the high seas by popular author Miranda Jarrett.

And rounding out December is *Counterfeit Laird* by Erin Yorke. This charming tale about the people in a small Scottish village who trick American businessman Creag Blake into believing he is the long-lost laird is sure to please readers—especially when the sparks begin to fly between Creag and the old laird's granddaughter, Jeanne....

All of us at Harlequin wish you a happy and safe holiday season and best wishes for the new year!

Sincerely,

Tracy Farrell
Senior Editor

THE VIKING

MARGARET MOORE

Harlequin Books

TORONTO • NEW YORK • LONDON
AMSTERDAM • PARIS • SYDNEY • HAMBURG
STOCKHOLM • ATHENS • TOKYO • MILAN
MADRID • WARSAW • BUDAPEST • AUCKLAND

ISBN 0-373-28800-X

THE VIKING

Copyright © 1993 by Margaret Wilkins.

This edition published by arrangement with Harlequin Enterprises B. V.

® and TM are trademarks of the publisher. Trademarks indicated with ® are registered in the United States Patent and Trademark Office, the Canadian Trade Marks Office and in other countries.

Printed in U.S.A.

Books by Margaret Moore

Harlequin Historicals

A Warrior's Heart #118
China Blossom #149
A Warrior's Quest #175
The Viking #200

MARGARET MOORE

says that the first great love of her life was Errol Flynn. "Naturally, I was devastated to learn that he died when I was three years old," she admits, but adds that her interest in historical romance writing developed from that early fascination. Margaret lives in Scarborough, Ontario, with her husband and two school-age children. When not in her basement at the computer, she enjoys reading and sewing.

To all the people at Harlequin who help make
my career a joy, especially Tracy Farrell,
Angela Catalano, Malle Vallik, Kathleen Abels,
and also Valerie Susan Hayward, who suggested
I submit to Harlequin Historicals

Chapter One

The curved prow of the Viking ship sliced through the water like the head of a great sea serpent. Muffled oars brushed through the shallow river. Inside the craft, men panted softly, hunched like trolls as they rowed.

"I do not like this," one of the men whispered. "Einar is as jumpy as a rat on a sinking ship."

Siurt nodded in agreement. The leader of the raiders usually stood as still as a stone at the stern of the longship. Now Einar was at the bow, shifting his weight as he looked toward the land.

Ull lowered his head as Einar's gaze swept over the crew and returned to the shore. "What does he expect to see over there?"

Siurt shrugged as he pulled, his huge arms straining. "We have never been this far inland, but Einar is not one to take chances."

"Then why did Svend stay behind?"

"You know the chieftain could not risk sailing after his horse threw him," Siurt whispered. "That is too bad an omen."

Einar walked down the middle of the vessel and ordered the crew to ship their oars. "Remember, the woman wearing a gold cross with three jewels is not to be harmed," he said quietly, "but brought to me."

Ull stroked his fiery red beard. "Why should we do that? You don't take women, Einar. And how do you know about this one, eh?"

Einar smiled with his lips, but his gray eyes were as cold as the blade of a sword left lying in the snow. "Why waste time fighting unwilling women when there is gold to be found? Slaves are more trouble than they are worth."

Ull laughed coarsely as his gaze went to the gold bands around Einar's neck, then to his wide silver armlet. "And why bother, with plenty of women wanting to share the mighty Einar's bed?"

Einar shrugged, but his hand went to his sword. "Ingemar keeps me content, for now."

"Then why do you want this woman?" Ull demanded, knowing he was questioning Einar at his peril, but more determined to understand why they had ventured so far into Saxon territory.

"Because I do. That is all you need to know." Einar turned and walked to the bow fighting to put aside his anger and think only of the raid.

He was not pleased to be here, so deep in the land of the Saxons. It was a great danger, but his chieftain had ordered it. To disobey would be taken as a signal by all that he was challenging Svend for leadership of the village, and that Einar had no wish to do.

He did not like relying on a Saxon traitor to show them the way. The man had promised a fire beacon, visible from the river to lead them to their destination, and that the village would be vulnerable, all the warriors gone. They were to take anything they wanted, provided they accomplished their task. And it was this task that angered Einar. There was no honor and no glory in the killing of a woman.

Svend, too, had hesitated when he heard what the Vikings were to do to earn all this treasure. However, he had agreed. He had obviously planned to do the disgraceful task himself, but the throw from his horse was a warning too potent to ignore, and so the responsibility fell to Einar.

Einar frowned darkly. Svend had surely imagined that a treasure of coins and livestock and slaves were awaiting his men, yet this seemed too much like a trap. Who could trust one who would betray his own people?

The Viking chieftain was wise and clever, but perhaps, for once, he was allowing greed to cloud his judgement.

Einar glanced at the night sky, grateful that they had missed the storms that usually beset the northern seas so close to winter. He whispered a brief prayer of thanks to Aegir, God of the Sea.

There would be rain before much longer, from the north. The Saxon had given them a span of three days in which to do this deed, and they were well within that time. Another week, and it might have been too treacherous to make the voyage across the open sea. Nonetheless, Einar wished the raid was finished and they were bound for home.

He heard muttering voices behind him and felt the growing excitement of his crew. For his men, taking this village would be as simple as plucking a dead chicken—if this was not a trap.

Einar spotted a fire, glowing palely on the hillside. He hurried aft and joined Lars, who was holding the steering board.

Einar pointed to the beacon wordlessly. Lars nodded and the longship turned as he guided it close to shore.

At a signal from Einar, the men began to jump over the side into the shallow water and climb up the riverbanks, making as little noise as possible.

Suddenly, a loud cry of alarm rent the darkness. Cursing, Einar spotted a figure racing away in the distance. He gestured to his men and they broke into a run.

The Saxon village was on a low rise upriver from the beacon. It was one of the largest Einar had ever seen, and surrounded by a wall of tall, thick timbers. Behind it, he could see a wood, and more hills in the distance. As they drew closer, Einar realized that the warning had given the villagers time to close a heavy wooden gate.

There were no men on the walls above, waiting with bows to shoot or rocks to hurl at the attackers. What was the traitor up to? Or had the warning been something the traitor had not foreseen?

But now it was time to concentrate on breaking down the gate. His men had raided many Saxon villages up and down the coast, and he had only to say the word before they began chopping down a nearby tree to use as a battering ram. They smashed the gate quickly and swarmed into the village.

It looked deserted. Einar cursed again as his men started breaking open the houses, searching for booty or villagers to take as slaves.

Einar gestured at his step-brother, Hamar, and Lars. Walking quickly through the settlement, he led them past the smaller houses toward the large hall the traitor had described. It was easy enough to see. When they reached it, Einar kicked open the door.

In the dim light from the smoldering hearth in the center of the floor, Lars and Hamar began searching for valuables. They found a cask of wine and, laughing, broke it open with their battle axes.

Einar ignored them. He was looking for the woman. The traitor had said she would probably be here, in one of the storerooms that had a secret hiding place dug in the dirt floor. He saw a curtain and pulled it aside, then entered, pushing away a chest as he looked for a wooden door.

No door, but he saw a pair of dirty feet behind another chest. He went toward it, reached down and pulled up a boy by the back of his tunic.

"My father is the thane!" the lad cried, striking Einar with his fists.

The boy looked about twelve years old, almost grown, but there was still more child than man in his face. Although Einar saw desperation in his eyes, he recognized what the boy was experiencing. It was the anguish of a weaponless warrior who wants to fight but lacks the means.

Einar smiled, yet before he could question the boy, something moved in the shadows and a female voice cried out, "Let him go!"

He turned quickly as a woman moved out of the shadows, long dark hair loose about her face. A large cross studded with three jewels hung around her neck, shining dully in the dim light, and she held a sword so heavy he was not sure she could lift it. Another smaller child huddled behind her slender body.

Einar had found the woman he was to kill. The traitor's wife.

He took a step forward. In that moment, to his great surprise, the woman lifted the sword. She called out a warning, but Einar only smiled and took another step. He knew now where the boy got his bravery.

The woman pushed the other child behind a chest, then looked at Einar again, her hands clenched tightly around the sword.

He grinned. The woman was courageous. He had no doubt that she would try to strike him with that sword.

He took another step toward her. Her face was half hidden by her dark hair, and he wanted very much to see it. At that moment, she raised her sword and ran at him.

Einar stepped easily out of her path. The woman stumbled and turned toward him again. By now, Hamar and Lars were both standing in the doorway, watching.

"I do not think she likes you," Lars called out.

"I think you are right," Einar replied coolly.

"It is just as well. Ingemar would not be happy to hear you have a new woman," Hamar added with a deep chuckle.

The woman came at Einar again, and this time he jumped back as the blade narrowly missed his hand.

"Go!" the woman called out to the children. The boy hesitated for a moment, then grabbed the other child's hand and made a run for the door. It was useless, for Lars and Hamar caught them before they got out. The boy struggled in Lars' grasp, but one cuff from the Viking's big hand made him stop. Hamar picked up the other child, a little girl.

Now the woman crouched low, a look of panic in her eyes, her teeth bared like those of a trapped animal. With surprising strength she held the sword high. "Let the children go, or I will kill you!" she cried out.

Einar decided he had had enough. He lunged for her and crashed with her to the ground, the sword, knocked free, skittering across the floor.

As she lay beneath him, he could see her face clearly for the first time. She was beautiful, as beautiful as any woman he had ever seen. Her long hair was the color of a raven's wing, her eyes the blue of the sea in spring, her lips... Her lips were ruddy and full, begging for a man's kiss.

"Please, do not hurt the children!" she pleaded.

"They will not be harmed," he answered, watching her eyes widen in surprise when he spoke her language. "They will not be harmed," he repeated, wanting her to believe him.

She nodded, then closed her eyes tightly and shuddered as he ran his hand over her body. She was as shapely as she was beautiful.

When she opened her sea blue eyes, they were filled with tears. "Please," she whispered, "do not let the children see my shame."

Einar stared down at her. She fought like one of Odin's handmaids to protect her children, only asking, when the battle was lost, that her children not see her humiliation.

Suddenly, he regretted that he had made this brave woman plead.

He hoisted her to her feet. The woman tried to strike him with her free hand, but he caught it easily. "No."

She stood still, not fighting him but keeping her gaze on the silent children.

It would be a waste to kill this woman. Better to take her. Svend would surely agree.

He began pulling her toward the door. "Bring her children, too," he said as he passed Lars and Hamar.

The traitor had wanted assurances that his children would not be harmed. No doubt he would pay a fine ransom for them. As for his wife, all he need know was that she was no longer his concern.

Outside, it was obvious that the villagers had fled to safety. The rest of the Vikings had gone on a rampage, gathering up everything they could carry and setting the deserted buildings on fire.

The huge, pale-haired Viking dragged Meradyce toward the ship. Terrified and exhausted from her futile fight, she could barely make her legs move. Indeed, she would have collapsed on the ground if it were not for the children.

The younger of the other two men carried Betha, who was too frightened even to cry as she stared at the curved blade of the man's battle ax nestled around his neck, the haft hanging down over his chest.

The older Viking with dark hair and a thick beard had one hand firmly clamped on Adelar's arm as the boy marched stoically beside him. If only Adelar had not run back, determined to fight the men who would dare to attack his village, they might all have been safely away. Even now, Meradyce knew by Adelar's glances at the man's sword that he was planning to try to get hold of it.

She hoped Adelar would see the hopelessness of such an action. She was sure the Vikings would not hesitate to kill him if he so much as touched one of their weapons.

The Viking's grip tightened on her wrists, his fingers like iron bands, and she bit her lip to keep from crying out in pain.

In the light from the flames of the burning buildings, he looked like a demon. He wore a helmet with a nose guard that cast deep shadows over his eyes. The helmet fit close about his head and over his ears, so that only his beardless chin and full lips were exposed. Long, unbound hair brushed his broad shoulders. In his free hand he carried a huge ax, which he swung back and forth as he walked. His mouth was grim, his long strides relentless as he led them away.

She scanned the village as he pulled her onward. Mercifully, she could see no bodies. The cry of warning had given the others time to escape to the caves.

How had the Vikings known the men were gone? Or had it been luck? And how had the blond one come to know her language?

When they drew near the Viking ship, Adelar suddenly wrenched his arm free.

With a cry, Meradyce twisted away from the Viking's grasp. "Run, Adelar!" she shouted, drawing the other man's attention for a necessary moment.

Adelar disappeared into the woods.

"Thank God!" Meradyce whispered fervently. Then she realized that the blond warrior no longer had his hand on her. She could run, too...

"Adelar!" Betha wailed.

Meradyce did not move. She would not leave little Betha to the mercy of these men.

There was a loud cry, and Adelar came sprinting from the forest. Before she could say or do anything, he threw himself at the tall Viking.

"Let them go!" the boy shrieked. "Coward! Barbarian!"

The man held Adelar by his shoulders.

"No" Meradyce cried, running forward and grabbing the Viking's muscular arm. "Do not kill him!"

The Viking looked down at her hands, then lifted his head. His eyes gleamed and his lips twisted into a grin. "The Saxon thane should be proud of you, and his children."

He let go of Adelar. "Now get on the ship."

Before he could touch her again, Meradyce took Adelar's hand in hers and went toward the man holding Betha, taking the little girl from him.

"We must go," Meradyce said softly, and she led the children to the longship.

On the shore, the Viking leader pulled off his helmet and stared at Meradyce as she turned to face the burning village.

His eyes were ringed with soot. She had heard both Viking men and women decorated their faces. How fiendish it made his face, with its strong cheekbones and lips that were pulled back into something she took to be a smile.

She moved back as other Vikings began loading the vessel, and sat down, drawing the children close. Even if the Viking had said they would not be harmed, they would probably be sold into slavery.

Meradyce knew what happened to slave women. If she was sold to a slave dealer, he would have to wait until every Viking had had his pleasure of her.

A sob escaped her, making Betha look at her with wide, terrified eyes. Meradyce fought to control herself. She must be strong.

"It is all right," she said softly, embracing Betha gently. "Your father is a great thane. They will not harm you."

Adelar gave her a fierce look. "They had better not. Or you, either. If I had my sword..."

"No, Adelar!" Betha cried, grabbing her brother's arm as if he had a sword at the ready. "You will be killed!"

Meradyce reached out and pulled him down beside her. "She is right, Adelar. There is nothing we can do against so many."

"But..."

"Nothing."

Betha began to weep again as Meradyce put her arms around them both.

By now the ship was filled with Vikings, all sitting expectantly.

The tall blond warrior jumped into the ship, a small chest under his arm.

At his shouted command the vessel began to move out into the river. He moved forward to stand by the dragon's head, his muscular body shifting with the movement of the ship as if he were a part of it.

Meradyce turned away, holding the children tightly against her, and watched the flames on the shore until they disappeared from sight.

"Holy Mother! Look!"

Kendric's gaze followed the man's pointing arm. On the horizon where his village lay, plumes of black smoke rose in the dawn's light.

With a cry, the Saxon thane raised his arm and signaled his men to follow. Kicking his horse into a gallop, Kendric fought to keep the smile off his face as they rode home.

When he had proposed taking his men on a cattle raid, everyone had believed that it was too near winter for the Vikings to venture far into the land of the Saxons.

That was true. It had taken more gold than he liked to think about to convince the Saxon chieftain to do this thing, but he would have paid even more to rid himself of Ludella.

No one would suspect that he had anything to do with this and certainly not that he had planned the attack for months, ever since he had learned that his wife had taken a lover.

Naturally he had contemplated sending Ludella home to her father when he had discovered her adultery with Orwin, one of his soldiers. But her father was a powerful *ealdorman,* a member of the counsel that advised the king. Ludella was very careful, and it was no secret around the village that her husband had an eye—and more—for pretty women. Ludella would surely make her father believe she was innocent, and blame Kendric for the lack of faithfulness and respect in their marriage.

Not for the first time, Kendric wondered if Ludella had seen him when he wrapped his arms around Meradyce after his daughter's birth, and if she had guessed that he felt more than simple thankfulness for the midwife's presence. Had that been the reason Ludella took a lover?

Surely not. Meradyce had not understood that there was more than affection in his action.

And everyone knew that Meradyce wore her chastity like armor. It would not be an easy thing for any man to entice her into his bed.

Nonetheless, he would be free to woo Meradyce with the promise of marriage. Surely that would break down her barriers.

Not that he *would* marry her. She was nothing but a midwife, however skilled. He would find a richer woman from a powerful family before he would wed again. After all, he was a handsome, wealthy thane who would certainly be an *ealdorman* one day.

Now he would have to find an excuse to kill Orwin. Trust Ludella to pick such a common fellow, but it would be easy enough to be rid of him.

The Saxon warriors reached the hill that overlooked the ruined village. Kendric could see people moving about the burned out shells of the houses.

He had not paid the Vikings to destroy the buildings, but he was vastly pleased. He had wanted to rebuild the town for a long time, with stronger buildings and a finer hall for himself. The penny-scavenging merchants had always protested, but now they would have no choice.

Kendric could see no corpses. Good. If he had one fear about making a bargain with the Viking chieftain, it was that the Vikings would not do as they said. After all, Vikings broke their word nearly as often as they gave it.

What the Viking raiders had not known was that Kendric had insured that Selwyn, the Saxon merchant who had acted as go-between, would not just light the beacon, but would also sound the alarm when the Vikings landed. That had given his people time to hide in the caves nearby.

All except Ludella. She would surely have taken the opportunity of his absence to meet with Orwin. She would be gone most of the night, he knew, but would come back before dawn, lest the villagers gossip. She would be caught outside the walls of the village, or forced to hide in the storeroom. Either way, she would be unable to reach the safety of the caves. The Vikings would find their prey easily and know her by the crucifix she always wore. Then they would kill her.

He led his troop down the road and into the village. Dismounting, he surveyed the damage. People began to crowd around him, each telling about the horrible raid in the night.

"Kendric!"

He gasped and slowly turned around. Ludella, her eyes red from crying and the smoke, her wide, narrow mouth a hard slash in her face, came toward him. "You *bastard!* This is all your fault."

He put his hands on his hips, silently cursing each and every Viking to the everlasting flames of hell. "What do you mean? How could anyone guess they would attack when it is so close to winter?"

"Find them!"

"What? They are probably far out to sea by now."

Ludella walked up to him and for the first time he saw the desperation in her eyes. "You must find them! They have the children."

"Oh, blessed savior, no!" Although he hated his wife, Kendric cared for his children—at least his son.

Ludella nodded, tears beginning to fall down her sooty cheeks. "Yes. And Meradyce, they took her, too."

Kendric stared at her, his mouth open. Then he closed it. "Why were you not with the children?"

Ludella's face paled beneath the soot. For the first time in her life, she was truly frightened of her husband. She knew he would kill her if she told him she was already in the caves when the raid began, meeting her lover. "Meradyce said she would bring them to the caves," she lied.

His gaze raked her body and she held her breath, wondering for the hundredth time if he suspected she was unfaithful. "Where is your crucifix, wife?"

She reached for it, but she had given it to Meradyce to keep for her. "Lost, in the hurry to escape."

But what mattered now was not her, or her husband, or her lover. As much as she despised her husband, Ludella loved her children. "Kendric, you must go after them."

He shook his head sorrowfully. "We cannot. We do not know where to look." Which was true. Only Selwyn knew, and he would be far away by now. He would not have tarried after calling out the alarm. "Nor can we risk setting out to chase them."

If it was dangerous for the Vikings, with their ships and skills, to sail this late in the year, it was twice as dangerous for the Saxons.

His plan was fast becoming a disaster. His wife was still living, the woman he desired gone, and his children with her.

"But they will be killed!" Ludella wailed.

Kendric didn't think so, knowing that Meradyce was with Adelar and Betha. She would tell the Vikings whose children they had taken, and the barbarians would know how valuable a commodity they had as long as the children were unharmed.

What Meradyce's fate would be he could easily guess. Unfortunate, but perhaps that, too, would help to keep his children safe.

"I do not believe they will hurt the children," Kendric answered, stroking his beard. "They will surely be ransomed. No doubt we will find out how much money they want soon."

Ludella narrowed her eyes. "How?"

Kendric cursed himself for a loose-tongued fool. He could not tell anyone about Selwyn, but he was sure the Vikings would send their ransom demand by Selwyn.

"They will want a large sum. They will find a way, for that much money."

He turned away, ostensibly to listen to one of his soldiers, but really to ignore his wife.

His mind was already planning vengeance. He would prepare his men and pay whatever necessary to build the finest ship in Saxon waters. He would make Selwyn tell him exactly where the Viking village was, and in the spring, he would find his children. Then he would make that savage Svend pay for breaking his word.

Chapter Two

If they had not been in Bjorn's finest vessel, with Lars to man the steering board, they might have all joined Aegir in his hall under the sea. The waves were high and the wind from the north as cold as a frost giant's breath. No one was happier than Einar to enter the *leden*, the area between the outer islands and the coast of home. Here the water was calmer, for the islands acted like a wall against the sea.

He was even more pleased when they reached their fjord. Although it was close to nightfall, he gave a relieved sigh and grinned at Lars.

His friend, also weary from the journey, smiled back. "By Thor's thunder, I will be glad for a hot meal and some good ale!"

Einar nodded, then glanced at the Saxon woman. She was wrapped in a leather bag used for storing goods and weapons by day, and for sleeping in by night.

He did not think she was asleep. Indeed, he doubted she had slept much during the whole of the rough voyage. Not only was she obviously terrified of him and his men, but the children had been very sick from the motion of the vessel.

The young ones lay huddled under his fur-lined cloak, which he had given them during the storm. Even after that, any time he had so much as looked at her, the woman averted her beautiful face.

If she had heard all the stories told about Vikings, she was surely afraid he would rape her. The other warriors were probably wondering why he had not. They considered raping a captive woman fine sport, bragging of their scratches and bites. They also claimed a raped woman was an obedient woman.

Einar preferred his women as filled with lust as he was, although this time, he had been tempted to take her, willing or not. Once, when the storm began to abate, he had even allowed himself to envision the Saxon's eyes shining with desire for him. But only once, for he had already decided she would be a gift for Svend, to thank him for giving him command of this vessel.

He had taken a great risk disobeying his father's order to kill her. Any Viking chieftain would suspect that a man was trying to take command by such an action, and perhaps some among his men secretly thought that was what Einar planned to do.

He sighed softly. He had lost count of the number of times Ull had hinted that Svend was getting too old to be the chieftain, implying that Einar should take his place. Ull could not seem to understand that Einar would sooner end his own life than be disloyal to his father.

Surely his gift would dispel any such fears his father might harbor. It would also be the best way to keep the other men from fighting over her.

She was worth fighting over, even now. Nothing could hide her astounding beauty, and Einar knew the exquisite shapeliness of her body.

And she was capable of great passion—at least of one kind. He had seen it in her face as she fought to protect her children.

The marvel was that she was able to subdue that feeling when the battle was over, obviously sensing that further resistance would be in vain.

Would that more of his warriors could calm themselves as quickly! Instead, they squabbled like children over slaves and booty, without reason or control.

Einar looked at her again. His blood began to race, quickening to heat in his veins. There was nothing to prevent him from taking her here and now. Svend would not care. If anything, he would wonder why any son of his had not taken her already.

And yet . . . he wanted to see not terror in her eyes, but desire. He did not want to force his way between her legs, but for her to open herself to him.

What if he were to keep her?

Hamar jumped up from his place in the bow. "Gunnhild!" he called out, waving to a woman on the shore.

"Get down," Einar barked at his brother.

Hamar turned, scowling, but said nothing. He was very proud of his pretty young wife, who was about to bear him a child. When he thought Einar was not looking, he waved again.

Einar moved down the ship and cuffed Hamar on the ear. "You may be my elder brother, but *I* am the commander of this ship. Do not forget it."

Hamar frowned. "Then you will give me the same respect on land."

"Of course, elder brother." Einar grinned broadly.

Lars and most of the other men hid their smiles. Einar and Hamar's mock quarrels were not unfamiliar, but all knew that both meant what they said. Svend's two oldest sons demanded—and got—the appropriate respect not only from the whole village, but from each other.

"There is Ingemar," Lars called out.

"Huh," Einar grunted. He had seen the blond woman standing beside Gunnhild. Ingemar was getting a little too demanding lately, talking about becoming his wife.

He did not want another wife. One had been quite enough.

Still, Ingemar was an interesting lover and would surely be grateful for whatever presents he cared to give her from this raid.

The longship drew up to its mooring and the men began to unload. Einar waited, trying to ignore the Saxon woman—and his growing desire to keep her.

Meradyce struggled out of the leather skin and took hold of the children's hands, making sure that they stayed close beside her as the Vikings began to disembark.

She tried not to look at the men, but at the ships moored nearby. There were five piers, and at each there was a vessel. None were as long and low as this ship; most looked heavier and more solid, and Meradyce wondered if the voyage would have been better in such a craft.

The constant movement of the ship had made the children very sick. They hadn't been able to eat since the voyage had started four days ago, and she had spent most of her time nursing the children. Now they all were weak and exhausted.

At least the horror of the storm was over. The hull of the vessel had twisted in the high seas. Chill winds had lashed out at them, and the waves had been almost as high as the carved dragon at the front of the ship. They had been drenched with salt water and miserable with cold, sickness and fear.

Once, when the storm was at its worst, when Meradyce was sure death was at hand, the Viking leader had turned and looked at her. She had seen the strain on his face, and the weariness, but he had no fear.

Perhaps because the Vikings were noted seamen, perhaps because she was too frightened to feel anything more or perhaps because he had not harmed her, she no longer felt afraid. Not of him, and not of the sea.

After the ship had entered calmer waters, the crew had begun to stare at her more and more, especially two red-haired men who looked enough alike to be brothers. The *way* they looked at her filled her with dread. She was certain that if they had been the ones to find her in Kendric's hall, they would have paid no heed to the children or her plea, but would have raped her on the floor of the storeroom.

The leader finally walked to where she sat huddled with the children. "Stand up," he ordered.

She obeyed, holding tightly to the children's hands.

"Will they be able to walk?" he asked, gazing at her steadily.

"I . . . I think so," she replied.

Before they could move, the Viking reached down and picked up Betha. He went to take Adelar's hand, but the boy stepped forward unaided.

"Follow me," the man ordered with a slight grin on his face. He led them to the middle of the ship, where a wide plank went down to the pier.

As Meradyce climbed over the side of the ship, she looked up at the rocky hills surrounding the narrow bay. She had heard it said that the Vikings' land was as cold and barren as their hearts.

When her feet touched the dock, she stumbled and nearly fell, saving herself by leaning against a large barrel of water.

Someone giggled and Meradyce looked up. A tall, pale-haired woman stood a little way ahead, laughing at her.

The Viking had gone on with the children. Adelar was having difficulty walking, too, but the Viking didn't wait.

"Stop!" Meradyce called out.

The Viking turned to her slowly, a smile on his face that she found as insulting as the woman's laughter.

She might be his captive, but for now, she had some pride left. She lifted her chin and took a step.

The ground was steady, she realized at once. It was only that she was used to the motion of the ship.

He was watching her. The children were watching her. That woman was watching her. Pressing her lips together, Meradyce took another step. Then another. Concentrating, she managed to walk almost normally.

The woman laughed again and called out something. The man nodded at Meradyce and replied. Then his voice dropped as he spoke to the woman.

Meradyce did not pay much attention. Instead, she looked at Adelar and Betha, who were deathly pale. She hoped that rest and small portions of food would soon set them right.

At last, and with a toss of her long hair, the tall woman smiled and walked away, pausing to look at them over her shoulder.

"Please," Meradyce said when the woman was gone, "is there some place they can rest?" She gestured toward the children.

The Viking nodded and continued on his way, leaving her to follow as best she could. He led her up the steep hill to a village. There was a low wall around it, and inside were several long wooden buildings. Smoke drifted slowly from holes in their roofs. It was a small settlement, and Meradyce wondered how such a place could muster a fighting force like the ship full of men who had burned her village.

Unless what she had heard was true—that many Viking raiders were farmers who went to sea in the summer months. It seemed incredible. But if that was how *farmers* could fight, it was no wonder that the Saxons sought to appease them with gifts.

They came to a huge longhouse. From outside, she could hear raucous voices and what sounded like the howling of wolves.

Einar pushed open the door and waited a moment until his eyes got used to the smoky dimness of the interior. Already most of his men were half-drunk, and some had started to sing.

Entering, he set the little girl down on the nearest bench. The boy sat beside her. Einar turned to make sure the Saxon woman was behind him. She was.

By now, he knew that she could mask her feelings, but although he knew she was afraid, she did not seem terrified. And when she looked at him, he thought he saw some trust in her blue eyes.

But she belonged to Svend.

Not yet. *Not yet.*

He went to a cauldron of warm water hanging from the rafters over one of the two hearths in Svend's huge longhouse. He washed quickly, telling himself that he must give the woman to his father. There really could be no other way.

"Einar!" Svend called out, raising his drinking horn.

Einar took the woman by the arm and pulled her to the center of the hall.

"Well, my son, a successful raid, but no slaves, eh?" Svend's eyes narrowed when he saw the Saxon and the cross around her neck. "What is this?"

Einar let go of the woman who should have been dead. He knew, as they all did, that while the chieftain looked too old and fat to fight, Svend could still defeat any younger man stupid enough to put his prowess to the test.

Einar walked forward until he was close to Svend, so that only those very near to his father—and therefore his most trusted friends—could hear his words. "This is the woman the Saxon wanted killed, but as you can see, it would have been a foolish waste."

Einar went behind her, then grabbed her dress and tugged it tight, so that her voluptuous body was apparent to all.

In a louder voice, he said, "She is my gift to you, Svend. Her children are for ransom."

Svend's eyes, and the eyes of every other man in the room, filled with lust. Einar let go.

Svend heaved himself out of his chair and came toward him. "By Odin, she is a fine woman, Einar!"

The Saxon woman was trembling, but she made no sound.

Svend slapped Einar on the back, almost knocking him over. "I thank you for your gift, my son, but I do not think my wives will!"

The rest of the men burst out laughing. Einar did not. Nor did Svend.

Svend surveyed the children. "Hers, eh?"

"Yes. They are the children of the Saxon thane."

"By Odin, he will be angry—but he will surely pay much to have them back. Clever of you, Einar, to think of that."

Einar got a good look at his father's eyes and knew Svend was not as pleased as he appeared.

"You take her. My gift to you for bringing the ship back safe, eh?" Svend returned to his heavy oak chair.

Einar stared at his father, then nodded and took the woman by the arm. As he led her to where the children were sitting, he felt a twinge of doubt. Perhaps he should have killed her. His father was displeased, and now Einar could see the jealousy on some of the men's faces, especially Ull's.

He was more troubled by his father's reaction. Einar had disobeyed his orders and broken the bargain with the Saxon traitor. It was not like Svend to reward disobedience, even if he thought it justified.

But his father's hidden anger and confusing action were not the main source of Einar's discomfort. He was beginning to feel that this woman had some kind of hold upon him.

He told himself it was only that he dearly wanted her body—no man would feel otherwise.

He spotted Ingemar sauntering toward him with a drinking horn and smiled at her.

"Yes, Einar?" she said, giving the Saxon woman a long, slow stare. "What would you . . . like?"

"That drink, for now," he replied.

Ingemar leaned way over and handed the horn to him. With a grin, he plunged his hand down her loose gown and caressed her breasts. He had been too many days without a woman.

Ingemar's breathing quickened, and he knew he had only to wink to have her meet him outside.

The little girl beside him coughed and he pulled his hand away. "Can you bring some bread and drink for the children?" he asked.

Ingemar licked her lips as she nodded. With a triumphant look at the Saxon woman and a toss of her blond hair, she turned and walked away.

Meradyce surreptitiously watched the Viking beside her. She understood enough to know that she had been offered to the old man, who must be a thane here. Apparently he did not want her.

Meradyce did not know why, nor could she guess. All she knew was that she was vastly relieved that the man had not taken her.

If she had to belong to any man here, she would have picked this one beside her. On the ship she had begun to realize that he was different from the Viking warriors she had heard about. He had not raped her or hurt her in any way. He had given the children his cloak, when surely he must have felt the need for it. He had treated Adelar with wisdom, perhaps even some respect for his boyish pride.

Here among his own people, he seemed like every other drinking, lusting Viking, his face hard and cold, his manner rough, but she still believed he would not harm her. She had been shocked when he brazenly shoved his hand down the fair-haired woman's dress, but from the resulting look on the woman's face, Meradyce didn't doubt that this was not such an unusual act for him, at least with that particular woman.

Meradyce became aware that the Viking was looking at her. She could feel his gaze like fingers along her spine and tried to ignore it—and him.

The woman came back with bread and gave it to her with a hostile stare. Meradyce had encountered jealousy before, and recognized it instantly.

Perhaps this woman was the Viking's wife. That thought brought little comfort, for although that might mean he still would not touch her, she would be just another captive, to be bought and sold like any other article.

She kept all her small hopes and great fears to herself, however, as she broke the bread. With gentle words and soft cajoling, she persuaded Adelar and Betha to eat.

"I want to go home," Betha said softly, her dark eyes filled with fear.

"So do I, but we must stay here for a while, until your father can come for us," Meradyce replied softly, hugging the little girl tightly as she looked around the room, noticing for the first time the fine tapestries that covered the walls. They were probably stolen, and were surely only used to provide some measure of warmth against the cold walls, not admired for their beauty or workmanship.

"Come," the Viking said suddenly, standing and yanking her to her feet. At once, the men in the room began leering, shouting and grinning like simple-minded fools.

Meradyce did not move. She did not want to go with him, and she was afraid to leave the children alone. Betha held onto her dress. Adelar jumped to his feet, his hands balled into fists.

"Bring them," the Viking said gruffly.

She did not say anything, nor did she look at him as she took the children's hands in hers and followed him with faltering steps that had nothing to do with her days at sea.

He led them outside. It was now night, and even colder than before. She shivered and picked up Betha, whose teeth were chattering.

The man brought them to a house not far from the chieftain's hall. He drew back the skin that covered the door and gestured for her to enter. She hesitated, then complied. He had not shamed her in front of the children before. She hoped he did not intend to do so now.

There was another woman, an older woman, inside. "Einar!" she called out, coming forward.

"This is my mother," the Viking said. "She is a Saxon, like you."

Meradyce glanced at him as she put Betha down, then at the woman. So that explained how he came to speak her language.

A young girl with thick, red-gold hair walked toward them from the back of the building, staring at them with large green eyes. The girl did not speak, but Meradyce had the impression that there was a very clever mind behind the impassive face.

"That is my daughter," the Viking said.

Meradyce had never imagined Vikings having mothers and children. The idea made them seem a little less vile.

"Who are they, Einar?" the older woman asked, smiling warmly.

"Captives. For ransom."

Meradyce looked at him. Ransom! It was better than slavery, but why did he think...

Because he had found them in the thane's hall.

Kendric would pay, at least for his children.

The old woman walked forward and looked at Adelar gravely. "You must have had quite a time capturing this fellow. He looks like a fine warrior."

Adelar gave the woman a skeptical look. Meradyce was tempted to warn her that he abhorred being treated like a child.

"Is this beauty your sister?"

"Yes," Adelar replied.

"Are you tired?" she asked Betha gently.

Betha, who clutched Meradyce's hand tightly, nodded. "Yes."

"The children will stay here, Mother."

Meradyce jerked her head to look at the Viking. Adelar stepped toward her protectively.

Suddenly Einar heard Hamar calling. "Olva! Olva, are you here?" he shouted as he rushed inside.

"What is it?" Einar demanded, surprised by the panic in his brother's voice.

"It is Gunnhild. She is having the baby!"

Einar looked at his mother, his brow wrinkled with concern. Helsa, the village midwife, and a selfish old woman, had died three months ago, taking her secrets with her.

"Olva, can you come?" Hamar pleaded.

Einar saw his mother's uncertainty.

"I do not know if I can be of much help," she said sympathetically, "but I will come."

"Is it the pregnant girl?" the Saxon woman interrupted. "Is she in labor?"

Everyone turned to stare at her. Olva gave her a questioning look. "Yes. Her time has come."

"I will help."

Einar frowned skeptically. "What does a highborn Saxon woman know of any birthing but those of her own children?" he asked, his voice mocking and cold.

The boy gasped. "Meradyce is not—" he began loudly, until he saw the expression on Einar's face.

"Not what?" Einar demanded, understanding dawning as he realized, for the first time, that the children did not closely resemble the woman who had risked her life for them.

The boy looked around, panic in his eyes. "Nothing! I meant nothing!"

Einar watched as the Saxon woman went to him, a gentle, soothing smile on her beautiful face.

"I am sorry, Meradyce," the boy whispered.

"It does not matter," she replied quietly, putting her slender arm around his shoulders.

"She is not what?" Einar asked again.

"I am not their mother," the woman said, turning to confront him. "I am a midwife."

"You are the wife of the Saxon chief. You wear the cross."

The woman's hand flew to her neck. "Kendric's wife was not in the village. She left this in my care."

"Einar, what is going on? Is Olva coming or not?" Hamar implored.

Einar asked himself if he believed the Saxon woman. Was she merely a village midwife, or the wife of a Saxon lord?

She wore the cross. And she looked like a lord's wife, with her proud, erect bearing and regal beauty. She might be lying, trying to escape. Where did she think she could go?

Sweet, gentle Gunnhild, the wife his brother adored, needed help, and if this woman *was* a midwife...

Einar made his decision. "Keep the children here," he said to his mother, then he told Hamar what was happening before taking the Saxon's slender hand in his. "This way."

As they hurried through the village, the Saxon plied Einar with questions. "Where is the woman who usually helps at these times?"

"Dead."

"Did she have medicines she used? Could I see them?"

"Yes. No one has gone near her house since she died. They were afraid of her."

"Good. They will not have disturbed anything. Ask him if his wife is bleeding."

Einar did so, quite amazed at the cool, calm tone of the woman at his side. If she was a man, I would want her for an ally, he thought.

"Ask him if the water has broken."

He did. "Hamar says not yet."

"And the pains? Is there much time between them?"

They arrived at the bathhouse outside the walls of the village, just inside the woods and near the river.

"What is this place?"

"It is the bathhouse. All our women give birth here."

She said nothing, but began to follow Hamar as he ducked inside the small wooden building. She hesitated, realizing Einar was not entering.

"I will need your help," she said.

"What for?"

"I must talk to her. Ask her questions."

"Very well," Einar said sullenly, following her inside.

Hamar had heated the stones until the room was like an oven. He knelt down near Gunnhild, who lay on the floor, her face contorted with pain. She managed to smile when she saw him, but when she noticed the Saxon woman, her brow wrinkled with puzzlement.

Briefly Einar explained, and as he did so, he watched the Saxon. She put her ear to Gunnhild's stomach, then felt her belly gently, but in such a way that Einar could believe she was a midwife.

"Tell her not to worry. Nothing is amiss. I know— I have attended the births of fifty children."

She saw his cynical expression. "I helped my mother from the time I was nine years old, and I have traveled to many villages."

Einar told Gunnhild.

"Is this her first child?"

"Yes," he replied.

Meradyce nodded. "I thought so. Tell her that the child is lying in the best position, but it may be some time yet."

He did, then turned away when Gunnhild's face twisted in agony.

"Tell her she must breathe like this when the pain comes." Meradyce demonstrated the technique. "Tell her!"

He spoke quickly.

"Ask her to stand up."

Einar stared at her. "What?"

"Tell her to stand up. She should walk."

"That is not right."

"How many births have you attended?"

"None, but—"

"It could be many hours yet, since this is her first. Walking will help. Help her up and then leave us, both of you."

After the men had assisted Gunnhild to her feet, Einar touched Hamar on the shoulder and nodded in the direction of the door. He wanted nothing more than to be gone from here.

When they were at the door, the Saxon spoke again, her tone like a chieftain's. "I will need a small log about this size." She made a circle with her thumb and forefinger. "It is for rolling on her back. It will ease the pains. Find one."

Einar nodded and obeyed.

As the first glow of dawn tinted the horizon, Einar sat in front of the bathhouse, trying to ignore Gunnhild's cries as she struggled to give birth. Across from him, Hamar sat glumly, slowly and quietly drinking himself into a stupor, unmindful of the cold, damp morning air.

The woman Meradyce had been right. It had been several hours since he had brought her to the bathhouse.

Einar closed his eyes. Drink would not help him forget the last time he had sat like this, waiting helplessly.

That time, though, it had been *his* wife, giving birth to his daughter. And when it was over, his wife was dead. He wondered if the Saxon could have helped Nissa, but dismissed the thought. It was better she had died.

Meradyce came out. She had tied back her long hair, but tendrils had escaped and clung to her sweat-dampened brow. The sleeves of her dress were rolled up, exposing white, slender arms. "I need you," she said, motioning him to follow her inside.

He did so, but he would rather have jumped into a snake pit.

"Tell Gunnhild that everything is going to be over very soon."

Speaking swiftly, he tried to avoid looking at Gunnhild's tired, sweat-streaked face.

"Tell her, when I say 'now,' she should bear down and push as hard as she can."

Gunnhild groaned, and in an instant Meradyce was beside her, one hand on her stomach.

The pain seemed to subside.

"Tell her."

As he spoke, the woman went around to Gunn-hild's feet, keeping her hand on Gunnhild's rotund belly. "Tell her I see the head! Tell her the baby has...dark hair!"

He did, averting his gaze.

"Now!" Meradyce cried.

Einar bolted from the room. Once outside, he took deep breaths of the fresh, cool air.

Hamar roused himself. "What? Is something happening?"

As if in answer to his question, a baby's squalling cry pierced the air. Then stopped. Einar and Hamar stared at each other until they heard women's laughter from inside the bathhouse. They sighed with relief.

Meradyce opened the door and smiled at Hamar, but when she looked at Einar, the smile disappeared from her lips. "Tell him he has a big, healthy son. His wife made me lay him on the ground."

Quickly, Einar told Hamar, who pushed past the woman and went inside.

"He will decide if the baby is well-made and if so, he will pick him up," Einar said to her, reflecting that her smile had been more beautiful than anything else about her.

"And if he thinks the child is not?"

"He will give him to the sea."

The Saxon frowned, then went into the bathhouse.

Hamar came out, his grin stretching from ear to ear. "This is a wonderful day, Einar! A son—and he is as fine as Balder!"

"What will you name him?"

"Eric. Eric Hamarson. A good name."

"Yes, a good name."

Hamar slapped Einar on the back. "That woman was a gift from Freyja! Gunnhild can not stop talking about her—except to admire our son, of course. She says she is even better than Helsa, and Gunnhild should know. She was always there when her brothers and sisters were born."

"Yes, it was a good thing."

"Einar?"

"Yes?"

"What are you going to do with her?"

"That is no concern of yours."

Hamar looked away. "No, no, I suppose not."

The baby began crying again, and Hamar grinned delightedly. "Listen to him! He is a strong one!" With that, he went inside to see his wife.

Meradyce came out a few minutes later, wiping her brow with the back of her hand. "She should rest in there for a little while, then her husband can take her home."

"Good."

Meradyce swayed slightly as she looked at the Viking, her vision blurred from exhaustion and hunger. While she was assisting Gunnhild, the need to help had overcome her physical discomfort. Now the strain struck her like a wave. She struggled to subdue her weakness, but to no avail. Her legs gave out and she sank to the ground.

The Viking lifted her in his strong arms and held her against his hard chest. He began walking, and she knew he was taking her to the village.

Just as she knew she had no strength left to fight him.

Chapter Three

When Meradyce awoke, she realized immediately, and with great relief, that the Viking was sitting at the far side of the longhouse, away from his huge bed.

She closed her eyes, hoping he would think she still slept.

"Are you hungry?"

She looked at the man whose name, she now knew, was Einar. In the dim light from a single wick floating in a dish of oil, she could see that he wore a different tunic, a dark one of fine wool that exposed his muscular arms. Around his neck a gold necklet gleamed, and he had a silver band around his upper arm. His breeches were of wool, the bottoms covered with fur held on by wrapped lacing.

Wordlessly, he pointed to a stool near the fire burning in the hearth in the middle of the floor. She got out of the bed slowly. She still had on her dress and she said a silent prayer of thanks.

He said nothing as she sat down, but began rummaging in what appeared to be a storage chest. He brought out some bread and a bottle of wine, something surely taken from one of their raids along the Saxon and Frankish coasts.

He handed her the bread and she began to eat hungrily, wondering how long she had slept. As she ate, she felt strength returning to her body.

Glancing around, she knew she was in the Viking's house. It was very much a warrior's dwelling. There were wall coverings like those in the larger hall, but they were dusty. The bed had many pillows and finely woven blankets as well as fur coverings, and she didn't doubt it was the piece of furniture he used most. Weapons seemed to be everywhere, some hanging from the timbers that held up the roof. The hearth didn't look as if it had been swept in days, and the only other items of furniture were the stools they sat on and the chests that lined the walls.

Two huge dogs lay near the door, as still as statues except for an occasional twitch of their tails. They were the ugliest dogs Meradyce had ever seen, but they watched the Viking with what looked like devotion.

If only she could manage to get one of the weapons, she thought, a dagger or something she could lift easily... She was still tired, but if she had a weapon in her hand, she would have the strength—and the knowledge—to use it. This would not be the first time she had struggled against a lustful man.

But if she did manage to escape the Viking, could she find the children and take them, too? Then what? Where could they go?

Nowhere. She would have to bide her time, submit to what she must and try to discover how they could return home.

* * *

Einar watched the Saxon chew the bread and sip his wine, all the while wondering what was wrong with him. He was not behaving like a warrior, serving her food and drink.

Even worse, he had acted like a coward while Gunnhild was giving birth, running from the bathhouse as if he were a scared child.

He took another drink. What was he, a boy or a man?

Wasn't this the most beautiful woman he had ever seen, with a body even finer than Ingemar's? Why did he not strip her clothes off and satisfy his burning curiosity to see her naked body—and then do what any Viking warrior would have done long ago?

She was his woman, his property, to do with as he pleased. He must be getting weak. Her feelings should be of no concern to him.

Einar tossed his drinking horn into the corner and stood up. The dogs also rose, but at one gesture from their master, they lay back down.

The woman paused, the wine bottle halfway to her mouth.

"Put it down," he said slowly, staring at her luscious full lips stained red with wine.

She did not move.

"I said, put it down!" He used the tone of voice in which he gave orders aboard ship—the tone of voice that made battle-hardened warriors jump to do his bidding.

Still she did not move.

He strode toward her and yanked the bottle from her hand, throwing it against the wall and shattering it. "When I tell you to do something, *anything,* you will do it!"

He hauled her to her feet. And then his mouth crushed hers in a fierce kiss.

She was limp in his arms, as limp as a wet piece of rope. He pulled back and looked at her. Her eyes were closed, and her lashes were wet with tears.

He was a Viking warrior and this was his slave, to do with as he pleased. How she felt should matter nothing. Once before he had let himself care for a beautiful woman—and the result had been disastrous.

He grabbed her gown and tugged, tearing it and her shift from her body in one move. Then he stepped back and let his gaze travel over her.

She made no move to cover herself as a tear fell on her cheek.

He was a Viking warrior and this was his woman. A woman as lovely as anything a man could imagine. A woman whose skin was smooth and white and perfect. Whose breasts were round and full above a narrow waist. Whose nipples puckered in the chill air of his house as if with desire. Whose legs were shapely and slender, like her arms. Whose dark hair fell like a waterfall around her.

Desire flared in his loins. He picked her up and laid her on his bed, forcing himself to ignore the terror in her eyes as he stood back to strip off his tunic.

And yet . . . and yet, he did not want to take her this way. She was as proud as any man, as beautiful as a goddess. She had helped Gunnhild, when she could have kept silent and left his brother's wife to suffer.

He could not take her against her will.

"Einar!"

With a curse, he turned toward the door.

"Einar!" Svend called again as he entered the house.

Einar saw the woman cover herself with a fur out of the corner of his eye.

Svend glanced at her, raising an eyebrow. "Too late, am I?"

Einar said nothing.

"Hamar and Gunnhild feel that this woman should be rewarded. They tell me she is very skilled in matters of childbirth. They have asked me to set her free, and since Helsa is dead and there is no one else in the village to take her place, I have agreed."

Einar took a step closer to his father, wanting to argue. The woman was his! He had found her. He had brought her here.

"I am glad you agree, my son. I know Ingemar will be pleased with my decision."

Svend began to leave, then turned back. "You shall be responsible for her, Einar. A woman like that needs a man's protection. If you were any other man, I would tell you to marry her, but I know I might as well ask you to slit your own throat." He smiled. "A man should be married, Einar. If you change your mind, that would be a good thing. If not, make sure no man touches her against her will. We need her." He paused on the threshold. "And *never* disobey my orders again."

Einar frowned. He should have known his father would find a way to punish him for daring to defy him.

Perhaps it was just as well. And there was always Ingemar to join him in his bed.

Meradyce watched the two men, inching slowly backward as she held a fur over her nakedness. Had this older man come to take her, too—or only to watch? Perhaps he regretted his decision to give her to Einar. She had heard that the Vikings fought over almost anything. Maybe they would fight for her.

She had been a fool to believe that this Viking was different, to even begin to feel safe. And yet, he had looked at her with respect, then turned away when she was helpless to fend off his attack.

The older man left. Einar pivoted on his heel, looking at her with a strange expression on his face. "You are free," he said.

She gaped at him, not believing his words.

"You are free," he repeated.

He reached down and began picking up the shattered pieces of the bottle, his muscular back gleaming in the light. "Svend has given you your freedom for helping Gunnhild," he said as he straightened.

"Truly?" she asked.

He looked at her with his cold gray eyes. "I never lie."

"Then I am free to leave?"

"Out of my house, yes."

"But not this village?"

He raised an eyebrow as he gazed steadily at her. "Where were you thinking of going?"

"Home."

He chuckled harshly. "Not unless you want a worse voyage than before. We cannot sail that far before spring. And how do you intend to pay for your passage?" He smiled, a slow, impertinent smile.

"I have many skills."

"I am sure you do."

She averted her face to hide the sudden heat of embarrassment that flooded through her at his tone. "I will earn money for our passage. How much will it cost?"

"Our?"

"Mine and the children."

"The children stay."

She stared at him, aghast. "What?"

"They are still to be ransomed."

She lifted her chin. "I will not go anywhere without the children," she said defiantly.

He frowned. "But they are not yours."

"I was taking care of them. They are still in my charge."

There was a long pause as he turned away and drew on his tunic. Finally, he spoke without looking at her. "I admire your loyalty."

Meradyce had been flattered many times, by many men, but never had a man's words affected her as his did at that moment. She was sure he did not say such things lightly, and somehow, she sensed that he admired loyalty very much indeed.

She told herself that what she thought about him was unimportant. All that mattered was that she must find a way to go from this place and take the children with her.

"You can stay with my mother, and so will the children." As he faced her, he ran his gaze over her and grinned wickedly. "Do you intend to remain in my bed, Saxon? If so, I would be very happy to join you there."

Blushing furiously, Meradyce clambered quickly out, holding the fur over her body. She looked at her torn gown.

Einar went to one of the chests along the wall. Lifting the lid, he took out one of the most beautiful gowns she had ever seen. It was a rich red color, intricately embroidered around the neck. "Here." He tossed the garment and a woven belt at her and they landed on the bed beside her.

Meradyce felt as if she was delirious with a fever. One minute she was frightened nearly to death, certain he was about to rape her, then he told her she was free. He made no secret of his unsatisfied lust, but he was letting her go. He had stripped her naked, and now he was giving her the most lovely garment she had ever had in her life.

She picked up the gown without a word. He rooted around in the chest and held out a shift of fine white linen. "If you want it, take it."

She would sooner go near a mad dog.

As he flung the shift at her, he laughed again, this time a deep rich sound that filled the room. "When you are ready, I will take you to my mother's house."

He sat on one of the stools. It was clear he had no intention of leaving while she dressed, so she struggled to put on the shift while keeping hold of the fur.

He watched her with the hint of a smile curling his lips. "I see you are indeed a woman of many skills."

She frowned and dressed as quickly as she could. When she finished tying the belt, he rose slowly, his expression suddenly serious. "No man is to so much as touch you without permission. If any man does, tell me. Svend has told me to protect you, and I will."

Surprised, she regarded the tall fair-haired warrior standing before her and wondered just how much she could trust his words.

Completely.

She knew it at once. She could trust this barbarian more than any man she had ever met, because he respected her more than any man she had ever met.

He went toward the door. As she sidled past the dogs, he grinned. Meradyce would never have believed a Viking warrior could seem boyish if she was not seeing it for herself.

"Have no fear," he said in a patronizing tone. "They will not move again until I tell them to."

His vanity emboldened her. She stood perfectly still and held out her hand, making low, soothing sounds in her throat. The dogs inched forward, then stood up and licked her palm.

Einar crossed his arms and frowned before grunting a command that sent the dogs back to where they had been before. Without a word, he strode out of the house and through the village, not even checking to see if she followed.

Meradyce smiled, silently blessing her father for teaching her such things as she followed Einar to his mother's house.

The moment Betha and Adelar saw Meradyce, they hurried to her. Betha hugged her tightly.

"She is to stay with you and Endredi," Einar said to his mother. "Svend has given her her freedom for helping Gunnhild in her labor."

"Truly, Einar?" Olva asked, smiling warmly.

He nodded and answered gruffly, "She is under my protection."

He turned to leave, glancing at Meradyce.

For an instant, Meradyce couldn't breathe. The look in his eyes! That mingling of restraint and regret and pride she had seen only once before in her life, on Paul's face before he had gone away from her.

It was impossible. She had imagined it.

She had cared deeply for Paul, whereas this man had stolen her away from her home.

He had taken the children, but kept them safe.

He was going to rape her, then he had stopped, even though she was helpless before him.

He was a Viking. Whatever else he was, whatever he made her feel, he was—he must be—her enemy.

Chapter Four

Meradyce woke with a start and stared at the smoke-darkened roof above the platform in Olva's house. She lay still as the memories of the past few days flooded through her mind. The raid on her village, the terrible voyage, the men . . . the Viking.

Surely she had imagined the expression in the Viking's eyes last night. It was like sacrilege to see any resemblance between that barbarian and gentle Paul.

Gentle, but not weak. If anything, Paul had been too strong, so filled with inner power that he could deny what they both felt because of a vow to be as much like Saint Paul as possible. She had pleaded in vain that she knew of many priests who married.

"I have made my vow and I will keep it," Paul had said, but before he left her, she had seen that same look in his eyes. Regretful, but determined to do what he believed he must.

Paul had kept his vow until the day he died.

No, this Viking was not like Paul. He was iron where Paul was gold. He was a pagan, primitive in his lust where Paul was a saint, spiritual in his denial.

Nonetheless, warmth throbbed through her veins at the memory of the Viking, half-naked and filled with desire for her, and she was ashamed. She tried to remember Paul's pale blue eyes but could only see gray eyes ringed with black.

Restless and dismayed, she turned onto her side— and realized that Betha was not beside her, as she had been in the night. Opening her eyes, she saw the Viking's daughter, Endredi, sitting beside the fire in the middle of the floor, stirring something in a pot hanging over it.

"Where are the children?" Meradyce asked, getting out of the bed.

There was a strange stillness about the young girl. To Meradyce she looked about Adelar's age, but her manner made her seem older.

Endredi stopped stirring and spoke softly in the Saxon tongue. "Olva took them to see the goats while she milked."

"What time of day is it?" Meradyce asked. She had worn her shift for sleeping and now pulled on her gown.

"Near noon."

She had slept a long time, but she felt rested for the first time since the horrible night the Vikings had taken her. She inhaled the delicious aroma coming from the pot. "What are you cooking?"

"Stew. Would you like some?"

"Yes. It smells wonderful."

Endredi did not smile at the compliment, but merely reached for a wooden bowl. She spooned out a rich broth filled with chunks of meat. Meradyce sat on a stool beside her and began to eat.

The stew *was* wonderful, and not just because Meradyce was very hungry. The meat was cooked to tender perfection, the broth was thick but not lumpy and spiced just enough to bring out the flavor in the meat.

Endredi pushed the wood in the fire, moving it and the coals to the sides of the hearth so that the bottom of the pot would not overheat and make the meat burn. Then she sat back and stared at Meradyce.

Meradyce found Endredi's unwavering scrutiny nearly as hard to bear as that of her father. Nonetheless, she ate as if nothing was amiss, occasionally glancing at her silent companion. The girl did not resemble her father. Her eyes were green compared to his gray, her hair more red than gold, her face round where his was long and lean. She was not a pretty girl, but her features would grow more striking with age.

She wore a pleated shift with a drawstring at the neck such as Meradyce had never seen. Over this, she wore two large panels of less fine cloth. The panels were held on by straps and fastened at the front by large, round brooches.

When Meradyce finished, she set the bowl down. "Thank you."

Endredi smiled, a slow, slight smile. Meradyce sensed that she had been given a great and rare compliment, and it filled her with unexpected pleasure.

Endredi took the empty bowl and went to a bucket near the entrance, where she rinsed it clean. Her movements were swift and deft, but careful. Meradyce noticed a loom leaning upright near the door, the weights holding the threads dangling nearly to the floor so that the weaver could stand while working. The pattern of the cloth being made was a brilliant red and blue, and she could tell, even from here, that the weaving was very fine and even.

Endredi saw where she was looking. "Grandma and I are working together. She makes good cloth."

"Who made the stew?"

Endredi began to blush and lowered her eyes shyly. "I did."

"Then you are a good cook. Your father must be very proud of you."

The girl turned away suddenly, but not before Meradyce saw the pain that flashed across her face.

Whatever the trouble between this girl and her father, Meradyce told herself, it did not concern her.

Endredi sat down a few minutes later and handed Meradyce a drinking horn filled with mead. "Gunnhild has already been asking for you. She wants to give you a present."

Meradyce smiled. Perhaps the gift could be used to help pay for passage, and it seemed, when Endredi spoke, that the awkwardness of the last few minutes had passed. "The birth was easy enough," she said.

"Gunnhild did not think so."

"That is because it was her first. She will soon forget the pain."

"Really?"

"So I have been told."

Endredi poked at the fire without moving anything. When she spoke, she did not look at Meradyce. "Do many women die giving birth?" she asked.

Meradyce thought a moment. She had seen nothing of Endredi's mother. It was possible the woman had died in childbirth, which would explain the girl's question. "Sometimes they do, if the baby is not lying properly or the bleeding can not be stopped."

Endredi did not respond, and her long red-gold hair hid her face.

The girl rose slowly. "I am to take you to Helsa's house. My father said you wanted to look at her things."

"Yes, I do. I did not have much time before, but I think she has several medicines. There is no other midwife close by?"

Endredi shook her head.

"Was Helsa usually paid in goods or coin?"

Endredi looked at her questioningly.

"I plan to earn my passage home."

"Then you may ask for whatever payment you like, but the women will be sorry to lose a midwife."

"I could teach someone else to take my place," Meradyce offered. As much as she wanted to get home with the children, she had no wish to leave any woman without the help of a midwife.

Endredi said nothing. She nodded again and led the way out of the house.

As they walked through the village, Meradyce wished she had a cloak. The air was chill and damp and the sky dark with clouds.

But more than that, she wanted the extra covering, for the dress Einar had given her was too tight. The men stared at her as if she was walking through the village naked. One of the red-haired men she remembered so well from the ship was sitting on a huge horse, perhaps waiting for someone at one of the nearby houses. She ignored him as they passed, but she felt his gaze upon her.

Meradyce entered Helsa's longhouse at the far end of the village with relief. Although it smelled musty, at least she was hidden from curious eyes.

She was even more relieved when she began looking through the clay vessels and small wooden boxes. The midwife had many medicines. Obviously the Vikings from this village traveled or traded far, for some of the herbs were quite rare. If it had not been for Paul's teachings, she would not have known what some of them were.

Endredi stood by the door, watching silently as the woman carefully opened each vessel, tasting some by licking the tip of her finger, putting it in the powder and then putting it to her tongue. Others she merely sniffed.

Endredi was trying to understand why her father had taken this woman. He set little store on beauty, easily ignoring comely slaves other men brought back to sell to traders from the south.

Her father had said many times that slaves were a bother he could do without. He would rather look for easily portable objects.

Endredi also believed that her father would take no slaves because Olva had told him of the misery she had endured as a slave in a rich Saxon's household.

Why *had* her father taken this woman?

The Saxon was clever. Her eyes flamed with intelligence and understanding.

She was loyal and brave, for the children had told Endredi how this Meradyce had fought to keep the Vikings from taking them. The boy Adelar obviously admired her very much indeed, and little Betha adored her.

The Saxon was kind. She had offered to help Gunnhild, and apparently had tended her with no heed to her own tiredness. Gunnhild had said several times that she had been convinced that the woman was a goddess in disguise, she seemed so full of vitality and good cheer, despite her hardships.

Endredi had listened without saying much, but she was certain her father had not touched the Saxon, not that way. She had overheard men say several times that they believed Einar too proud to have any woman who would not jump into his bed willingly.

Perhaps her father had taken the woman because he sensed, as she did, that the Saxon was not afraid of him. This was nothing short of a marvel to Endredi, who held her father in complete awe. One glowering look from him was enough to make her want to cry, assuming he did look at her. But she knew her father abhorred cowards.

Suddenly the woman gasped, drawing Endredi's attention. "This is wonderful!" she exclaimed, holding up a small wooden chest. "I have only seen this herb once before, in a monastery."

Endredi tried not to shiver with fear. She knew what a monastery was. It was where the priests of the Saxons lived in luxury. The Saxons paid the priests vast sums, or the priests would cast an evil spell on them and condemn them to eternal flames.

Endredi fingered the amulet of Thor's hammer around her neck. She wanted nothing to do with anything from a monastery.

As for the other medicines, Endredi decided that she would watch the Saxon carefully and try to learn. She had no hope of beauty, but perhaps if she was skilled in medicine, her father would not dislike her so much.

Endredi sighed softly. If the Saxons had stolen *her,* she doubted her father would even notice. And he certainly would not care.

At first Adelar had been interested as Olva told them the names of all the goats. Betha was very happy, for she loved animals. She had found a kitten near one of the storehouses just beyond the pasture and now she played contentedly with it.

As Adelar watched his sister, he longed to be home again. Or so he told himself. He frowned and fought the memories of the recent weeks. The squabbling and bickering, the angry words in the night, the whispered accusations, his mother's tears. How Betha would put her hands over her ears or run to find Meradyce. How he would, too.

Meradyce was his friend, his nurse, his comforter—and he had wanted to save her from the

Vikings more than anything else in his life. But he had failed, although now she was free, whatever that meant coming out of a Viking's mouth. He could only hope he could keep her safe.

He hoped his mother was not too distraught. Surely she would know, as he did, that as long as there was a hope for ransom, the greedy Vikings would not kill them.

His father would pay whatever the barbarians demanded, for all of them.

Olva started milking, occasionally squirting the warm, white liquid at the kitten's mouth, which made Betha giggle. Then another old woman joined them, chattering away in the strange language the Vikings spoke.

Adelar tried to listen, to see if he could understand any of it, but the women talked too fast.

He looked around. The pasture was closed off by a low rock wall. Outside it was a pine wood, although not a thick one, for it was easy to see the path through it.

Two men, carrying bows that were slightly longer than their arms and quivers of arrows, walked past the wall toward the wood. Adelar looked at them in surprise. The Saxon warriors always spoke of the Vikings' battle axes and swords. He did not know they used bows.

A voice called out, and the men quickened their steps.

They must be practicing shooting, Adelar thought. Quickly he glanced around. Olva was still talking to the other woman and milking. Betha was teasing the kitten with a corner of her dress.

Adelar climbed the low wall and hurried after the two men. He hid behind a tree at the edge of a large, bare field. A group of men stood nearby holding their bows. They looked strangely uncomfortable, as if not familiar with the weapon in their hands. One man stood a little ways ahead, his bow drawn. Adelar looked down the field.

He could see several arrows stuck in the ground between where the men stood and the small tree they were aiming at.

Suddenly a hand grabbed the back of Adelar's tunic. "What have we here, then?" a familiar voice asked in Saxon, turning Adelar toward him.

The Viking named Einar let go. Adelar did not stumble and was glad he had not as he stared up at the man's face.

The man was not angry. If anything, he was amused.

Adelar did not like to be laughed at. By anyone. "Your friends are poor shots."

The man's eyes widened a little. "They are not used to it."

"Bows and arrows are only good for hunting, anyway."

"Are they?"

Adelar kept his gaze on Einar's face, but he was surprised. It had never occurred to him that a bow could be anything other than a sport weapon, at least for noblemen. But clearly this barbarian had another idea.

Suddenly Adelar realized that the Viking might be right. In a battle, did it matter what was noble if you were trying to win?

"Would you care to join us?" the man asked solemnly.

Adelar nodded, very pleased not only that he was being asked to join, but because of the way the Viking looked at him. There was no smile on his lips or laughter in his eyes.

When they reached the group of men standing in the field, Adelar tried to ignore their hostile looks. He was sure it was only because he was with Einar that they remained silent.

Einar retrieved a weapon from one of the smaller men and held it out to the boy. "You may try this, if you like."

Adelar nodded and took it in his hands. It was a very fine one, of strong, supple yew. Einar handed him an arrow.

The other Vikings began to laugh.

Adelar set his stance and drew back on the bowstring, taking aim carefully. Again, the Vikings burst into raucous laughter, but Adelar ignored them. To hit the tree was too important.

He let the arrow fly. It went straight and true, striking the tree with a dull thud.

Adelar smiled. He had been blessed, he knew, with a good eye and a strong arm, and he had never been more glad of it than at this moment.

"Well done, my young Saxon," Einar said, and Adelar heard the true respect in the man's voice. He grinned and held out the bow.

"No, I think you should keep it. On one condition."

Adelar waited. The Viking came closer, his hands on his hips. "Promise me you will not use it against me."

Adelar thought about the request. This man was the enemy of his people, a ruthless Viking who had stolen them away from home. But he had not hurt Meradyce or Betha.

Adelar gazed into the steady gray eyes watching him. "I promise."

In that moment, a bond was made, for Adelar, although only a boy, did not give his word easily.

Einar nodded and spoke to the other men, who were not laughing anymore.

Suddenly Betha ran up and grabbed Adelar's arm. "What are you doing here?" she whispered, almost crying. "I thought you were lost!"

Adelar shook off his sister's hand. "I was tired of looking at goats."

Olva arrived and looked at Einar.

"He joined us in our practice. He is welcome to stay."

If Olva was surprised, she kept it from her face as she turned to Betha. "Come with me, little one. Adelar will remain here with Einar."

Betha let Olva lead her away. She knew Adelar would be safe with Einar. Although he was a Viking, she thought he was a good man, and by some instinct she could not have described to anyone, Betha always knew when someone was good. Or bad.

There was something else she had realized about him. He sounded the way Meradyce did sometimes, as if he was very sad and lonely. When Meradyce sounded like that, Betha always found an excuse to give her a hug.

But Betha did not think anybody ever hugged Einar.

Ull turned to Siurt with a frown. "What do you make of that, eh?"

Siurt looked at the Saxon boy standing beside Einar. "He is good with a bow."

Ull snorted with disgust. "It is a weapon for children, that is all. No true Viking would use it. You cannot see the eyes of the man you are fighting."

Siurt shrugged. "You are right."

Ull's gaze went to Einar. "He likes that boy, too."

"Maybe because he does not have any sons of his own."

Ull nodded and stroked his beard thoughtfully. "Good thing, too." He leaned closer to his younger brother. "It will be hard enough as it is, with all Svend's other sons to contend with."

"Einar still has no wish to become chief?"

Ull's face showed his disgust. "No. The men would flock to follow him. Everyone knows Hamar is too weak and Svend is too old. And Svend's other sons are too young. But Einar! Even I would gladly follow him."

"But he does not want to become chieftain."

Ull gave Siurt a sidelong glance. "Then another man must."

After filling a large basket with medicines, Meradyce and Endredi left Helsa's house. Meradyce saw no sign of the red-haired man and sighed with relief as they walked through the village.

As they entered Olva's longhouse, Meradyce gasped. It seemed to be filled with women. She looked around for the children and finally spotted Betha sitting contentedly on a low stool, stroking a sleeping brown kitten. There was no sign of Adelar.

Olva called out from the back of the long, low building, then pushed her way through the throng. "Meradyce! As you can see, everyone has heard of you already."

"Where is Adelar?"

"With Einar."

Meradyce wondered what the Viking would want with Adelar. He was only a boy, although, at twelve years of age, he was fast approaching manhood. Or thought he was.

Dread flashed through her as she remembered something she had overheard Kendric and the other men talking of once. They were whispering about the Vikings and how they probably amused themselves for long days at sea when they were without women.

Her face must have betrayed something of her fear, for Olva spoke quickly. "He is safe with Einar."

Meradyce nodded, but she went to Betha. She had long ago learned that Betha's intuition regarding a person's true character was infallible. To her relief, Betha smiled and said simply, "Adelar likes Einar. He wanted to stay with him."

Meradyce returned the smile. Glancing around, she saw Gunnhild sitting on one of the sleeping platforms, nursing her infant son. Gunnhild's face broke into a smile when she saw Meradyce looking at her. It occurred to Meradyce that Gunnhild was a very pretty young woman, something that had not been obvious when she was in her labor.

Gunnhild spoke.

"She is thanking you for your help, and she brought you this." Olva picked up a lovely piece of fabric from beside Gunnhild and opened it out. It was like Endredi's shift, pleated around the top and with a drawstring to pull it close about the neck before falling straight to the floor. The sleeves were also pleated. It was a beautiful garment.

"Tell her, thank you."

Olva did, then spoke to Meradyce. "The women are relieved you have come. They have all been worried about bearing children since Helsa died."

"I will be happy to help them, if I can."

She went toward a very young woman who stood off to one side, wringing her hands nervously. She did not seem to be much older than Endredi, although she was obviously very far along in her pregnancy.

The girl stood absolutely still as Meradyce felt her belly. The baby moved suddenly, and Meradyce smiled. "Olva, tell her the baby kicked me. What a strong one!"

When the girl heard Olva's words, she smiled shyly and spoke quickly.

"Asa wants to know if she bears a son," Olva said.

"Tell her I cannot be sure, but she is carrying the child high, and her hips have not widened very much. It could very well be a boy."

Asa smiled when Olva finished speaking, but Meradyce paid no attention. She was still feeling the young woman's belly. Something was unusual. She put her ear to the woman, listening carefully. Then she stood back. "How long?"

"She is about seven months," Olva said.

Now Meradyce was sure. Twins. There had been too many feet, and the girl was very large if she had nearly two months yet. "Tell her, if she feels any unusual pain, anywhere in her stomach or back, she should send for me at once. That baby is strong, and many times the strong ones are impatient to come out."

Meradyce was lying, but she had no wish to worry the young woman. Twins often arrived early and were too small to survive. Still, there was also a good chance for healthy children, so it would not do to alarm her.

Olva passed on the words, then faced Meradyce. "I told her Einar's little brother will be just like him. Einar came nearly a month soon—and strong! He hit my mouth with his little fist when he was only a few days old and made me bleed!"

Meradyce had already moved on to another woman, but she paused for a moment. How could that young girl be bearing Einar's brother, if Olva was Einar's mother? Surely she must have misunderstood.

Then she remembered the Viking notions about divorce and men having several wives at the same time. Clearly that was true.

She decided it was pointless to waste time trying to understand Viking customs. Einar's parentage or any other relations were of no interest to her.

For the rest of the afternoon, she examined the pregnant women, trying to see if there would be problems or if all would go well.

All the Viking women seemed in good health. She recommended that they eat as much as they liked, especially of vegetables, since it was well known that vegetables strengthened the blood. They would not eat what they considered bad luck, however, just as they would do everything they could to ensure healthy children, including wearing amulets. Such superstitions were probably pointless, but Meradyce knew that if they made the mother more confident, they would not be harmful, either.

Toward evening, when the longhouse was nearly empty, Olva stood at her loom, weaving. Betha, having let her kitten go outside, watched in fascination at the speed with which the older woman worked. Endredi was cooking the evening meal, and a delicious aroma emanated from the cooking pot.

Meradyce smiled at the remaining woman, whom Olva had introduced as Reinhild. She had borne a baby since Helsa's death and wanted to make sure there was nothing amiss with either her infant or herself. They were both well. As Reinhild turned to leave, Meradyce heard a sound at the door and straightened.

It was Einar. He strode in carrying a chest she recognized from his house. Before she could ask about Adelar, the boy pushed past him and ran up to her, a large bow in his hand. "Look, he gave it to me. And I am the best shot—better than all of them!"

Meradyce nodded, wishing she could disappear as Einar walked toward her, all too aware of Reinhild's presence and her curious stare. She pretended to be fascinated by the bow.

"Hamar wants me to thank you again," Einar said as he put down the chest.

She did not look up or speak.

"You need more clothes," he said gruffly. "That gown is immodest."

She raised her eyes. "If my garments are immodest, I do not see that I can be held accountable. You did not allow me the opportunity to collect my things before you dragged me away."

She caught Olva's surprised expression out of the corner of her eye, but chose to concentrate instead on the man in front of her. It *was* his fault—and his fault that she felt like an item on display in a market stall.

Not only that, but if Viking women were like Saxon women—and after meeting them this afternoon she was convinced women were much the same everywhere—the news of Einar's gift would spread through the village like water down a steep hill. Once again she would be the subject of gossip and speculation. Even here, she would not be spared.

Einar's lips twitched. "So now I am making amends."

Mercifully, he said no more, but turned and left.

Olva resumed her weaving, but Reinhild gaped at Meradyce as if she had gone mad, and Endredi looked shocked. Betha smiled.

Adelar frowned. "Meradyce," he said urgently, "Meradyce! I was even better than him! Meradyce!"

"Yes, Adelar, I heard you. Good for you."

Meradyce looked at the bow in Adelar's hands, but he knew she didn't care, not really. She was thinking about *him*, the Viking.

The Viking wasn't worthy of her. She was a Saxon, after all, even if she wasn't from a high-ranking family. A beautiful, kind, wonderful Saxon.

And she was the love of young Adelar's life.

Chapter Five

After the evening meal, Einar, Svend and Hamar sat in the chieftain's longhouse, their drinking horns in their hands.

"One hundred pieces of silver is not enough," Svend said quietly before taking a gulp of strong ale.

"We took everything of value in the village, Father," Hamar answered, his voice equally subdued. "It will be difficult enough to get the hundred pieces."

Svend belched loudly before answering. "The man paid five hundred to have his wife killed. Surely his children—his *son*—is worth at least that much."

"Perhaps we could ask two hundred for the boy, fifty for the girl," Hamar suggested.

"He must have rich relatives," Svend said. "Let us ask for five hundred for the boy, one hundred for the girl."

"I still say that is too much. Better we get a small ransom than none at all. If it is too high, the Saxon might be willing to let us keep the children. After all, he wanted his wife murdered."

For the first time, Einar spoke. "He would not want his son killed. The boy is everything a man hopes for in a son."

Hamar glanced at his brother in surprise, then quickly away.

Svend reached for his drinking horn, looking at his tall, fair-haired son. *He* was a son for any father to be proud of—and so was Hamar. Einar was bold and clever, Hamar cautious and wise. They made a fine pair to rule his land when he went to Valhalla. "How much should we ask, then?"

"One thousand pieces of silver."

Hamar sucked in his breath as Svend leaned back in his chair, eyeing his son. "And if the man cannot pay, we kill the boy?"

"No."

Svend raised his eyebrows as if astonished, but inwardly he was pleased. For too many years he had feared that Einar cared nothing about having a son. After his wife had died bearing a daughter, everyone had expected Einar to remarry, and soon. It was no secret that any maiden in the village would have gladly taken Nissa's place—and any one of them would have made a better, more faithful wife.

Nissa had been beautiful, with long hair like spun gold. Every warrior had envied Einar when he wed her, until Nissa made it clear that she hated to sleep alone when Einar was away. It was a good thing she had died in childbirth, for surely a man as proud as Einar would have killed her for her infidelities.

It was a pity Endredi's eyes were exactly like her mother's.

But now here was Einar, filled with admiration for an enemy's son. And not only that—Svend was sure his handsome son was being driven nearly mad with desire for the beautiful Saxon woman. Nothing else would make Einar disobey an order. Svend understood the feeling all too well.

Indeed, Svend would have been more disappointed if his son *had* been able to ignore such a lovely woman. A skilled woman. A woman who would surely bear fine children. She would make a perfect wife for Einar. "And what of the boy's sister?"

"Ask fifty."

"And if the Saxon refuses to pay even the fifty, I suppose we could sell her to the traders from the south. She is a pretty child."

"Olva likes her."

This time, Svend *was* surprised. Einar barely seemed to notice his daughter was alive, but now he was concerned about this foreign girl, even though he was trying to make it sound as if he wanted her spared for Olva's sake.

"Very well," Svend said, deciding. "We ask one thousand pieces of silver for the boy, fifty for the girl. If it is not paid, we tell the Saxon we will sell them as slaves. Now, what of the woman?" Svend asked the question casually, but he watched Einar's face closely as he spoke the words.

"She wishes to sail home in the spring," Einar replied. "She thinks she will earn enough for her passage, so we can take her with the children, if the Saxon pays."

"Huh." Svend took another drink. "Then we should see that she teaches someone what she knows about childbirth before that. Endredi would be a good choice."

"Endredi is too young."

"Endredi is nearly a woman," Hamar pointed out.

"If you do not wish it, so be it," Svend said calmly. "Or perhaps you are planning a marriage for your daughter?"

Svend had to struggle to keep a smile off his face when he saw Einar's expression. No doubt his son wanted to think time stood still. It was good to remind him that he wasn't growing younger or immortal like the gods. "Perhaps Ull?"

Einar jumped to his feet. *"What?"*

The men in the hall looked up from their food. "Sit down, my son," Svend said with a deep chuckle. "Merely a suggestion, and I see an unwelcome one."

Einar glared at his father as he sat. "I agree to let the Saxon teach Endredi."

"Good," Svend said, taking a drink so that he would not laugh.

Einar would never have agreed unless he was given a worse alternative, but Endredi was a very clever, compassionate girl, according to Olva. She would make an excellent midwife, he concluded.

"Who will take the ransom message to the Saxons?" Hamar asked after a short pause.

"Since Einar speaks the Saxon tongue, he will go to Hedeby. There is yet time for such a short voyage before winter. Find the man who brought us the Saxon's first message. He will know how to get our demands to him."

Einar nodded.

"What if they only offer to ransom one of the children?" Hamar asked.

"It will have to be both or neither," Einar said at once. "The boy will not leave his sister."

"How can you be so sure?" Svend demanded.

"If I were the boy, I would feel the same." Einar took another drink, avoiding Hamar's and Svend's scrutiny. He knew they were surprised by his interest in the Saxon children, but so was he.

It was true that Adelar was as fine a son as a man could want. Einar had admired the boy's bravery in the Saxon village, seen his efforts to hide his illness at sea, been impressed by his attempts to protect the woman and amazed by his skill with a bow. This afternoon, as the shooting practice continued, he had been filled with envy for the Saxon thane, and a sudden yearning for a son of his own.

For years he had not felt any urge for a son. His experience of married life had been one of anger and pain, and he would not marry again. He had had many women, but none of his offspring—except Endredi—had survived beyond the first year. After a time, he had hardened his heart and told himself he had no need of sons.

Now he knew that was not true. Perhaps the gods had sent this boy to be his son in the place of a child of his body.

But his heart knew differently.

The gods had sent a woman worthy to be the mother of his children.

The *skald* took his place in the center of the hall, ready to begin. The other men settled themselves comfortably and prepared to enjoy the bard's poems of gods and great heroes. As the old man spoke, Einar tried to pay attention to the words and not think about Saxons at all.

Suddenly he was aware that Ull had come to sit beside him. "Reinhild tells me you gave the Saxon woman a gift this afternoon," he said loudly.

The old man turned to see who had interrupted him, and the hall fell silent.

Einar turned slowly to Ull, raising an eyebrow. "I did," he replied, "and I still have plenty of fine clothes and jewelry to give as gifts to women who please me. But tell me, Ull, why have you taken to gossip? Have you nothing more important with which to occupy your time?"

"Do you want her?"

Einar smiled coldly. "Perhaps."

Ull narrowed his piglike eyes, clearly not certain how far to push Einar.

He wisely decided not too far. He went back to drinking, and the storyteller, with a sour look at the red-haired man, resumed his tale of the theft of Thor's hammer.

Einar took another long drink of strong mead. It was no man's business but his if he had given the Saxon a gift. Nonetheless, he wished there had been no witnesses to his generosity.

He was responsible for the Saxon woman, and she needed garments. He did not want her parading around the town in that dress she had on today. It was too tight, showing any man who glanced at her the contours of her shapely body. If he did not want to waste time protecting her—as Svend had ordered—she would need more appropriate clothes to wear.

He had not expected to find other women in his mother's house, but he might have known the ones having babies would rush to see a midwife.

Unfortunately, he seemed to have stopped thinking clearly the minute he found the wench in the Saxon village.

He looked around the hall. All Svend's warriors were there, listening and drinking. Several women were also there, serving the ale, Ingemar among them.

She stopped to fill Einar's drinking horn again, smiling at him, her eyes filled with lust. He said nothing, but he watched her swaying hips as she walked slowly over to Lars.

Ingemar was pretty. The Saxon was beautiful, of course, but as frigid as the mountains of ice that floated down from the far north. This afternoon she would not even look at him, except when she dared to upbraid him.

His lips curved up at the memory. How her eyes had glistened with boldness! No other woman had ever defied him as she did. She spoke to him as an equal, and he suddenly realized he enjoyed it very much.

He reminded himself that women were only necessary for physical pleasure. He should get Meradyce out of his mind completely. Forget she even lived.

Ingemar went past again, but this time Einar caught her arm and pulled her down onto his lap. He kissed her fiercely, one hand around her waist, the other traveling up her leg.

Ingemar pulled back, laughing. "Now that is more like the Einar I know! I was beginning to fear you were some troll in disguise."

"I would be happy to prove to you that I am a man."

She smiled at him as she entwined her arms around his neck, moving her buttocks in such a way that he was filled with desire. "Please do," she whispered in his ear before beginning to nibble on the lobe.

Desperate to prove that he could forget the Saxon and that his lust had nothing to do with her, he picked Ingemar up and carried her from the hall.

The *skald* was not pleased that his tale had been interrupted again. Because it was Einar, however, he said nothing and merely waited until the warrior had carried the woman outside.

Watching Einar stride from the hall with Ingemar in his arms, Lars suppressed a sigh and took another drink. As long as Ingemar wanted Einar, he had no hope of marrying her. He would have to keep his desire a secret, for now.

Ull, seated across the room, saw Lars' half-smothered sigh and the way his shoulders slumped as Einar went out.

He nudged Siurt. "Einar should learn to be more discreet," he said with a sly smile.

* * *

Meradyce lay awake on the pallet in the longhouse. Used to living alone, she was easily disturbed by the small sounds of others sleeping.

Carefully, she removed Betha's arm from across her neck. It was late, very late, but she could still hear the boisterous sounds of the men in the large hall. She still could not get used to the Vikings' singing, which sounded like the howling of starving dogs.

Olva's longhouse was stuffy, too. Surely if she was cautious and careful, she could risk going outside for a moment of fresh air.

Quietly, she eased her way off the sleeping pallet. She wore one of the shifts from the chest Einar had brought, but the air was chilly, so she pulled on a woolen gown she had found. Then she went to the door and peered out.

It seemed that everyone in the village was either asleep or in the chieftain's hall. Moving cautiously, she stepped outside and went around to the back of the longhouse.

The moon was high in the sky, casting light over the buildings and making odd shadows. Meradyce found a large stone to sit on and watched the few clouds move against the huge white orb.

A sense of peace stole over her. A little way beyond the low wall she could see the river leading to the fjord through a band of trees. The moonlight looked like silver, glimpsed through the shadows of the leaves.

Sometimes even a cold, rough place could be beautiful.

Sometimes even a cold, rough man could be kind.

She sighed and pulled her knees up, hugging them to her chest. She still was not sure what to make of Einar. At one moment he looked as if he wished she was gone, the next he was bringing her gifts. She wished she could ignore his existence, yet at the same time felt grateful knowing that he was her protector.

It was all too familiar to be dependent on a man's protection. At home, that man had been Kendric.

She knew that he had wanted her. More than once he had made that very clear, like the time just after Betha's birth when Ludella lay sleeping nearby. He had come up behind her, his strong arms snaking around her waist.

If he hadn't been the leader of the village, she would have done more than twist away and pretend that his gesture was one of relieved happiness and thanks for her help.

But he was the leader of the village. And she was no fool. She knew that every man who lived there or even visited surely guessed Kendric's interest—and so left her alone.

She had to admit that she felt safer with the Viking. With Kendric, she had always felt he would expect to be rewarded for his concern someday. At least the Viking seemed to find protecting her troublesome and kept his distance.

What would have happened, she wondered, if Kendric had been the one to take her, have her at his mercy, alone in his house?

She shivered again, and this time not from the cold. If the circumstances had been reversed, she was sure Kendric, like those other Vikings, would have shown no mercy.

She looked at the ground. The true difference between Kendric and Einar was that Einar, although a barbarian Viking, respected her. Kendric, a Saxon thane, merely lusted.

Perhaps that was why she had answered Einar the way she had that afternoon, in front of Olva and the others. At first she had wanted to pretend he was not there, but she could not. Her mind warned her not to anger him, and yet she had felt curiously free to . . . to *scold* him.

His surprise and his near smile had been worth the risk.

What was she doing, thinking like that?

She should not be thinking of him at all.

She began to shiver, but she was not ready to go back inside just yet. With another quick look around to make sure no one saw her, she got up and walked to the wall. Climbing over it, she made her way toward the river.

The water lapped quietly against the rocky bank, and Meradyce breathed in the familiar smell of pine trees. If she closed her eyes, she could almost imagine herself back home. For a while this afternoon, among the women, she had felt that way, too.

Women were very alike when it came to bearing children. They all wanted healthy offspring. They all tried to guess whether they bore a girl or a boy, especially if it was a first child.

She was relieved that there was only the girl bearing twins to concern her at the moment. She would watch the girl—Asa—and be ready the moment she went into labor. The longer she could hold that off, the better. And fortunately, Helsa had possessed some medicines that could slow the labor and might even stop it.

The moon disappeared behind some clouds, and Meradyce knew she had stayed there long enough. Now she would welcome Betha's little body warm against hers, and hopefully sleep would come.

When she climbed over the low wall, she paused. She could hear sounds coming from nearby, strange, panting sounds that she had never heard before. A dog, perhaps?

She stayed still, listening. Not a dog, for there were hasty, quiet words being gasped out.

Two voices. A woman. And a man. Einar.

Cautiously, she went slowly forward, keeping in the shadows. When she came to the side of Olva's house, she peered around the corner. Then she gasped, her hand flying to her mouth in surprise.

Einar was there, all too recognizable. And a woman—the tall, blond woman—with the bodice of her gown pulled down to her waist and her skirt lifted to her thighs. His head was down, his mouth on her naked breasts, and one of his hands caressed her exposed leg as he pressed her against the wall.

Meradyce turned away. She should leave. Go back to bed.

She peeked around the corner again. She knew, of course, how babies were made, but she had never actually seen a man and a woman together.

Her breathing began to quicken, her blood to rush through her veins. What would it be like, to be in Einar's arms?

The woman's legs went around Einar's waist, and he thrust against her. The woman moaned softly, her head thrown back. Her hands clutched Einar's shoulders tightly as she cried out.

Flushing with shame that she had watched, Meradyce stepped back, then turned, determined to return to Olva's house.

And found herself staring at a man's chest.

His lust satisfied, Einar moved away from Ingemar's willing body.

Ingemar pulled up her bodice and tied the drawstring, an equally satisfied smile on her face. "You could not even wait to get me to your bed, Einar?"

He grinned. "No."

"Shall we go there now?"

"If you like," he said, adjusting his breeches. He had no wish to find Ingemar beside him in the morning, but she had fulfilled a need, and letting her keep him warm tonight was not such a bad idea.

Ingemar looked at him with a far from friendly expression. "If you don't want me, tell me."

Oh, that game again, he thought. "Of course I do."

"To make love to."

"Yes."

Ingemar tied the knot at her neck slowly. It was time she caught a husband, and she liked Einar very much. Not as much as Lars, perhaps, but Lars was not a chieftain's son.

And Einar was an amazing lover, as well as a fine warrior who always brought home the best booty. He would make a good husband, if any woman could ever drive Nissa and her adulteries from his memory. It was true he could be cold and distant and arrogant, but surely that was Nissa's fault.

Ingemar decided it was time to see how the wind filled her sails. She had been sure she was close to snaring Einar until he returned with that Saxon witch. "You want me in your bed, but not to marry?"

The look on Einar's face was cool and indifferent. "Ingemar, I have never said I would marry you."

"You just like to play with me."

He reached out and pulled her close. "Yes, just as you like to play with me. Shall we have some more games tonight, my beautiful Ingemar, before I sail for Hedeby?"

"The other women say you think that Saxon wench is more beautiful," Ingemar said, with pouting lips. She was well aware that pouting emphasized their ruddy fullness. "And they say you have given her a whole chest of clothing."

Einar chuckled as his arms encircled her in the chill night air. "You should also know, then, that Svend has put her in my care. She cannot run around naked, or I would have to fight half the men in the village over her. I do not want to waste my time." He began to kiss Ingemar's neck. "I have other ways I would rather spend it."

Ingemar arched backward, enjoying his caresses and convinced there was yet a chance for a marriage with the chieftain's finest son. She drew back slightly. "Why do you go to Hedeby?"

"To arrange a ransom."

"For the Saxons?"

"Yes."

Relieved and happy, Ingemar kissed Einar passionately. The Saxon would be ransomed, then gone. No other village woman could compete with Ingemar for beauty—and surely Einar already appreciated her other talents!

Lost in her dreams of marriage, Ingemar suddenly heard a low cough behind them.

Einar opened his eyes, his lips still on Ingemar's, and saw Lars standing at the back of the nearest building, his hand on the arm of the Saxon woman.

To his surprise, Einar felt himself blush as he let go of Ingemar and stepped away. "What are you doing here?" he demanded in Saxon.

When she did not answer, he asked the same question of Lars.

"I found her behind here," Lars replied.

"It was a good thing it was not Ull or one of the others who saw her," Einar said to Lars as he went closer.

Glaring at Meradyce, he continued in the Saxon tongue. "Do you not realize how stupid it is to wander around the village alone?"

He was angry, very angry. But Meradyce had seen the guilty start he gave when he saw her, and then the way he let go of the woman. The knowledge that he was embarrassed gave her a strange sense of exultation. She returned his stare calmly. "I could not sleep. Nor could you, I see."

He reached out and grabbed her arm, pulling her close. By Thor's hammer, now she looked less sure of herself! He grinned slowly and whispered, "Did you enjoy what you saw?"

She tried to move away, but he held her tight, and in the moon's bright light, he realized she was blushing.

"I saw nothing!"

"Liar!" he whispered, chuckling. He let go of her and she stumbled back. "Do not even think of doing anything that foolish again. You are lucky it was Lars who found you and not . . . someone else."

He turned to Lars. "Take her to Olva's house."

Lars nodded, his glance straying to Ingemar, reminding Einar that Ingemar was waiting.

"Sleep well, my friend," Einar said.

Lars nodded again, took hold of the woman's arm and began walking toward Olva's house.

Einar went back to Ingemar. "Come," he said, heading for his house. When he reached it, he kicked open the door and tugged Ingemar inside.

Einar spent the rest of the night in Ingemar's arms, telling himself he didn't care that the Saxon woman had seen them making love. He was sure she had, even if she denied it. If he wanted to make love to every woman in the village, it was none of her concern.

Maybe she had imagined herself in Ingemar's place, her arms clutching his shoulders, her legs around his waist pulling him in farther and deeper, her soft moans filling the quiet night, her back arching, thrusting her breasts closer to his lips...

When he took Ingemar again, Einar kept his eyes open so he would not forget whose body he was enjoying. He owed Ingemar that much.

Chapter Six

Over the next few days, Meradyce began to feel a part of Olva's household, although she remained on the fringe of life in the Viking village. She tended to such women as needed or wanted her help, and the rest of her day she spent inside Olva's longhouse.

Betha usually stayed near her, except for a few times when she ventured out in Endredi's care. She often helped the older girl, or Olva, when she was not playing with her kitten.

Adelar, however, had been spending more and more of his time in Einar's company. At first Meradyce had been concerned. Not for his safety—Adelar was worth far more alive and unharmed—but she wanted to know why the Viking kept Adelar with him. He was kind and generous and even respectful to Adelar, although the boy was the son of an enemy.

Looking up from the wool she was combing for Olva, Meradyce glanced at Endredi as the girl sat near the hearth, preparing the evening meal. Perhaps Einar allowed Adelar to be with him simply because Adelar was a boy. It would be unfortunate if he preferred the company of another man's son to that of his own daughter, but not unusual.

It *was* unusual that Einar apparently had no other children. She knew full well that he didn't lack for female attention—she blushed hotly every time she remembered that night when she had seen him with Ingemar—and it seemed incredible that a man that virile had only one child.

It occurred to her that perhaps he had other women, and other children, in another village.

She frowned as she remembered that Adelar had gone down to the fjord with Einar to watch the men load a ship. Still, there were many ships in the fjord, and just because Einar was involved did not mean that he was leaving....

Adelar came into the longhouse, his face a picture of curiosity. "Where is Einar going?"

Meradyce kept her eyes on her work.

"Hedeby," Olva said, pausing in her spinning.

Meradyce saw Endredi's surprised face as she hesitated for a brief moment in the preparation of the evening meal. The girl went back to work quickly, but Meradyce had seen her sorrowful eyes. Obviously, Einar told his daughter nothing of his comings and goings.

"Where is Hedeby?" Adelar demanded, coming closer to stand near Meradyce.

"Five days' sail to the south."

"Is it a town?"

"A big one."

"Why is he going?"

"To trade."

"When will he be back?"

Olva shrugged. "When he gets back. It is hard to know. It depends on the trading, I suppose."

Meradyce forced her hands to keep combing and her voice to sound unconcerned. "I thought it was too near winter to sail any more."

"Not to Hedeby. It is not so far across the open sea."

Meradyce nodded. A new realization had sent all thoughts of other women and children from her mind.

If Einar was gone, who would protect her?

Perhaps he would have his friend, the man named Lars, stay behind. "Do all the warriors go?"

Olva shook her head. "No." She gave Meradyce a shrewd look. "Have no fear. No one would dare give Einar any cause to fight. Einar takes his duties and his responsibilities very seriously indeed."

Meradyce smiled slightly. Although Olva was the Viking's mother, Meradyce felt confident in Olva's estimation of the men in the village. Surely no one would want to challenge a warrior like Einar.

But there was one man who might dare.... "The red-haired man, does he go, too?"

"She means Ull," Endredi explained as Adelar hunkered down beside the hearth. His hand reached for a piece of bread, but Endredi slapped it. Adelar moved away.

"Ah." Olva frowned slightly. "No, he never goes on voyages that are just for trade. He *claims* it is unbecoming a warrior to act like a merchant, but everyone knows it is because most merchants get the better of him in a bargain."

"Is your son a good trader, or does he agree with this Ull?"

Olva grinned. "Einar likes to win, whether in a fight or in trade. And he has been taught by the best at both." Her grin disappeared. "Maybe if Einar was not so good at everything, Ull would hate him less."

Meradyce paused in her work. "Ull hates Einar?"

Olva began weaving again. "Perhaps hate is too strong a word. But they have always competed with one another." She looked at Meradyce, her meaning unmistakable.

Meradyce turned away to hide the flush stealing over her face. She had no wish to be the prize fought for by two men, especially two Vikings. She wished she was as homely as a sow.

"Einar can beat anyone," Adelar said decisively. "Could I go to Hedeby, too?"

"Certainly not," Meradyce answered quickly.

"Why not?"

"I need you here."

Adelar nodded, apparently satisfied. "When do we eat?"

Olva laughed softly and put the spun wool into a basket. "Boys are all the same. When do we eat? I am hungry!" She went up to Adelar and gave him a squeeze. "We will ask Endredi to make some fish stew, will we?"

Betha looked at them, her face full of dismay. "I do not like fish!" she whispered to Meradyce.

"I think Endredi's fish stew will be very special. Let us try it. We do not want to hurt her feelings."

Betha looked doubtful, but Meradyce knew the little girl hated to hurt anyone's feelings.

Endredi gave Betha one of her rare smiles. "Do not worry, I will make a special bit for you, Betha, with only a *little* fish."

Meradyce smiled her thanks to Endredi, but the girl merely nodded and went back to work.

Meradyce sighed softly. She had learned from Olva that Endredi's mother had indeed died in childbirth. That was all the information Olva had offered, and her pained expression had prevented Meradyce from questioning her any further. Nevertheless, she thought she could guess why Einar ignored his daughter: he blamed her for her mother's death. He must have cared for Endredi's mother very much.

Meradyce sighed again, which made Betha get up and come to her, her face grave.

"Are you sick?" Betha asked quietly.

"No, dearest, I am only a little tired."

Betha nodded and enveloped Meradyce in a loving embrace.

Einar entered an inn in Hedeby and scanned the room. Sure enough, the Saxon named Selwyn was there, barely discernible behind a table in a dark corner. As usual, he had a mug of ale in one hand and a serving wench in the other.

The other patrons, men from countries scattered over the known world, looked up from their dice or their friends to stare at the Viking giant filling the doorway. He held his ax loosely in one hand, and a huge sword dangled from his belt. His shoulders and arms seemed enormous, and his eyes were ringed with black.

Quickly their attention went back to their games and their drinks, lest they inadvertently offend the golden-haired warrior.

Einar walked over to Selwyn's table and sat down, adjusting his sword and laying his ax out in front of him. The serving girl's eyes widened, but she smiled when she realized Einar was looking at her.

"Ah, Einar!" Selwyn said with a grin that exposed his few remaining teeth. He pushed the wench away. "Later, my lovely. There's other business to be done first."

The girl gave both men an impertinent grin and walked off, swaying her hips.

Selwyn watched her go with an appreciative chortle, then turned to Einar. He liked the tall blond Viking, as much as a Saxon could like any Viking. For one thing, Einar and his men had increased Selwyn's personal wealth. For another, Einar was one Viking whose word you could trust. "Well, my friend, what can I do for you, eh?"

"I want you to take a message to the Saxon Kendric."

"The thane? The leader of the village a band of no-good, berserker Vikings sacked and burned after taking his children?"

Einar smiled slowly. Selwyn must have found out about the children in his own secretive way. "The same."

Selwyn leaned forward. "I take it we are discussing ransom?"

"Yes."

Selwyn frowned. "It's too risky to make such a journey now. The winter..."

Einar waited patiently as Selwyn continued to protest. Once Selwyn knew the amount of the ransom, Einar had little doubt that the Saxon would swim to Kendric if necessary, in order to collect a large percentage for acting as go-between.

Finally, when Selwyn obviously thought that Einar had heard enough to appreciate the magnitude of the task, he got down to business. "Exactly what amount of ransom are we talking about?"

"For the boy, one thousand pieces of silver. Fifty for the little girl."

Selwyn's eyes widened, then narrowed. "And for the woman?"

"Nothing."

Selwyn slumped against the wall. "Nothing?" He frowned. "I think you're making a big mistake there, my friend. Kendric would pay plenty..." He stopped when Einar lifted his hand and casually rested it on the shaft of his ax. "She's alive?"

"Yes."

"Well, that's good, that is. Kendric will pay a bag of silver for her."

"Why?"

"I heard she was the most beautiful woman in the country."

"What else?"

Selwyn took a long gulp of ale. "She is the best midwife for miles around."

Einar shifted impatiently, wondering what the greedy little man was trying to hide. "There is something more, is there not, Selwyn?" he demanded.

"Well, Einar, there are only rumors..."

"What rumors?"

"There are rumors Kendric..."

"What?"

"Kendric was very fond of her."

Einar leaned closer. "*How* fond?"

Selwyn shrugged. "Fond."

Suddenly Einar reached across the table and grabbed Selwyn by his tunic. "A man can be fond of his dog or his horse. *How fond?*"

Selwyn's eyes were wide with fear, and when he spoke, Einar had no doubt that he was telling the truth as he knew it. "I heard Kendric wanted her for his mistress, but she wouldn't have him, not while he was a married man."

Einar let go of Selwyn's tunic and gestured for the serving wench. "More ale," he muttered when she sauntered over.

Selwyn rubbed his throat. "Of course, she might have been playing a very clever game. Kendric likes women and the village gossip is that he will soon be made an *ealdorman* and a powerful man. Maybe she wanted to inflame his desire before she—"

"She will not be ransomed."

Selwyn stared into his ale. "Perhaps you are right." His gaze flicked to the Viking. "She will not be worth nearly so much, now, I take it?"

"Enough about the woman."

Selwyn shrugged and finished his mug of ale.

"How soon can you get the message to Kendric?"

"Hard to say, hard to say. Depends on the weather. Some ships are still going from the south over that way, but not for long."

Einar knew Selwyn was only trying to increase his own payment. "Tell him we will come in the spring with the children."

Selwyn nodded, his small eyes looking more like a ferret's with each passing moment. "And me, Einar? How much do you offer me for the risks I will take?"

"A hundredth portion of the ransom."

Selwyn grinned. "That is fair. That is fair."

"Tell him if there is treachery, he will regret it."

The Saxon smirked and once again spoke in a conspiratorial whisper. "You are sure about the woman, Einar? Even if—well, Kendric was not very pleased to hear she was gone when he got back, I heard. Might as well try ransoming the woman, too. After all, she may still be worth something as a midwife."

"Will he pay for his children?"

"Yes, yes, of course he will."

"What is he like, this thane?"

Selwyn looked at his empty mug. When Einar had paid for another drink, he replied, rubbing his beard. "Pretty well off, I would say. Ambitious fellow, though."

"He is an old man?"

"About your age, I would guess. Good-looking, too. Excellent fighter, so I hear."

"His people—they follow him gladly?"

"Well, he is clever." He gave Einar a sidelong glance. "You didn't get many slaves, did you?"

Einar's hand gripped his ax tightly for a moment. "What do the people say about *her?*"

"Proud, very proud. She will not mix with people. Some say because she's proud of her looks. Others, proud of her skills. They're all a little afraid of her, I think." He leaned across the table, his mouth twisted into a leer. "What do you say, Einar? Was she proud when you dragged her off to your ship?"

Einar had heard enough. He stood and looked down at Selwyn. "Tell the Saxon what I want for his children, and then tell him he should have taken the woman while he could. She is . . . very pleasing. I will not send her back."

Einar turned and walked away, sure that Selwyn would deliver the message just as he had spoken it. Let the Saxon believe he had lost the woman he wanted to the Vikings. Kendric was a traitor to his own people, and from Selwyn's expression it was clear that Kendric had betrayed them, too, by posting a sentinel. Let him lay awake imagining Meradyce in another man's arms.

It would be small recompense for Kendric's treachery—and Einar's own sleepless nights, laying awake, thinking of her, knowing that she was close by. . . .

He stepped out into the bustling streets of Hedeby. It was a large and well-fortified town, surrounded by a wall that joined a vast earthwork stretching all the way to Hollingstedt on the Northern Sea as a defense against attacks from the south. The earthen wall around Hedeby had but two gates. Those—and the harbor—were the only way into the town, which stood on the border of the Frankish kingdom.

The town itself seemed huge, noisy, smelly and crowded to Einar. He hated places like this, filled with strangers, thieves and foreigners. He much preferred the quiet of his own village, where he knew everyone and they knew him.

Hurrying along, he headed toward the inn where he had left his shipmates. He alone dealt with Selwyn, for he alone was in Svend's confidence and spoke the language of the Saxons fluently. It was just as well, for Einar had no wish for his men to engage in fighting more than necessary—and they would have.

"Einar!"

He turned and looked down a narrow lane, then grinned when he saw a plump man bustling up to him.

"Einar, my lad! Well met! How do you fare?"

"Thorston! You old thief! What are you doing here? I thought you would be home by now!"

"So did I, boy, so did I!" Thorston clapped a friendly hand on Einar's shoulder, reaching up to do it. "I had a chance to buy some fine wine for a bargain price, but it meant I had to stay another few days. Tell me, how is your mother?"

Einar smiled warmly at his mother's second husband. Like Hamar's mother before her, Olva had divorced Svend when he brought home another woman from a raid.

Einar had been a youth of fourteen when Olva married Thorston, after several months of arduous pursuit. He knew she cared for the round-faced merchant very much, even though Thorston spent several weeks of the year on trading voyages. Secretly Einar thought that was one reason his mother had agreed to marry him: she still maintained quite a bit of independence. And when Thorston returned, there was always a joyful reunion.

"She is well, but I think you should be prepared for a scolding. You know how much she worries when a journey is delayed."

"Are you staying at Nils' or on the ship?" Thorston asked.

"This time I sleep on the ship."

"Just wondering, Einar," Thorston said with a broad grin. "I know Nils' daughters would gladly find room for you."

"Thank you for your concern, but they are too skinny."

"Not the youngest one. She is as ripe as..."

"I will have to tell Olva about your knowledge of Nils' daughters," Einar said, keeping a straight face.

"Now, Einar, I am only joking! Say, I suppose there is room on your vessel for a few casks of wine, eh? Then I can get home that much faster."

"How many are a few?"

"Twenty—maybe thirty if I can talk the fellow down a bit more... Let us say forty."

Einar chuckled. If there was a way to make ten silver pieces into twenty, Thorston knew it. Because of his stepfather, Einar was a very wealthy man. "I think we can manage that. Anything else?"

"Not much. Some cloth, jewelry, some spices."

"It is a good thing we did not come to trade ourselves."

"No? Then what brought you here?"

"Ransom."

"Really? Tell me all about it. And tell me about Olva. Will she be very angry this time, do you think? I bought her the most beautiful brooch I could find, just in case."

Einar told him about the raid and the guests staying in Olva's house.

Einar did not tell him how beautiful the Saxon woman was, nor about the jealousy that had filled him when he learned that the Saxon leader who had wanted her was young, handsome and rich.

As Einar spoke, Thorston masked his surprise as well as he could. Einar—bringing home a woman! Perhaps the young man was merely becoming more like his natural father as he aged, but Thorston did not think so. This woman must be something special.

Einar went on to speak of Olva and of life in the village. He said nothing about Endredi, but Thorston did not expect him to and knew better than to ask.

Thorston had planned on staying a few more days in Hedeby, but he immediately decided that, for once, he would forgo some profit. He had to see Einar's woman.

Chapter Seven

Meradyce smiled at Asa. "Everything seems very well indeed."

"But I am so big!" the girl complained softly, her brow wrinkled with concern. "Svend will think I am going to be as fat as a . . . as a pig."

"All women think that. You will be slender again."

The young woman did not look convinced, but she said nothing more as she walked to the door of Olva's house.

"Watch how you go! Be careful not to slip in the mud," Meradyce cautioned.

The rain had finally stopped, after days of lashing wind and storms, but the ground was still treacherous.

Meradyce went back to grinding up some herbs. Olva and the others had gone down to the fjord, for a ship had been sighted.

Einar and his men had not yet returned from the place called Hedeby, no doubt due to the weather, and Olva was hopeful that it was Einar's vessel moving slowly through the fjord.

Meradyce told herself she didn't care who it was. Their comings and goings had nothing to do with her, although if the children wanted to watch, there would be no harm in it.

She heard someone enter and turned around, expecting to see Olva or Endredi.

It was the man named Ull. His unkempt mane of red hair straggled about his shoulders, and his bulk made the room feel as tiny as a goat's shed.

"What . . . what do you want?" Meradyce asked as he came toward her.

He answered in his own tongue, his voice low and guttural.

Meradyce forced herself to look at his face. He grinned, which made him seem a little less fierce. Then he put his hand to his abdomen and belched.

Meradyce hid her smile. Wind! What did they expect, when they drank ale by the buckets? Nevertheless, she supposed she could prepare something to sooth his stomach. Something that would taste horrible, to pay him back for all the discomfort he had caused her by staring at her.

She kept her back to him as she found the appropriate herbs and mixed them together in a small bowl. When she was finished, she turned around and held out the bowl, gesturing for him to drink it.

He took it but came closer, saying something quietly, still staring at her.

Meradyce took a step back, her heart beginning to pound with dread. Where was Olva? Where was Endredi?

Why had Einar gone away?

Ull reached out and grabbed her hand. She opened her mouth to scream, then realized he was putting something metallic in her palm. It was a small, circular brooch made of silver.

She glanced at his face as he nodded and spoke again.

Suddenly there was another shadow in the room. "What in the name of Odin's eye is this?" Einar roared, glaring at Ull.

Ull spun around. Then he grinned like a cat in a barrel of cod. "She is making me feel better."

Einar strode into the room, trying to ignore the Saxon woman, her lovely eyes lighting with recognition, her luxuriant hair, her beautiful lips parted as if to greet him. "What are you doing here alone?" he demanded.

She straightened her slender shoulders. "I am not alone."

"So I see. I told you not to walk around the village by yourself."

"I was not walking around. Ull came here. What was I supposed to do, push him out the door?"

She knew Ull's name! How many other men's names did she know?

"Unfortunate weather, Einar, keeping you from home so long," Ull said.

Einar swiveled toward him, dearly wishing he could smash Ull's smug face into the ground. "Yes, it was," he replied. "But I am here now."

He faced Meradyce. "What did he want?" he demanded in Saxon.

"I was making a potion for him."

Einar noticed the bowl in Ull's hands. "Take your medicine and go."

Ull seemed in no particular hurry to leave, however. "How was business in Hedeby? Profitable, I trust?"

"Yes—not that it is any concern of yours. Just as this woman is no concern of yours."

Ull shrugged his shoulders. "I felt ill, so I came to see her. Surely there is no harm in that—unless you are going to make her your woman."

Einar clenched his teeth, but his voice was calm when he spoke. "You know as well as I that Svend has said she is not to be harmed."

"I was not thinking of *harming* her, Einar. Svend did not say she could not marry. She would make a fine wife." Ull sauntered toward the door.

"You already have two fine wives."

Ull paused on the threshold and turned. "Nothing the matter with having three."

"I do not think she would agree. The Christians only have one husband."

Ull smiled. "If she agreed to be my wife, Einar, I would gladly divorce both Ilsa and Reinhild. Now, I must be seeing to my horses. Good day."

As Ull strolled out, Einar's hands balled into fists.

Suddenly he felt a soft touch on his arm. Her hand. On his arm.

He whirled around. Her eyes widened as if with fright and she backed up a little.

Thor's hammer, why should he always feel like a vicious brute when he was near her?

"What did he say?" she asked.

Einar moved away. He could think better when he wasn't near enough to touch her. "He says he would like to marry you."

A horrified expression came to Meradyce's face, which pleased him greatly. "I told him I did not think you were interested."

"No, I am not."

Einar thought it would be best to avoid the subject of marriage. "What did he need the medicine for?"

To his surprise, and even greater pleasure, she smiled. "Wind."

Einar grinned back. Wind! Only Ull would think of courting a woman by coming to her with that excuse!

She was still smiling, and for the first time he looked at her not as a beautiful woman, but as a companion sharing a joke.

"He will not like his medicine," she said softly. "It will taste horrible."

"He deserves it."

She flushed. "It will also..."

"What?"

"He will need to be near a bucket."

This time Einar threw back his head and roared with laughter.

And then he realized something else. She was laughing, too. No, not really laughing. She was *giggling*, like a young girl.

He thought it was the most wonderful giggle he had ever heard. He fell silent, to hear her better.

Meradyce stopped giggling and looked at him, her eyes still filled with the happiness of shared laughter.

He went toward her. Suddenly, everything changed. Meradyce saw his expression alter from simple joy at her to desire. A hunger came into his gray eyes, and this time, she felt an answering need within herself. Passion, strong and primeval, began to throb though her body in a way she had never experienced, so potent that it was almost frightening.

The door opened and Endredi came inside, breaking the current that seemed to flow between them as she paused awkwardly on the threshold.

Einar spun around. "Where were you?" he demanded harshly as he glared at his confused daughter.

"I . . . I was down at the ship. Did you not see . . ."

The poor girl was trembling with fear. Meradyce hurried to her, frowning at Einar. He had no cause to be so severe with her.

Einar caught Meradyce's accusing look and knew she thought he was being unduly unkind. Already it seemed she had forgotten her fear of Ull, but if Endredi had been here, Ull would never have dared to linger.

Or maybe the Saxon had not been afraid of Ull at all. Maybe she had only been afraid of discovery.

Perhaps she was just like Nissa.

At that moment, Thorston bustled in the door, carrying a large box. He greeted Einar, who did not reply as he pushed past him on his way out the door.

The plump little man shrugged, then his round face beamed with a wide smile as he came toward Meradyce and Endredi. Olva, Betha and Adelar followed close behind.

The man set down the chest before giving Endredi a fatherly embrace. Then he began to stare unabashedly at Meradyce.

"This is my husband, Thorston," Olva explained with a warm smile. "He came home with Einar from Hedeby—and about time, too!"

The man winked at Meradyce and said something she could not understand.

"He *claims* he found too many bargains." Olva grinned. "As long as it was that, and not women!"

Thorston seemed to guess what she was saying, for he gave Endredi a wounded frown before launching into another spate of talk.

Meradyce went and sat beside Betha, who was busy delving into the chest.

Olva's husband! She hadn't expected that. He certainly looked like a pleasant man, but now the house would be even more crowded.

It suddenly seemed as if the winter was going to be very long indeed.

"You did not say she could not marry one of us," Ull said for the tenth time, getting even redder in the face as he glared at Svend.

Svend gave a disgruntled sigh. He should have known a woman like the Saxon wench would be trouble, especially with a malcontent like Ull about. He doubted that Ull was seriously interested in the woman. Oh, like every man in the hall, he probably wanted to bed her, but Svend was also sure that Ull wanted to make divisions in the village.

Unfortunately, Ull had friends among the warriors, who would back him as long as the trouble was nothing more serious than a woman. At least he did not have friends who would help him seize power.

"Svend said she was free," Einar replied, still as cool as the first breeze of winter as he sat beside his father, his legs slung over the arm of the huge oaken chair he had brought home from a raid.

Svend cleared his throat. Maybe *he* should have married the Saxon woman. His two older wives would not have cared—but Asa would have been upset.

He glanced at Einar. His son was trying very hard to look as if the woman's status was merely a question of law.

"I was not trying to take her against her will," Ull said, clearly wondering why Svend was letting Einar answer for him.

"You had no business coming anywhere near her," Einar said coldly.

"I am a free man, she is a free woman. Why not?"

Svend raised his hand, ready to deliver his judgment. "The woman is free, as Ull says. So I say this. She may be courted as any free woman."

"Am I still responsible for her, then?" Einar demanded.

Svend shook his head. "No. *I* will be."

Ull looked surprised, but said nothing. He was free to pursue the woman, but he had wanted to do so mostly to aggravate Einar. Now Einar had no reason to be involved—and if Ull offended the woman, he would offend not the chieftain's son, but the chieftain himself.

Einar shrugged his shoulders and lifted his drinking horn. It mattered nothing to him if some other man wanted the Saxon. He watched Ull swagger away to another part of the hall.

On the other hand, Ull did not deserve to win so easily.

Ingemar, standing near the doorway, smiled. Einar need not go near that Saxon cow anymore. Of that, she would make sure.

"Enough talk about women," Svend bellowed. "Where is the storyteller?"

As the poet took his place, Einar noticed Lars sitting not far off and gestured for his friend to move closer. When he did, Einar leaned toward him. "I want to ask a favor of you, old friend."

Lars grinned. "What?"

"I want you to court the Saxon woman."

Lars looked at him, obviously appalled. "Are you mad?"

Einar sat back and grinned. "You cannot tell me you do not think she is beautiful."

"Beautiful she may be, but I am not interested in coming between you and Ull."

"What do you mean?"

Lars looked at his friend intently. "Einar, do you think I am stupid? You want the woman yourself."

"I do not."

"Fine. Lie to yourself."

"It is no lie. I do not want her—or any woman in particular."

Lars looked away. "Why not let me help you by courting one of your other women? Ingemar, perhaps."

Einar laughed loudly. "I need no help with Ingemar!"

Lars shrugged and spoke quietly. "Then you get no help from me."

"I want Ull to have some competition. He already thinks too highly of himself."

"He is not the only one."

Einar was surprised by the bitterness in his friend's voice and looked at him. "Are you saying I am as conceited as Ull?"

Lars smiled as if all were well. "Not as conceited, but you do not suffer from a poor opinion of your abilities. I will say, Einar, that if you truly want Ull to have some competition, you should court the woman yourself."

"Come outside. I need to speak with you," Einar demanded gruffly.

Meradyce pulled her covers up to her chin and stared at him. He was beside her bed, wearing his long fur cloak.

"Why outside?" Olva demanded from her bed across the narrow room. "Einar, are you drunk?"

"I am not drunk. I want to speak with her *alone*."

Thorston sat up. "It is cold out there."

Betha stirred beside Meradyce, who glanced at Adelar, asleep on his pallet. Unless she wanted them awakened, she had better comply.

She began to get out of her bed carefully, so as not to disturb Betha.

"Really, Einar, could this not wait?" Olva whispered.

"No."

His mother clucked her disapproval, but lay back down. So did Thorston.

Meradyce drew on her gown and her shoes. Einar went to the door and went out. She followed.

Once outside, she wrapped her arms about herself. The night was very cold, and she could see frost in the moonlight. If she was any judge, it might even snow before much longer. "Well, what is it?" she asked. She was not going to walk far away, not at night. Not with him.

He turned to her, but his face was in shadow and she could not see his eyes. "Svend has decided that you may be courted."

"What? What do you mean?"

"Have you never been courted before?"

"Yes, I have." Which was true. A few men had asked her to be their wife. "But I have no wish to be courted."

"Especially by a Viking," he added.

"By *any* man."

He tilted his head quizzically. "Do you not like men?"

"Generally, yes."

"That is good."

"But I do not want to marry," she said quickly, nervous at the tone of his last words.

"Every woman wants to marry."

"Not me."

He came a little closer, and she hugged herself even tighter. "Why not?"

"Because . . . because I do not." Her teeth began to chatter. "It is cold, and if you do not mind, I would like to go back—"

He took off his robe. "Put this on. I want to know why a woman does not want a husband."

"No, thank you. I do not have to explain myself to you. I just want to go back to bed."

He stepped forward and put the cloak around her. It smelled of ale and old leather and salt water, but it was warm. "If there is going to be trouble, I should know."

"What kind of trouble?"

"Competition, among the men."

"And as my protector, you are concerned."

Einar did not answer.

"You need not be. I have no desire to marry, so there should be no competition."

"Maybe they will think I only want to keep you for myself."

At his softly spoken words, she wondered what it would be like to be courted by a man like Einar, but she quickly tried to dismiss the notion. "I will not marry."

He heard the resolve in her voice. "Why not?" he asked, even as he told himself it should not matter to him. "Why not?" He went closer, wanting to see her eyes.

She looked at him steadily. "It would not be just. I cannot give any man my heart."

"Perhaps your heart is not what a man would be interested in."

She turned away, but he put his hand gently on her arm. When he spoke, his voice was low and serious. "You could have any man you wanted, and all his wealth. Is that not enough?"

"Perhaps for you a body in the bed is sufficient. I would want more than that from a husband—but it would not be fair to ask for what I can no longer give."

"What are you saying?" he demanded, needing to know what other men had been to her. "You are not a virgin?

Meradyce did not flinch or try to move away, but her eyes shone with scorn and defiance. "That is all you understand. I have loved and been loved in a better, purer way."

Filled with anger and jealousy and an overwhelming dismay, Einar pulled her to him and kissed her fiercely, his mouth plundering hers. He would make her forget her other men.

For one instant, he thought she was going to respond, but she stood unmoving, unyielding, unfeeling. With an oath, he let go of her, raising his hand.

"Will you strike me now, Einar?" she asked in a voice as cold as the water of the fjord. "Is that how you intend to make me want you?"

He lowered his hand with a mighty effort and shrugged casually. "I do not want you. I have plenty of women, and I do not think you would be worth the effort."

With that, he turned and disappeared into the night.

Chapter Eight

Einar sighed as he closed his eyes and leaned against the wall of the bathhouse. The rocks were well-heated, and he had just thrown another ladle of water over them, sending steam into the air.

Hamar sighed, too. "This is wonderful. Life is good, Einar. A fine wife, a healthy son—what more could a man want, eh?"

"A fast horse, a faster ship, piles of silver, two women in your bed, both doing their best to arouse you...."

Hamar looked at his handsome brother. He was not sure if Einar was serious or not until he saw the grin on his brother's face.

"A fast ship, maybe, for you, I grant you."

"And the women. Do not forget the women."

Hamar sat up. "I do not believe that, Einar—or why would you argue with Ull over the Saxon wench?"

"I like to argue with Ull. It keeps him in his place."

"Huh," Hamar snorted.

This time Einar opened one eye. "You do not think she is worth arguing over?"

"Maybe. If I were not already married, definitely. I am just surprised you do, that is all."

"How is your son?"

"Thriving. What a grip he has, too!" Hamar gave Einar a sidelong glance. "If you do court this woman, will it be to marry her—or just to annoy Ull?"

"To annoy Ull."

"It is a fine thing to have a son, Einar."

"You sound like Svend." Einar stood up. "Ready for the river?"

Hamar rose. "If you are."

With a yell, they burst out of the bathhouse and ran the short distance to the river, where they dove in. The water was freezing, so they ran out again with another yell, and laughed together as they threw themselves down on the bank.

Only then did they notice the women doing some washing farther down the river. The village women were used to such a sight, but Einar saw at once that Meradyce, a bundle of wet cloth in her hands, was standing close by. Obviously she had completed her washing and was returning to the village, until the sight of two naked men dashing for the river had halted her progress.

Einar watched her face redden as he stood up, facing her boldly.

The Saxon ducked her head, not looking.

"You are offending her," Hamar chided, chuckling. "Can you not see she is embarrassed?"

"If the sight of a naked man is too much for her, she should not come near the bathhouse," Einar said with a laugh.

When Meradyce saw Einar's brazen grin and heard his mocking tone, she stopped. She did not know exactly what he had said, but she did not have to. It was enough to know that he was making a jest at her expense.

Perhaps he thought she blushed because she had never seen a naked man before, but with her medicinal skills she had been called upon to tend many wounds—and she had seen more than one warrior with nothing to clothe his body.

She thought she had intruded where she had no right, but a glance at the other women made it clear they were amused, not appalled.

Except for the blond woman named Ingemar. She was watching intently, a smug smile on her pretty face.

Meradyce stood her ground and, returning boldness for boldness, surveyed his body slowly, remembering well the night he had looked at hers.

She began at his feet, up his long, muscular legs, past his genitals, his chest, his shoulders and ending with his face. Then her gaze returned to the portion of his body below his waist and above his knees. "It is a very cold day, I see," she said. "You should take care you do not catch a chill."

To her delight, his derisive expression faded and he marched past her to the bathhouse.

"What did she say?" Hamar demanded as he followed Einar. "Well, what?"

Einar yanked on his clothing. "Nothing important."

Ingemar watched the men leave, then went back to her washing, pounding her dirty linen against the rock as if it was Meradyce's head. Ilsa, working beside her, had also watched the confrontation between the Saxon and Einar with dissatisfaction.

"I tell you, it is disgusting!" Ingemar said. "Comes here and makes eyes at our men! The slut!"

"Walking around with her snoot in the air like she was the queen of the Saxons—when she ought to be sweeping my hearth like any slave!" Ilsa added, her voice even more strident than usual as she wrung out a shift as if she was wringing the neck of a chicken.

Reinhild swished her soiled linen in the river. "Soon it will be too cold to do any washing," she said, hoping to change the course of the talk. She liked the Saxon woman, but more importantly, she knew the village needed her.

The other two women ignored her. "You are absolutely right," Ingemar said. "I think Svend's finally in his dotage. Why should she be treated any differently than any other captive? She is not noble, nor even a thane's wife or daughter. She is no better than a serving wench."

"Sh!" Ilsa hissed as Asa, heavily pregnant, came slowly down the path toward the river, a small basket of wash balanced on her hip.

"It is good to have a midwife," Reinhild said.

"You had your son without one," Ilsa replied defiantly.

Reinhild nodded, but Ingemar could see the younger woman did not realize the threat the Saxon presented to her. "Imagine—Ull and Einar fighting over her like two children," she said sorrowfully. "Of course I know Einar does not really want her, but you know how he likes to goad Ull—who seems to want the Saxon very much."

Reinhild frowned and Ingemar suppressed a satisfied smile. Reinhild was Ull's newest wife. Her greatest weakness was her sensitivity about her lack of physical beauty, even though every woman in the village considered her the most likable of Ull's women.

Ilsa was better-looking, but she had the tongue of a born complainer, as Ull and everyone else had discovered when he brought her home from a neighboring village. Nothing ever suited her. Some people had wondered why she didn't divorce Ull when he married Reinhild, but others said it was because she knew no other man would take her.

After calling a greeting to Asa, Ingemar leaned nearer and whispered, "It is only her beauty, you know. Take that away, and no man would really want to be bothered with her."

"It is too bad we cannot cast a spell of ugliness on her," Ilsa muttered.

"If only she would leave the men alone!" Reinhild sighed.

"I have just thought of something we can do," Ingemar said, smiling.

The other women moved closer to hear.

Meradyce looked at the woman who ran into the house. Ingemar's eyes were filled with tears and she was wringing her hands in distress. She spoke quickly, gesturing at Meradyce.

Endredi turned to her. "It is one of the children. He has fallen and hurt his leg. It is bleeding a lot."

Meradyce was on her feet in an instant. "I will come at once." She paused. She might need Endredi to act as translator, but if there was a lot of blood ... "Wait here until Olva returns with the children. Then ask her to come."

Endredi nodded as Meradyce picked up the first basket she found. She did not know what she would see when she reached the child, so she threw in several small bags of medicines. Some would dull pain, some would stop the flow of blood, some would draw poison from a wound.

Then she followed Ingemar outside, practically running to keep up with the tall woman as they went to a house at the far side of the village. Ingemar ducked under the covering over the door, and so did Meradyce.

She looked around as she straightened. "Where is the child?" she asked the two women who were waiting there.

Einar was on his way to the shipbuilding yard when he heard the scream. A woman's scream. He took off at a run. When he reached the village, he saw a curious crowd gathered outside Ull's house. There was no one screaming now.

He ran to the house and tore the covering from the door.

Ull was not inside. Ilsa and Ingemar rose slowly from the center of the floor where they had been bending over something. Reinhild stood sobbing in the corner, her hands over her face.

Before Einar could speak, he realized it was a person on the floor. A woman. Meradyce.

He went nearer as Meradyce stood slowly, then he gasped when he saw what they had done.

Her hair, her long beautiful hair, lay in masses on the ground. Her face was streaked with dirt, her gown torn. She must have struggled against them, but they had shorn her head as if she were a sheep, leaving each strand of hair no more than a finger in length.

Einar looked at Ingemar, the knife still in her hand. And Ilsa, a satisfied smile on her thin, pinched face.

Meradyce glared at Ilsa and Ingemar. "Tell them," she said slowly and deliberately, "that if they ever touch me again, I will kill them."

There was no doubt in Einar's mind that she meant the words as, with her head held high and shoulders straight, Meradyce walked out of the longhouse.

He heard the shocked murmur of the waiting crowd, but he smiled. Slowly. Coldly. "She said she will kill you if you touch her again. She means it—and if she does not, *I* will."

Ingemar took a step toward him, her eyes pleading. "She is causing too much trouble—"

Einar held up his hand to silence her. "You will never serve me wine or food, or even speak to me again."

Then he left them, going out into the street. Far ahead he could see the Saxon, but to his surprise, she went not to Olva's house, but to his.

Ignoring the crowd of curious onlookers, he followed her quickly. When he entered his house, she was standing with her head lowered and her arms crossed, her back to him.

"Did they hurt you?" he asked softly.

She whirled around to face him—and he was even more surprised. The look in her eyes reminded him of a berserker, a Viking warrior who worked himself into a frenzy before a battle.

"I want Endredi," she said fiercely. "Here. Now."

He stared at her as she barked her commands. "What?"

"I said, I want Endredi. Right away."

"Perhaps my mother—"

"I want no sympathy. I want Endredi. She knows how to keep silent." Meradyce glared at him, willing him to fetch his daughter.

Selwyn had spoken the truth about Meradyce. She was a proud woman—and at this moment, her personal honor and her sense of justice were completely outraged.

She had done nothing to deserve the women's attack. She had not asked to be brought here. If anything, she had only tried to help the Viking women.

But she *was* here, and although she had sought only to do good, her shorn locks were their thanks. If these women wanted a reason to hate her, she would give them one tonight!

Einar frowned. "I will see that they are punished."

"No. I will deal with this."

"You are only a woman—"

"So are they!" She paused for a moment. "Ingemar I know," she said, for the first time not blushing at the memory of the night she had seen her with Einar. "But why did the other women help her?"

"They are Ull's wives."

Meradyce nodded. "I see. Now fetch me Endredi."

"Are you sure—"

She stamped her foot impatiently. "Yes, I am!"

With that, Einar left the house and went to find his daughter.

"Einar?"

Einar looked up as Ull sat beside him in Svend's hall.

"I am sorry about what my wives did."

"You should be."

"I will beat them later for it."

"Keep them away from her from now on."

Ull leaned a little closer. "Does she look—"

He stopped as a woman came into the hall. Einar sat up and stared. All the men in the hall turned toward the door.

It was Meradyce. She had washed what remained of her hair and now it curled around her face, brushing her pale smooth cheeks.

The women had no way of knowing that without the weight of length, Meradyce's hair curled. In fact, the curls were extremely flattering around her lovely face.

Tonight she wore an exquisite blue gown that made her eyes look even more like the sky in summer, and she had a small, round silver brooch pinned to her breast. Einar knew the gown had not been in the chest of clothes he had given her. She must have ransacked the other chests of booty in his house, but it looked so perfect on her, he did not care that she had taken it without his permission. He didn't recognize the brooch, but that had probably come from his house, too.

As she came forward, he—and every other man—saw how the gown clung to her shapely body.

In her hands, she held a silver vessel. She glided toward Ull and Einar as they stared at her.

With an enticing smile, Meradyce leaned forward, giving Einar an even more tantalizing view of her breasts, then picked up his drinking horn and filled it with wine from the container.

Einar did not care that she must have taken some of his finest wine, as well. He felt as if one of the goddesses was acting as his serving maid.

Then, to his great displeasure, she did the same for Ull.

When she straightened, she smiled again at them, one slender, graceful hand reaching up to brush a curl that fell across her face. "If Svend has decreed that I may be courted," she said softly, "I am willing."

Her long, slender fingers touched the brooch. "Thank you for the gift, Ull."

Einar wanted to kill Ull, right then and there.

"And thank you for the gown, Einar." She ran her hand over it, drawing their attention to her shapely body, as if they needed any assistance to notice.

She smiled at them both once again, then turned and walked slowly from the hall.

For the rest of the night, Einar said nothing to Ull, even though Ull continued to drink great quantities of mead as he sat beside him. Nor did Einar speak when the *skald* chose to recite the tale of the cutting of Sif's hair.

Sif, Thor's wife, had been sleeping when the evil god, Loki, crept in and cut off her long golden tresses. In the legend, Thor told Loki he would break every bone in his body unless Sif's hair was replaced. Loki, fearful of Thor's power, went to the dwarves for help. They had woven a wig of spun gold that grew like real hair.

But Loki had contrived to trick the dwarves, too, and his evil plans multiplied until one dwarf finally sewed Loki's mouth shut in revenge. Loki removed the stitches, but he had been humiliated. Not seeing that he had been the one who began all the trouble, he continued to conspire against the other gods from that time on.

Svend and the others cast wary glances at Einar and Ull as the bard spoke, clearly wondering if this hair-cutting would lead to a division among the village like that of the gods. But Einar only stared stonily ahead, and Ull kept draining his drinking horn as if he had a monstrous thirst.

Einar was trying to decide how to handle Mera-dyce's challenge, for a challenge it definitely was. He had long ago decided that no woman was worth fighting over. Nonetheless, her action had filled him with anger, after the surprise had passed.

It was foolish to goad him and dangerous to goad Ull. What did she think she was doing?

Finally Ull asleep, his head falling forward onto his chest. Einar stood up and nodded at Svend, then walked from the hall, mindful that every man's gaze was on him.

The night air was cold and damp, with a brisk breeze from the north. He could taste the salt in the sea wind and wished he could go on a voyage. A long one. Anywhere.

He entered his house and stopped in his tracks.

The Saxon woman turned around, the blue garment in her hands and another, plainer one on her body. "I came to return this," she said, not meeting his gaze.

He took one step toward her. "Why did you do it?"

Her head snapped up, and he saw she was unrepentant. "Do you think this is the first time I have been punished because I am beautiful?"

He had never considered that.

"I am tired of the injustice. Tired of the whispers, the jealous looks, the gossip. Tired of men treating me as if I were a piece of jewelry or cloth."

"This is your method of vengeance?" Even as he asked it, he knew it was true. And he knew how she felt. He, too, had seen jealousy in men's eyes, men who thought Svend favored him only because he was the chieftain's son. Men like Ull.

"Partly," she said as she turned away and put the gown on one of the chests.

"And the other part?"

She turned to face him squarely. "How does a Viking want to die?"

"Fighting," he answered.

"Why?"

"To gain entrance to Valhalla and feast with the gods."

She nodded slowly. "To get victory, even in the moment of defeat."

He had never thought of it that way before.

Then, for the first time since he had known her, he saw defeat in her eyes. "I cannot fight any more. I cannot win. I had hoped . . ."

She looked away and sighed deeply before raising her eyes to him again as she squared her shoulders. "There is a part of me no man can ever touch, but if I cannot avoid marriage, I will choose. I will have a measure of victory in defeat, if that is all I can hope for."

He went toward her. "I do not think you are defeated. What you did tonight was not the action of a defeated foe, but a warrior."

With a mixture of pleasure and relief, she saw the look of sincerity and admiration in Einar's face. After she had returned from the hall she had wondered what had come over her to behave so boldly and turn her anger into such an action. She had never done anything like that in her life. She had tried to convince herself that she had simply wanted to show those women that they could not shame her. She had done nothing to be ashamed of.

Now, at this moment, with Einar looking at her, she knew the real reason she had done it. She wanted him as she had never wanted a man. She wanted him in a way that was like a physical hunger.

She meant what she said about a part of her that even Einar would never be able to touch, just as she had meant it when she said she had no heart to give. That part of her belonged to Paul and his memory.

But now, when Einar gathered her in his arms, she did not resist. Could not. And when his lips touched hers, passion leapt to life inside her, a passion so long dormant that it was as if she had never fully lived until that moment.

A man would have had to be dead not to sense Meradyce's intense response, and Einar was very much alive. He held her to him, deepening his kiss. His lips trailed across her cheek and she heard his low chuckle. "Shall we tell Ull he has already lost?" he whispered in her ear.

She felt as if he had slapped her. As if she deserved having her hair cut off. As if she was as weak as a child. "Why?" she snapped, pulling away.

She would not let him take her small victory away. Not even him.

He stared at her. "You want me. I know it."

"You kissed me. I let you. I have not let Ull kiss me. Yet."

Einar's brows lowered and his expression became so fierce that Meradyce was afraid. "You are playing a very dangerous game, Saxon," he said slowly.

"I did not set out the rules," she said, backing toward the door.

Suddenly his expression changed, grew lighter. "Very well. But perhaps I will not play. Go to Ull, if it pleases you. I shall be here, if you change your mind."

She was at the door.

"But do not enter again without calling out. I may not be alone."

Without another word, she went outside.

Einar slumped down on the nearest stool. It had taken a mighty effort to act as if he did not care what she did, or with whom.

He cared very much. He reached for a wineskin and took a huge gulp, staring at the folded blue gown.

He cared too much.

Chapter Nine

Olva lay beside her husband, whispering so that she would not disturb anyone asleep in the house. "I could not believe it when Endredi told me what had happened. Her beautiful hair! And then to go to Svend's hall!"

She felt Thorston shake with silent laughter. "I wish I had been there, to see their faces! I bet that fool Ull almost fell off the bench!"

"I am worried."

"About what? That she has gotten herself into deep waters by doing such a thing?"

"No."

"What, then?"

"I am worried that Einar will not win her."

"He has always gotten whatever he set his mind to."

Olva twisted on her side so that she could see Thorston's face. "I am worried that he will not even try."

"If it were any man other than Ull, I would agree. But he is the one man in the village who could make Einar vie for her. He would fight with Ull over an old bone."

Olva nodded in agreement, but her brow was still furrowed with doubt. "But you know Einar's never cared when it came to women, not after Nissa. Since then, he has always said no woman is worth fighting for."

"Do you think it is true, about Ull and Nissa?"

"Who knows? I can believe Nissa went with half the men in the village, even when Einar was at home. It was an evil day when he wed her."

"She was beautiful."

"So is the Saxon, and I do not think that sways Einar's opinion."

"But he does not treat her like any other woman. I saw that right off, in Hedeby, when he spoke of her. Or rather, did not speak of her. He was very secretive about the whole business. And then, he completely ignored Nils' daughters. Usually he teases and jokes and gets all their hopes up outrageously before he actually chooses one to take to his bed."

"*What?*"

"Oh, Olva, he is a man, after all. They are pretty girls and clean—"

"He never told me."

"You are his *mother.* How many men you know tell their mothers about their women?"

"*You* never told me about Einar and Nils' daughters."

"It's not my business."

"You men all stick together, don't you? Have *you* been with one of Nils' pretty daughters, Thorston?"

Thorston chuckled again and gave her a light kiss on the cheek. "I am flattered you would think they would have anything to do with me, especially when Einar is staying there. But if they asked me . . .''

"Why, you old—"

Thorston laughed and caught her hand before she slapped him.

Olva grinned. "You are awful, Thorston."

"You are not going to divorce me, are you?"

"Not tomorrow, anyway. But if I hear about you and another woman, I will don your breeches and walk through the village without a moment's delay."

"I am as faithful as an old dog, Olva."

She kissed him tenderly. "I know."

"You want Einar to marry this woman."

"Yes, I do. He cares for her, Thorston, the way I have never seen him care for another woman. And she would be good for him."

"Well, does she like him at all? He did steal her away from her home."

"I wish I could tell. She is so quiet and deep. That is why I could not believe what she did tonight. It did not seem like her at all. I cannot help hoping she did it because she does like Einar. He has been gentle with her, and he is a fine man."

"That is a mother talking."

"Well, it is true. He has never hurt a woman in his life, not like some I could name."

Thorston heard the bitterness in her voice and knew she was thinking of her early life among the Saxons. "They are probably dead by now, Olva."

"I hope they all rot in hell forever for what they did to my family. And to me."

"Yet you want a Saxon to marry your son."

Olva snuggled beside her husband, trying not to let the memories burden her. "Yes. I want Einar to marry her. She is kind and gentle and loyal. She had no reason to protect those children. They were not hers, after all. And yet I am sure she would die for them. You know that Einar prizes loyalty above all things. If only *he* could see her virtues!" She lay silent for a few moments. "I know he feels something for her. If he truly cared nothing for her, he would not look at her the way he does. He would not have given her gifts. Ingemar would not have felt driven to do something so terrible, either."

"So, we have decided he wants this woman, at least as much as he has ever wanted one, and maybe more. We are not sure how the Saxon woman feels about Einar, but maybe she cares for him a little, too. Whatever she feels, she is now a prize for Ull and Einar to fight over, if Einar decides to bother."

Olva sighed. "It sounds hopeless, when you put it in such a way. I suppose we will have to trust the gods."

Thorston patted her hand gently. "The Christian or the Viking?"

Olva smiled. "With Einar, we will need all the gods we can get."

Adelar stared at Meradyce, asleep alongside Betha in their bed, from his pallet on the floor. If it had been a man who had dared cut off Meradyce's hair, Adelar would gladly have shot him through with an arrow. But women . . .

He wondered if Einar was going to do anything about it.

Adelar wanted this terrible crime to be avenged, but as he glanced at Meradyce's sleeping form, he began to question whether he wanted Einar to do it.

Endredi said several of the Viking men wanted to marry Meradyce. She seemed to think this a great honor, but Meradyce would surely never agree to such a thing.

He frowned scornfully. No Viking would ever be good enough for a Saxon, not even Einar.

He heard Meradyce sigh in her sleep, and for a moment doubt assailed him. If Einar was not a Viking, would Meradyce want him?

He was a fine warrior and surely the only man among the Vikings who was even slightly worthy of her.

But Meradyce could never care for him, an enemy of the Saxons. No doubt she hated all the Vikings' attentions.

A firm resolve took possession of his heart. It was his duty to guard her from unwanted suitors, and keep her safe.

Still later that night, but well before dawn, Endredi woke and lay unsleeping.

Ingemar and Ilsa had done a terrible thing to Meradyce. It was not Meradyce's fault that Ull lusted after her, just as it was not Meradyce's fault that Einar had taken her from the Saxon village.

Ingemar could be hateful, especially if her jealousy was inflamed. Endredi had seen it before, when any

other woman so much as mentioned Einar in Ingemar's presence.

That was one of the reasons Endredi prayed to
Freyja that her father did not marry Ingemar.

As for Ilsa and Reinhild, it was easy to see who had
led whom. Ilsa was like an evil giantess, always com-
plaining, never happy. Some women whispered that it
was because she had no child to turn her thoughts
away from her discontent; Endredi doubted that even
a child could make much difference.

Reinhild was always kind to the girls of the village,
and was only a few years older than Endredi. Ull had
desired her for several months before Reinhild's father would agree. Reinhild had whispered to Endredi
that she wanted Ull, but only if Ilsa would divorce
him. Ull wanted to divorce Ilsa, Reinhild said, but
Ilsa's father was a powerful chief in another village.
Svend refused to allow the divorce, for if Ilsa went
home, her father might feel that Ull had shamed his
family, and violence would surely result.

Then Reinhild became pregnant by Ull. Svend ordered her father to consent, and Reinhild had married the man she wanted, although she also had to
contend with Ilsa.

If only he had been content with his two wives!
Unfortunately, Endredi had begun to fear that Ull was
going to ask her father for her as wife, too. He always
smiled whenever he saw her, or called out a greeting.

She did not know what her father would say. Although she knew he had no liking for Ull, perhaps
Einar would be pleased that she would no longer be
any concern of his. And Svend would probably say

that Ull was one of the village's finest warriors, so such an alliance would be beneficial for the whole village. The chieftain might even use her as a way to end the rivalry between the two men.

In the darkness, Endredi sighed. She wanted to feel some passion for the man she married. She had heard of that feeling in the tales the storyteller told, the emotion that would drive the gods to do great deeds for their wives. Many times, as she lay on her bed at night, she had imagined a hero doing a great deed for *her*.

Ull did not seem much of a hero.

If only she knew what Meradyce really thought about her father and Ull. It would be a good thing for her father to marry someone kind and warmhearted like Meradyce.

She had never seen him so concerned about another person in his life. When he had come to fetch her, his voice was harsh, but his eyes told her that he was very worried about Meradyce.

And she could not help but worry that if Meradyce wed Ull, things between the two men might get even worse.

Endredi frowned as another notion grew in her mind. Try as she might to believe Meradyce kind and guileless, was it not possible that she was *trying* to make trouble among the Vikings? After all, she was a Saxon. Perhaps she hoped to inflame old hatreds and jealousies, to divide the warriors.

No. Endredi would not believe that Meradyce was deliberately trying to make trouble. If that was so, there was no reason for Meradyce to help the women or teach Endredi about medicines and childbirth.

Endredi heard a sound in the stillness and held her breath, cautiously rolling over to look toward Meradyce.

She heard Meradyce sigh and wondered if she was awake, too. For a moment, Endredi was tempted to go to her, but she didn't. She would not know what to say, and perhaps the presence of Einar's daughter would give Meradyce no comfort.

Kendric frowned at the ugly little man standing before him. "What do you mean, nothing for Meradyce?"

Selwyn had bargained with enough merchants to know when someone was trying to hide his interest. Kendric was *very* interested in the woman and why she was not to be ransomed, although he kept his voice calm. No doubt it was because his wife was sitting right beside him, her gaze flashing between them as they spoke. "That's what they said. One thousand for the boy, fifty for the girl, not a copper coin for the woman."

Kendric leaned back in his chair. Ludella sighed, but there was no sincere regret in the sound. "It is a pity, of course. She was so beautiful..." She spoke as if the midwife was dead.

As he waited, Selwyn wondered if the woman Meradyce had been a virgin when Einar took her, or if this man had succeeded in seducing her, despite the gossip—and if his skinny wife had found out. That might explain her wish to dismiss the woman.

He would not be surprised if that was the truth. The Saxon thane was powerful and rich as well as handsome. Women probably ran to get in his bed—but if they were smart, they would know better than to brag about it. There was more than a hint of ruthlessness in Kendric's face, and surely he would not deal kindly with anyone who would give his wife cause to make trouble.

Selwyn wished he had seen the village midwife when he had traveled here the other time, before the raid. Kendric obviously cared what happened to her. Even Einar, who never took slaves, had wanted her. The Viking's eyes had narrowed with jealousy at the mention of the Saxon lord, although Einar had tried not to betray any personal interest. And he might have succeeded with a man less discerning than Selwyn.

Selwyn waited for Kendric to speak, certain the man would want to know more when his wife was not there.

The thane's wife put her hand on her husband's arm. She was not an attractive woman, and the desperation in her face made her even uglier. "We will pay for the children, will we not?"

Her husband gave her a look that told Selwyn how little he cared for her. "Of course."

Selwyn grinned. "Good. They'll come back with the children in the spring, since you've promised to pay."

"I will be ready for trickery," Kendric cautioned.

"You won't get it, not from Einar. He hates deceit," Selwyn added meaningfully. "Now, as to the matter of *my* payment, for all the risks I'm taking . . ."

"How much do you want?"

"Five hundred pieces of silver."

"What? Are you mad?"

"It's not easy dealing with those barbarians," Selwyn said in a wheedling tone. "They'd just as soon slit a Saxon's throat as talk to him."

"One hundred."

"Three hundred and fifty, my lord. I've already gone to a lot of trouble, sailing here. The weather was terrible, the boat leaked like an old wineskin—"

"One hundred and fifty."

"Say two hundred and we'll call it done."

Selwyn saw the thane's wife nudge him and knew the bargain was as good as sealed.

"Very well," Kendric muttered. "Fifty now, the rest when I have my children back."

Selwyn opened his mouth to protest but shut it when he saw the look in Kendric's eyes. "Yes, my lord."

Kendric frowned again at Selwyn, then turned to his wife. "We have other business to discuss," he said bluntly.

She gave him a dissatisfied look but stood up. "We will pay whatever they ask." She stared hard at Selwyn, as if she did not trust him to deliver the message to the Vikings properly. "I will see to the evening meal."

When she was out of earshot, Kendric spoke. "Why will they not ransom Meradyce?"

"Well, my lord, the Viking refused. He also said to tell you that you should have taken her while you had the chance, since she's very pleasing."

Kendric flushed, and Selwyn wondered if he should have kept Einar's words to himself. There were enough bad feelings between the Saxons and the Vikings. Still, discord was always good for trade, at least in weapons and slaves. "The Viking might yet be willing to bargain, my lord," Selwyn said slyly.

Kendric shook his head. "I am not."

Before the unpleasant but unfortunately necessary Saxon merchant could start whining again, Kendric waved his hand dismissively.

As the little man rose and made his way from the hall, Kendric sat thinking. He regretted that such a thing had happened to the beautiful Meradyce, but it had. He had desired her not only for her beauty, but for her virginity. Obviously the virginity no longer existed. As a slave to the Vikings, her beauty was probably diminishing every day.

He imagined Meradyce, stripped, helpless, being mounted by one of the muscular Vikings, and felt a pleasant tightening in his groin.

He stood up. There was no reason to yearn for Meradyce, and he had noticed a new serving wench in his hall.

Meradyce sat in the pleasing silence of Helsa's deserted hut. Endredi and Betha had come with her, but had gone to find Betha's kitten.

Meradyce sighed. It had seemed a very long time since she had been by herself. She had missed being alone. After all, that was how she spent most of her days at home.

Here, she felt as if she was constantly under scrutiny, like a rare ornament. More of the Viking men seemed interested in her, although she suspected few really thought they had any hope of competing with Ull.

Even Adelar had noticed the change and was concerned for her, which touched her heart. After she made it clear she had no intention of encouraging them, he began to relax his constant vigil. Nonetheless, she had avoided being by herself in case one of the Vikings should accost her.

Einar ignored her completely, and two days ago, Olva had revealed that Einar was no longer responsible for her. That duty had been taken over by the chieftain himself.

Determined to rid her mind of her worries, if only for a short time, she stood and began to search the far corners of Helsa's hut. She was sure she had found most of the herbs and potions, but there could be other things of use here.

Helsa had been most untidy. Mice had had a feast in the baskets and had eaten some things that they shouldn't, judging by the corpses. Wrinkling her nose, Meradyce went toward some larger baskets in the opposite corner, thinking they probably held linen.

Inside, she found clay jars full of liquid. She worked the covering off one and sniffed.

It smelled like apples. She dipped her finger in and took a taste. Yes, it was a drink made of pressed apples, a harmless beverage usually enjoyed in the autumn.

She got a cup and poured herself some. The fluid was clear and pale gold, its aroma reminding her of harvest time and long happy hours up in the leafy trees, picking fruit.

She sat on a stool beside a battered wooden table and drank. It was like tasting home.

Or as much of a home as she had ever known. Ever since her parents had died, she had been completely alone in the world. There were men who wanted to change that, but she knew it was only her physical beauty that intrigued them. None bothered with her feelings, her desires, her needs.

Paul had, but he could not—would not—marry her.

She drained her cup and raised her hand to her hair. If only her shorn locks would dissuade the men!

Unfortunately, this time she had brought on the attention herself. What a fool!

Her face grew hot as she remembered the look of surprise and desire on Einar's face when she had poured his wine in the hall. Was that why she had done it, to see that look of longing, knowing that this time she had some power? Some measure of control?

Perhaps.

She had another cupful. Was there anything so very wrong with what she had done? She could refuse the Vikings as she had refused other men. She could refuse Einar, too. She was free....

She thought she heard a noise and turned toward the door. The movement made her dizzy as she squinted to try to see who stood there.

Einar.

She started, but the man did not move or even blink an eye, and his shape seemed to shift before her.

She closed her eyes and shook her head, but that made her even dizzier.

She opened her eyes. The man had not moved.

"You are not Einar," she accused, not noticing how slurred her words were. "I have made you up, out of my head. You are a...a vision, or some such thing."

She stared down at the empty cup and giggled. "Oh, I know what has happened! This drink has fermented...I am *drunk!* I have heard of men seeing things when they have had too much wine, but I never really believed it till now."

She tipped the clay vessel forward. "Oh, I *have* had a lot of this." She frowned, then grinned. "I have never been drunk before." Her brow wrinkled thoughtfully. "It is not...unpleasant. I can see why men..."

She smiled again and shrugged her shoulders. "If I am drunk already, I might as well have some more. Especially since it makes me imagine a much more pleasant Einar than the real one."

She poured herself another cupful, ignoring the fact that some spilled on the table. She looked at the vision, which had not moved, then giggled again and shook her head. "Of course not, silly girl. If it is not real, it will stay right there."

She leaned back and almost fell off the stool before righting herself. "Whoops! How undignified—and we must always be dignified. Do you not agree, Einar-of-my-mind? Of course you do."

She narrowed her eyes. "You are too dignified to fight for me. Too dignified even to look at me, now that other men might woo me."

She took another large gulp. "You know, this is a delicious drink. I have not had it in a long, long time. Not since that harvest when those boys—who were they now? It does not matter. They chased me all around the orchard with wormy apples. I ran like a deer, I will tell you. They never did catch me." She giggled again and leaned forward, whispering loudly. "I went into the caves. You know, the ones the villagers hide in from you Vikings."

She took another drink and frowned. "You see, even then, the boys were chasing after me. How I hated it—and them! I just wanted to be left alone. Like now. I want to be left alone." She waggled her finger in the general direction of the vision. "I do. I do not want to be married."

She sighed and took another drink. "I did once. I wanted him, and he wanted me, too. But he had made a vow he could not break." She swirled the contents of the cup as she stared at it. "He only kissed me once. Just once... He said I could not understand. That he had obligations. I was fourteen. I knew what I felt."

She sat silently for a moment, then whispered, "I think."

After another drink and another thoughtful silence, she spoke again, more slowly. "Now I am not so sure." She glanced at the vision.

"I wanted him to kiss me, of course," she went on pensively, "but when Einar looks at me... when he touches me... I want to do so much more than kiss."

The vision moved slightly.

"I wish I could make you go away. Even if you *are* something I am imagining, I am doing too good a job."

She sipped some more of the drink. "I wonder what it would have been like, *living* with him. He did not laugh very much."

She gave the vision a sidelong glance. "Einar does not laugh very much—at least not around me. But he has a nice laugh. He is good with Betha and Adelar. It is too bad about Endredi, but I can understand . . ."

She crossed her arms on the table in front of her, frowning deeply. "I wish he had not made that vow." She slipped forward.

Her voice dropped to a soft whisper, and a sob escaped her throat. "I wish the Vikings had never come!"

The vision leaned closer.

"I wish I had never seen Einar. I wish he had never been kind to me. I never dreamed . . . I never thought . . . But when he kisses me . . . I am a fool. A ridiculous fool." She slipped farther forward. "I could not care for a Viking. I could not."

She closed her eyes. "I will pretend I am in the monastery garden again, with him." She pressed her eyelids more tightly, a frown creasing her face.

"What is wrong with me, that it is only Einar I see?" She put her head down on her arms. "And he does not care for me at all," she whispered sorrowfully.

She drifted into sleep as Einar went out slowly, a thoughtful expression on his very real face.

Chapter Ten

Einar tried to convince himself it was best to have nothing to do with the Saxon woman. No woman must ever again have any power over him. Her past and her feelings were nothing to him. He should feel no pity, no concern, no tenderness.

As he had listened to her secrets in Helsa's house, he had experienced an almost overwhelming feeling of compassion for her—until she spoke of another man. Then he had felt such fierce jealousy that it was as if Nissa lived again.

When he saw Ull or one of the other men walking toward his mother's house in the next fortnight with meat or ale or some other gift surely intended for the Saxon, he told himself he did not care. He would not give her any more gifts. He would not even talk to her. He would simply... ignore her.

Most days he took young Adelar with him when he went hunting or fishing or to practice fighting. It was only because he liked the boy and the boy seemed to want to be with him. If Adelar happened to speak of Meradyce, well, it was not important.

Adelar was pleased to be Einar's companion. For one thing, he was convinced by Einar's lack of interest that the tall Viking had no wish to marry Meradyce. For another, Einar was a great warrior and a good teacher. Adelar was learning many things about hunting, fighting and the Vikings themselves.

In return, Adelar told Einar about his father, the greatest Saxon lord in the whole land. With sly looks, he warned Einar that the Vikings had better think twice about invading the land of the Saxons in future. Einar nodded, obviously impressed, so Adelar told him more.

He spoke of his village, although, wise for his years, he never mentioned the secret caves nearby and the people who were their allies.

One day, Einar, accompanied as usual by his two huge hounds, took Adelar to see how a Viking ship was built.

They went to a large building that was near the edge of the fjord, close to the piers. It was bigger than any structure Adelar had ever seen, with an unusual row of posts along the outside connected to the roof.

Einar saw where he was staring. "If we put the posts outside, there is more room for the ship."

Adelar nodded as they entered, then halted as he gazed at the skeleton of an enormous longship, its curved prow shaped like a serpent. For a moment he was afraid, remembering the first time he had seen a vessel like it.

He conquered his fear as he realized that such ships were the greatest weapons the Vikings possessed, along with their knowledge of seamanship. He would study this vessel and learn what he could of its construction, ready for the day he would guard the Saxon shore.

This ship would be even larger than the warship that lay in the harbor. It had the shallow draft common to all Viking longships and the lean grace of a craft made to cut through waves the way a horse could gallop through a meadow. "Adelar," Einar said, "this is Bjorn, the best shipbuilder in the world."

The old man nodded a greeting as he came toward them, speaking in the slow, measured tones of one who thinks much but says little.

"He assures me the ship will be ready in the spring," Einar said with a smile. "He should know. He has been building ships since he was younger than you."

"Does he teach others?" Adelar asked innocently.

"Some things, but a good shipbuilder is always trying new methods." Einar tapped his chest. "Some must come from the heart. Bjorn says he just knows when something is not quite right."

"Oh," Adelar said as Einar went over to examine the vessel more closely.

All around them in the vast space, men were working on the huge ship. Some cut large timbers into planks, which were laid in an overlapping manner on the frame. As Adelar went closer, he noticed, with great surprise, that some of the lower planks were not attached with nails, but lashed onto the ship with what appeared to be tree roots.

"It makes the hull bend with the sea," Einar said, noticing the boy nearby.

"But doesn't it leak?" Adelar asked incredulously.

"A little," Einar admitted, "but it is best this way." His voice took on a thoughtful quality as he gazed at the longship. "You want the ship to move beneath you like a woman, responding to every movement, every—"

"I do not understand. A ship is not alive."

Einar looked down at Adelar with a slight grin. "It is not? Maybe that is why you Saxons build vessels that are only fit to wallow in a river."

Adelar frowned. He did not like anyone criticizing his people, but when he looked at the sleek lines of the Viking ship, he could not deny that the Saxons could learn a lot about seaworthy ships from the Vikings. "How many men will it hold?"

"Enough."

Adelar watched the men working. They seemed to know what to do without being told. A nod or a short word from Bjorn was all the direction they needed.

"Come," Einar said suddenly. "Let us go fishing."

Adelar glanced at his companion. He must have betrayed too much interest in the shipbuilding, for Einar seemed less than companionable.

But Einar had been edgy for several days, so maybe it had nothing to do with him.

Einar led him up a nearby hill to a deep pool in a stream that flowed down to the fjord, joining it in a lovely waterfall.

Einar reached into his tunic and produced a line with a bone hook on the end. He gave it to Adelar, then threw himself down on the bank and put his hands behind his head. "Fish," he commanded.

Adelar glanced at the man on the bank. His eyes were closed. Maybe all he needed was some sleep. Adelar sat as still as he could.

"Adelar?"

The boy looked at his companion with some surprise. Einar's gray eyes seemed to transfix him. "Yes?"

"Why does Meradyce not have a husband?"

Adelar had not been expecting that question, and he was not sure he liked it. "I do not know."

"Has any man asked for her?"

"I do not know."

"Has there ever been any man she seemed...to care about?"

"I do not know." Adelar's heart was beating rapidly. He stared at the water in the pool, feeling his face flush hotly. When he grew older, he would realize that what he was feeling at this moment was jealousy, but for now he only knew he did not like Einar's questions.

He began pulling up the line. "I want to go back."

Einar did not move. "What is the matter?"

Adelar shrugged his shoulders. "Nothing." He did not want anybody to know how he felt about Meradyce—and especially not Einar. "I am hungry."

"Have a drink from the pool. We will stay here for a while yet."

Adelar did so, then dropped the line in the water.

"She is very beautiful. I thought a woman like her would be married," Einar said offhandedly.

"Endredi said that man Ull keeps bringing food because he likes Meradyce."

"Huh."

"She would never agree to marry a Viking."

Einar looked at him, a slight smile on his lips. "No?"

"Do you want to marry her?" The question sounded innocuous, but Adelar held his breath while he waited for Einar to answer.

"No, I do not."

Adelar let out a sigh of relief.

"Why does she encourage Ull and the others?"

Adelar shrugged again, but now that he was sure Einar had no personal interest in Meradyce, he felt free to respond. "She does not. She is just the way she always is, but they will not stop."

"What do you mean, always is?"

"You know—polite and respectful, but that is all. I do not think she ever wants to marry." Adelar gave Einar a sidelong glance. "You are not married."

"No."

"Why not?"

Einar frowned before he answered. "Because I do not want to be."

"Maybe Meradyce does not want to be, either."

Einar grunted and closed his eyes. Adelar felt a little tug on his line and pulled it up. Nothing. He dropped it back. "Betha thinks Meradyce wanted to get married once."

"Who was the man?"

Adelar frowned. "I do not know, but I think he was a priest or worked at the monastery. Betha believes he died. But Betha is just a little girl, after all. I think she made it up."

Einar pulled up a long piece of grass and began to tie it into a knot. "What does your father think of Meradyce?"

"He likes her. Everybody likes her—except some of the women, but they are just jealous."

"Does she like your father?"

Adelar's brow furrowed with thought. "I suppose so. She respects him, of course, like everyone in the village." Suddenly Adelar's eyes narrowed. "Why are you asking me these things?"

This time it was Einar who shrugged, but Adelar leapt to his feet. "My father already has a wife!"

"Sit down, boy."

Adelar glared at the Viking, filled with a sudden fear as he remembered the bitter recriminations and irate words between his parents. "My father cares for my mother. Very much!" he cried, willing himself to believe it.

"*Sit down.*"

Reluctantly, Adelar obeyed.

"I merely thought that, if your father is everything you say he is, it would be natural to suspect that Meradyce might not be married because she is pining for someone she cannot have. Such as your father." Einar was speaking the truth, and the boy realized it.

"She has been like that since she came to our village. What she feels can have nothing to do with my father."

"She did not always live there?"

"No. She used to visit sometimes with her parents. When they died, she came to live in the village—and if she *did* care for a man, it was before that," Adelar finished decisively.

Einar looked at the sky. "It is getting late. We will fish for a little longer, then we must go back."

Adelar dropped his line in the pool. "Do you like Meradyce?" he demanded suddenly.

"I respect her."

"Then tell those other men to leave her alone."

Einar shook his head. "I cannot. That is not my place."

"You are supposed to protect her, aren't you?"

"Not any more. She is Svend's responsibility now." Einar hesitated, then spoke again. "Is she afraid of the men?"

Adelar sniffed derisively. "Certainly not. Meradyce is never afraid. She was not afraid of you, was she?"

Einar kept his views on that to himself.

"It would be easier for her, that is all," Adelar said.

"I cannot interfere. Men would think I was claiming her myself."

"Oh."

Suddenly there was a tremendous tug on the line. "I have one!" Adelar cried, jumping to his feet. Then he slipped on the wet grass and fell into the pool.

Einar quickly grabbed his tunic.

"I have him!" Adelar yelled as Einar hauled him out of the water, dripping wet. And he did have rather a large fish for so small a pool.

"Let us get back and clean it—and get you in dry clothes."

"I am all right. Just look at this fish!"

All the way to the village Adelar bragged about his luck and went over and over again the feeling when the fish took the hook.

Einar was not listening. He was trying to understand why he felt so pleased that Meradyce was not pining for the traitorous Saxon thane and why he felt so hopeful, knowing the man she had cared for might have been a holy man committed to his church—or, even better, dead.

"What in the name of Njord happened to you?" Olva exclaimed as the still dripping Adelar held out his fish.

"I caught this." He sneezed loudly as Meradyce hurried to him and put her arm around his shoulder, drawing him toward the hearth.

She cast an accusing look at Einar, who shrugged and said, "He fell in a pool. Nothing to be worried about."

"Look at my fish!" Adelar demanded, shaking off Meradyce's motherly embrace.

"It is wonderful," Meradyce said, "but you need to get into dry clothing."

"Is it dead?" Betha asked, her soft voice full of dread and horror as she sat beside the loom, a puppy in her lap.

"Of course it is," Adelar said with disgust at his sister's ignorance. "It has to be dead if we are going to eat it."

Olva beckoned to Adelar. "Come, young warrior, and get into something dry before you get sick." Adelar looked about to protest until Olva added, "And then no fishing or fighting for a long while, eh?"

As Adelar went toward Einar's mother, Meradyce returned to her seat by the hearth. She had been sewing and prepared to resume her task. Nonetheless, she was well aware that Einar still stood near the door.

"Do you like my puppy?" Betha asked, picking up her newest pet and holding him out to the Viking who towered over her.

Meradyce glanced up, noticing at once Betha's trusting smile and the puppy's discomfort. To her surprise, Einar smiled warmly.

He looked very handsome when he smiled.

Then he bent and took the puppy, and Betha's little hand. He walked with her to the hearth and sat on the ground, pulling her into his lap while holding the puppy gently but firmly in his hand. "He is a fine dog. What do you call him?"

"I named him Alfred, after the King. My father is going to be in the *Witan,* you know. They help the King decide what to do."

Meradyce kept sewing, but she was completely flabbergasted. She had no idea that Kendric thought he could achieve a place in the *Witan.* He was not of sufficient rank—or rather, not yet. She should have guessed his ambition would aim so high.

"Do you miss your parents very much?" Einar asked the child softly.

"Yes, but at least Meradyce is here."

"Yes, at least Meradyce is here."

Meradyce felt a pleasurable warmth diffusing her body at his gentle words. It was as if . . . as if he, too, was glad she was there.

Olva returned, having found some dry garments for Adelar. Her face lighted with a maternal smile at Einar and Betha. "You are just the same, you two, with your pets. Dogs, horses—and anything hurt. Always bringing something home to keep until it healed, he was. Remember the time you had the fish? What did you call it?"

Einar glanced at Meradyce and rolled his eyes. She couldn't keep a smile off her face at his mock dismay.

"Spotty," he answered.

Olva sat beside Meradyce and laughed softly. "Yes, that was it." She nudged Meradyce and grinned. "He found it in a stream. It got caught in some branches, and he came and took my best pot to carry it in. Imagine! I made him find some place else to keep it. Well, the next day Svend—I was still married to him then—came back from a short trading voyage. Einar stayed to watch them unload the ship, and I went to fetch some wood. We never thought to tell Svend about Spotty, so when I got back with the wood, there was poor Spotty, gutted and cleaned for supper!"

Meradyce tried desperately not to laugh, especially at Einar's comically downcast face.

"He would not speak to his father for a week," Olva finished.

At that moment, Endredi came inside. She began to smile. Then she saw Einar, Betha still in his lap, and she flushed as red as Olva's wool.

"Oh, Endredi! Here you are. Did you get some nice salted herring?" Olva asked brightly.

Einar got up, gently standing Betha beside him. Her puppy, now happily freed of his little mistress's caresses, ran around the house, sniffing everything. His expression hard and serious, Einar nodded at them and went to the door.

He had not said one word to his daughter. Again.

Meradyce had seen the hurt in the girl's eyes, and this time she could not sit by and remain silent. She followed Einar as he went out the door.

Night had fallen, and from the sounds coming from Svend's hall, it was obvious that most of the warriors were already inside. She glanced about and saw no one other than Einar as he went into his house.

With a determined tightening of her lips, Meradyce strode over to his house and entered. Einar had lit a lamp and was in the process of removing his tunic when he realized he was not alone.

"What in the name of—" He stared at her for a moment, then finished removing his tunic before he spoke again. "What do you want?"

"Why do you ignore Endredi?" she asked bluntly.

He turned slowly. His naked chest gleamed in the flickering flame from the oil lamp and his blond hair brushed his broad shoulders. The light made deep shadows on his face, so it was hard to see his eyes. "How I conduct myself is none of your concern."

"You hurt her, you know. She cares for you very much."

He tossed aside his tunic and reached for a wineskin, pulling out the stopper.

"I understand that you blame her for causing your wife's death, but it was not her fault," Meradyce said urgently. "You are making her suffer for something she could not prevent."

Einar took a drink before responding. "You seem so sure you understand," he observed coolly.

She took a step forward, her concern for Endredi's happiness overriding every other feeling. "I have seen this before, when a mother dies in childbirth."

"Do you know how much I loved Endredi's mother?"

Meradyce ignored a pang of jealousy. "I know it might be difficult, but could you not at least talk to Endredi?"

Einar came closer. "It is a torture to me, to even be near her."

"For Endredi's sake, I ask this."

By now he was very close to her, and she could at last see his eyes clearly in the dimness.

"You understand nothing."

Meradyce stared at him, speechless at the bitterness in his voice. He hesitated, then looked at her intently. "By the time Endredi was born, I loathed her mother."

"Why?" she asked softly.

"Endredi is not my child."

"But...you must have acknowledged her," she said, confused. Surely no Viking warrior would accept a child he didn't believe was his.

He laughed harshly. "My wife told me before she died that the child she bore was not mine, but Nissa lied as often as most people eat. I could not be sure, even then, that she was not lying about that. It would be like her, to want to..." He turned away.

"Hurt you?"

"Yes."

"Why?"

He shrugged his shoulders. "Why does any woman try to hurt her husband?"

"Because he has hurt her first."

He whirled. "You are so certain you know everything, Saxon! Well, not this time. I did nothing to hurt her. I cared for her—too much! Too late I discovered what she was really like. She was a *whore*. She went with any man who looked twice at her! She only married me because I was the chieftain's son, and because it would make other women jealous of her and more men want her."

She heard the pain beneath the bitterness, and her heart filled with sorrow. "I am sorry, Einar."

"So now you know why I acknowledged Endredi. So now you can go."

"Was that the only reason you picked her up?"

He glared at her. "Yes."

But she had seen him with Betha, and Adelar. "You are lying."

In the next instant he had grabbed her shoulders roughly. "No one accuses me of that," he said savagely.

It was too late. She was not afraid of him. She could never be afraid of him now. "You pitied the child, didn't you? So small, there on the floor, waiting for you to give her honor or shame."

He cast her from him. "Yes!" His voice fell as he turned his back to her. "Yes."

She went to him, reaching out to touch his arm. "Einar, I did not understand."

"Do you now?" he demanded, facing her. "Do you know how hard it is for me to be near Endredi, to always be looking for some piece of me—or other men—in her?"

The last remnant of resistance in Meradyce's heart melted at Einar's sorrowful words. And without her realizing it, her youthful adoration for a dead man disappeared.

She put her arms around Einar, wanting to give him comfort, wanting to understand his sorrow.

He sighed raggedly, his arms limp at his sides. "Now you know why I will never marry again."

She heard the finality in his voice, and tears sprang into her eyes. "Never?" she whispered.

He pulled away and looked at her, a questioning, hopeful expression in the gray depths of his eyes. Then he kissed her. Tenderly. Gently. Wonderfully.

She wanted him. Meradyce knew it now as surely as the sun rose each day. She wanted to be with him, to share his sorrow and his joy. To be his wife.

"Stay with me," he said softly as his lips traveled toward the tender skin of her neck.

If only she could be certain of his feeling for her, to know that it was more than lust.

"Do you want me for your wife, Einar?"

She drew back to see his eyes, sensing with triumph and happiness that the answer would be yes.

Before Einar could answer, he saw only the triumph and the power in a woman's eyes. "No, I do not."

He saw her shoulders sag with defeat before she twisted away from him. "I will say nothing to Endredi about her mother," she said as she marched to the door. "But she is no longer a child. You should tell her the truth."

"Meradyce!"

"I will not speak with you again, Einar."

"Then you will marry Ull?" He marveled that he could sound so unconcerned.

She lifted her lovely chin defiantly. "That is no concern of yours."

Then she was gone.

Chapter Eleven

Einar glanced at Lars as they sat in the bathhouse. "What do you mean, you are leaving?"

"Ingemar wants to go to Hedeby, and I am going with her." Lars' usual booming voice was quiet but determined.

"You will be returning before winter sets in, then."

Lars looked at Einar steadily. "No. We will not be coming back."

Einar stared at his friend in dismay. "You cannot mean that."

Lars nodded, his face grim. "Yes, I do. She says she will not stay here to be humiliated. I offered to go with her, and she agreed."

"The Saxon has done nothing to humiliate her."

"You do not understand, Einar. It is not the woman—it is *you.*"

"Me? How have I humiliated her?"

"You did not offer to marry her."

"I told her I was not going to marry her. It did not seem to make much difference before."

Lars shook his head. "By Thor's hammer, Einar, for a clever man you can be very stupid. She heard your words, but she hoped she could persuade you to change your mind, even after you brought the Saxon home. Rightly or wrongly, she is certain you will marry the woman, and she does not want to be here when you do."

"So take her to Hedeby, then. But come back. You are the best steersman in the village—and my friend!"

When Lars did not speak, Einar suddenly realized something else. "You care very much for Ingemar. That is why you are going. I did not know...."

Lars looked at him and smiled wistfully. "I have always wanted her, Einar, but I had no chance, as long as she hoped you would marry her."

"So marry her and stay here."

Lars stood up and tossed more water on the heated stones. "Einar, she is as proud as you are. She does not want to be near the Saxon."

Einar looked at his friend, certain now that his going was inevitable. "I am sorry you are leaving, Lars."

Lars grinned, but there was sadness in his eyes. "I wish it could be otherwise, Einar, but I have wanted Ingemar for a long time. If this is what I must do to be with her, then I will."

"Svend will not be pleased."

"I am not looking forward to telling him."

Einar leaned back against the warm walls. "He will be fit to chew his shield."

"I know." Lars leaned back, too. "So tell me the truth, now, Einar, since I am leaving soon. Will you take the Saxon woman for your wife?"

"No."

* * *

"Lars refused to stay?" Hamar asked incredulously. He did not want to believe that Lars would leave the village, but when Hamar saw the dismay and anger in his father's face, he knew it had to be true.

"I cannot believe it myself. Just because a *woman* wants to go!"

"He wants Ingemar."

Svend gave his son a scornful look. "Fine. Marry her. But by Odin's eye, he's the *man!* She should do what he says. I do not know what's happening to my warriors—you are all going soft!"

Hamar knew this was no time to remind his father that he had gone to great lengths to please all his wives and that he still gave them very generous presents, even the ones who had divorced him years ago.

"And now this ridiculous business between Ull and Einar."

"Einar does not seem particularly interested in the Saxon."

Svend glared at Hamar. "Are you blind? Have you not seen the way he watches that woman? Thor's thunder, he drools like a dog over a piece of meat every time he sees her! And Ull—he is acting like a lovesick boy!"

"Maybe she will pick Ull soon and be done with it."

"No woman would pick Ull over my son!"

Hamar smothered a smile. "No, of course not." He became serious. "But you know how Einar feels about marriage. What does Olva say?"

"What is that?" Svend said abruptly.

They could hear the murmur of a crowd outside. Without a word, they stood and went to see what was happening.

Ilsa strode down the center of the village. She wore a pair of Ull's breeches, her gown tucked inside the wide waist. She held them up with one hand, and the other hand swung out determinedly.

It seemed the whole village was watching the woman follow the procedure for divorce. Some in the crowd pointed and laughed while others frowned. Others looked worried, knowing this divorce could lead to a blood feud.

"Where is Ull?" Svend demanded.

Hamar shook his head. "I have not seen him this day. He is probably hunting."

"Stop Ilsa right now. Find Ull." His face glowering with rage, Svend turned to go into his hall. "And then get Einar and the Saxon woman."

A short while later, Ilsa, Einar, Meradyce and Ull stood in the chieftain's hall. Svend sat in his chair, frowning at the four people in front of him.

Out of the corner of his eye, Einar saw his mother push her way to a place where she could see.

"This must stop," Svend said forcefully, turning the full force of his glare on Meradyce.

Einar moved slightly, and the chieftain's gaze came to rest on his son. "Einar will marry the woman."

"That is not fair!" Ull cried. "You said she was to chose!"

Svend rose slowly. "Do you challenge me, Ull?" he asked, his powerful voice all the more terrifying for its quietness.

Ull shook his head. "I merely wished to remind you of your own orders."

Svend smiled coldly as he sat down. "You are right, Ull—but now I am changing my orders. She will be Einar's wife."

"I demand this decision be put before the *Althing*," Ull responded, naming the yearly session held to settle matters of dispute.

"I think no one else considers a marriage a matter worthy of discussion, by the *Althing* or anyone else," Svend answered calmly. "It is done, and I will hear no more about it."

During the talk, Einar gazed at his father as if paying no attention to the woman beside him. Now his wife.

He knew he could interrupt and tell Svend that he wanted no wife, but unless he wanted to challenge his father for the leadership of the village, he dare not disobey another order.

That was the only reason he was not protesting this decision, he told himself sternly.

It did not explain why his heart beat rapidly and the blood pounded in his veins, but he would not dwell on that.

"What is it?" Meradyce asked.

He saw the tension in her face even as he fought to keep his own expressionless. "You are now my wife."

"What?"

"Svend has just made me your husband."

"He said I was free."

"Not anymore. Now you belong to me."

Her eyes narrowed as she frowned. "Does this mean a Viking's word is only good until he decides otherwise?" she asked, her voice quiet but filled with scorn.

"It means that the chieftain has given an order and we must obey."

"What is she saying?" Svend demanded.

"She is thanking you for making such a fine choice," Einar replied.

"Good. That is settled then," Svend said, picking up his drinking horn.

Ull frowned, then marched from the hall as Olva stepped forward. "There is no time to prepare a feast!" She began to protest, until Svend held up his huge hand.

"Enough!" he roared. "They are married. That is the end of this!"

He wrinkled his bushy brows in puzzlement as he glared at Einar. "Well, my son, are you going to stand there or take your wife home and begin making children?"

Einar took Meradyce's hand in his and strode from the hall, pulling her after him.

Once inside his house—their house—he let go of her hand and turned to face her, wondering if he would see that passionate anger he knew she was capable of.

Her eyes betrayed nothing but mild contempt. "I see Saxons and Vikings have different ideas of honor."

"I had no choice in this either, woman."

"Then let me go."

"So you can go to Ull?"

"No," she said quietly, crossing her arms slowly. "So that I can be free."

"No, I will not. You are my wife." He walked across the room and grabbed his drinking horn. He had to do something, anything, as he fought to control himself. How could she be so calm? Could she not see that she was enraging him?

Meradyce's face betrayed nothing of her feelings, but inside, her emotions raged like the storm at sea. Part of her was filled with anger that the Vikings could give her freedom and then so easily take it away. Something had happened to make the Viking leader do it, but she didn't know what.

The other part, the part she was trying hardest to subdue, wanted to go to Einar and beg him to take her, even though Einar seemed upset at being ordered to have her for his wife. "Why did Ilsa have breeches on?" she asked after a long moment.

The suddenness of her question startled Einar. "She wanted to divorce Ull."

"Why?"

"Because of you, I would imagine."

Still Meradyce seemed calm, standing there so close to his bed. The sight of her filled him with nearly unbearable yearning, but he forced himself to sound as if nothing was amiss. "That would have meant trouble for the village."

"So marrying me to you ensures peace?"

"Yes."

She went slowly toward the bed. Desire pulsed through his body as he watched her.

By Thor's hammer, he wanted her! And more than that, he needed her in a way he had never needed a woman. Not as someone simply to share his bed, but as someone to share his life, to ease his sorrow and share his joy. A woman to bear his children.

This woman.

He dared not tell her. To do so would be to weaken, to show that he had lost control when she had not.

It took him a moment to realize that she was taking off her gown.

"What are you doing?"

"I am your wife. You will do as you planned all along. I will not fight you any more."

Her voice was low and scornful, and for the first time in his life, Einar felt defeat. "Stop."

Her hands hesitated at the drawstring of her shift and she twisted to look at him over her shoulder, her gaze resentful. "Why? Is this not what you want? My body, in your bed, to take your pleasure?"

Einar's hands tightened into fists. He had never before tried to explain his feelings to a woman, not even Nissa before he knew her true nature. "No." One word, but it took a great effort for him to say it.

She paused, and he saw uncertainty in her eyes.

He crossed the room to her. "What happened to the man you wanted to marry?"

Her eyes widened. Then her lips pressed together with anger. He did not care. It was a form of passion, at least.

"How do you know about that?"

Einar remembered her speaking of a monastery. "What was he, a priest?" he scoffed, sure by the look in her eyes that he guessed the truth. "Too holy to touch you, I suppose."

She glared at him. "Do not dare to speak to me of him, you . . . you barbarian!"

She lifted her hand to strike him, but he caught it easily, his grip tightening until she blinked back tears of pain. He let her go.

She scrutinized his face as she rubbed her arm. "Why, you are *jealous!*" she whispered incredulously.

"You are my wife now, Saxon. I will make you forget every man you have ever met!" With savage fury his mouth crushed hers, demanding that she respond. Let her dream of her priest while he had her body. If that was all he could get, he would at least take that.

She wrenched herself away. "Stop!"

He stood as if frozen in the ice of winter, only his heaving chest giving evidence that he was alive. They faced one another like two weaponless warriors on a field of battle.

She stared into his eyes, her gaze searching. He looked down, unable to look into her blue eyes anymore.

"Do you truly want me?" she asked softly.

He straightened. "What?"

"Svend ordered me to be your wife. You *told* me I was. I have to know, Einar. Do you really want me for your wife?"

"Yes!" He no longer cared if what he felt for her was weakness or strength. With one stride he reached her and in one motion took her in his arms. "I want you for my wife. I need you, as much as a man ever needed a woman! Meradyce, please, be my wife!'' he whispered.

His lips pressed down on hers in a kiss that said even more than his words.

Meradyce responded willingly, her lips crushing his in a fiery kiss. She had seen his feelings in his eyes, and she knew he meant what he said. Desire and triumph flowed through her body. Passion ignited within her as she pressed her body close to his.

The shields around them both had shattered. She knew it, felt it, reveled in the knowledge.

She wanted him, in every way.

She pulled away and with feverish hands attacked the lacing at the neck of his tunic. She could not resist the urge to press her heated lips to his neck or slip her hands inside his tunic and feel the hard muscles of his chest.

He moaned as his hands moved, one to clasp her tightly to him, the other to cup her breast. His thumb brushed over her nipple.

Meradyce gasped at the thrill of pleasure his hands aroused. She tugged at his tunic until he stepped away and tore it off. The light was dim, but she already knew every muscle, every contour. Her breathing quickened and she yanked at the drawstring of her shift.

The chill air touched her body, but it could not cool her. There was only one way. ''Einar, take me,'' she whispered.

He needed no urging, but her words thrilled him beyond measure. He would, soon, but not quickly. He wanted to enjoy his triumph.

He gazed at her lovely body, now waiting for him willingly, but only for a moment. He took her chin in his hand and tilted her face upward.

She did want him, as much as he wanted her. Slowly, he smiled, delighted that he had not forced her. To see her look at him thus was worth all the frustration and anger and pain. "Meradyce, take *me*," he said softly, lowering his hand to caress her.

She arched to his touch and suddenly he could be patient no longer. He picked her up and put her on his bed, then quickly rid himself of his breeches. He lay beside her, looking at her with sudden tenderness. Gently, he stroked her neck, her breasts, her stomach. "I will try not to hurt you."

She smiled at him, her eyes so filled with trust that he could scarcely breathe. "I know. I also know it will be a brief pain, only this once." She put her hands on his shoulders and pulled him closer.

He wanted to plunge inside her, to feel her body taking him, but he had loved many women, not a few of them virgins. He knew he should be careful with Meradyce. He forced himself to linger, caressing her slowly, letting his hands arouse her.

He kissed her, using his tongue to probe her willing mouth, gasping with delight when she began to return his kiss. He almost lost his self-control when she thrust her hips toward him in silent invitation.

He began to tease her nipple with his lips. Her breathing was fast, and small whimpers of pleasure escaped her. He moved his hand between her thighs, trying to wait.

But he couldn't. He had already waited so long....

He pressed his length inside her, watching her face to know if he was hurting her too much.

Suddenly she thrust her hips upward and wrapped her legs around his waist.

It was more than he could stand. All he knew now was the driving need of his body as he pushed inside her, seeking release. Her hands clutched his shoulders. Her legs tightened around him as she writhed under him, primitive and passionate. She cried out, her body as taut as a rope on a straining sail, propelling him forward to glorious completion.

Spent, he gently moved away. "Did I..."

She looked at him, a small, beguiling smile on her lips. "Not much. Husband." Her face grew serious. "Einar, would you have married me if Svend had not ordered it?"

He stared at the ceiling. "Would you have married Ull?"

"Answer my question."

He rolled on his side, one hand toying with a dark curl. "Are you going to be one of those nagging, questioning wives?"

"I want to know, Einar," she said softly.

"I do not know," he replied honestly. He pressed a kiss to her brow. "My experience of marriage was not pleasant. I had no wish to go through it again. Would you have married Ull, if I had refused?"

He heard her sigh softly. "It would not be fair, even to a man like Ull, to marry someone when your heart belongs to another."

He pulled her to him so that her soft, warm body was on top of his. "Do I have your heart, Meradyce?"

The look in her eyes told him everything.

Then, suddenly, Einar knew they were not alone.

Chapter Twelve

With one swift motion, Einar pushed Meradyce aside and stood up, his eyes scanning the longhouse.

"What is it?" Meradyce asked.

A small movement caught his eye. "Adelar?"

The boy stepped forward.

"What do you want?" Einar asked as he pulled on his breeches.

The blade of a knife flashed in Adelar's hand as he rushed at Einar. Einar caught him easily, falling with him unharmed to the ground, where the boy continued to struggle fiercely.

Meradyce hurried to pull one of the fur coverings around herself and went toward them. "Let him up."

Einar let the boy go and Adelar stood up shakily, his gaze shifting from Einar to Meradyce.

"Adelar, why did you do that?" she asked quietly.

He stared at the ground, his shoulders slumped.

"Adelar, answer me," she demanded.

Adelar lifted his head proudly. "If he has hurt you, I will kill him!"

Meradyce shook her head. "Einar would never hurt me, just as you would not."

He looked at her with surprise. "You do not want him for your husband, do you?" he asked urgently.

"Yes, I do," Meradyce answered.

"He is a Viking!" Adelar protested.

"I know," she said softly.

As Einar watched them, understanding dawned. The boy cared for her not as a mother, but as a lover. Einar marveled at Meradyce's wisdom, for she was treating the boy as if he was a jealous man, not an errant child.

And although a few moments ago he would have said it was impossible, his feelings for Meradyce deepened.

"Come with me," Einar said, putting on his tunic.

Adelar looked about to object, but Einar's words had the force of an order. Adelar obeyed.

Einar led him outside and out of the village, to the field where the warriors practiced fighting. The air was cold, but not uncomfortable. Einar was grateful, for it sharpened his sated senses.

He sat down on a rock and motioned for the boy to sit beside him. When he did, Einar said, "Your feelings—and your choice of women—do you credit. But she is too old for you."

Adelar glanced at him swiftly and somewhat skeptically.

"You are young. The best years of your life lie ahead of you. There will be many women before you find the right one."

"That is *your* way, perhaps. It does not have to be mine."

This was going to be more difficult than he thought, Einar reflected. "Why do you want Meradyce?"

"I do not have to tell you."

"Then I shall answer for you. Because she is kind, gentle, beautiful and clever."

"Why did you ask me, if you knew the reasons?"

"Because they are the reasons I care for her, too."

The boy's expression was hard and unforgiving. "If you care for her, why did you rape her?"

"I did not. I *loved* her." He faced Adelar squarely. "And she *loved* me. She chose me herself, Adelar. I did not force her."

Adelar jumped to his feet, his face filled with anger. "I do not believe you."

"Then I shall tell you myself."

Einar twisted around to see Meradyce walking toward them, dressed and swaddled in a warm cloak.

"Sit down," she said to the boy.

Adelar seemed about to disobey, but he sat down grudgingly. She sat beside him and looked at him steadily. "Adelar, I care for Einar very much. You know the kind of man he is."

"He is a savage barbarian—"

"No! That is your wounded pride talking. He is a fine warrior, as you would be. He is also honorable, loyal, kind. He did not take me—I gave myself."

"You may be able to forget who you are," Adelar said scornfully, "but *I* never will."

Einar saw Meradyce's pale skin flush pink. With shame?

"The Saxons are no better than anyone else," Einar said slowly and deliberately, glaring at the boy. "Do you know how we found your village, Adelar? Your..." He hesitated for a moment. "You have a traitor in the midst of your glorious people."

"You are lying!"

"I never lie."

"Then who?"

"Ask your father."

"I do not believe you!" Adelar cried, leaping to his feet. "I hate you! I hate you both!"

Before they could stop him, Adelar ran down the path toward the village. Meradyce began to follow, but the boy was far ahead, and she knew that he needed to be alone. She turned to Einar, worry on her features. "There was a traitor in our village?"

Einar nodded, pulling her into the comfort of his arms. "Yes."

"Who?"

"Kendric."

Meradyce gasped, horrified. "Kendric? But why? Why would he betray his own people?"

"He wanted us to kill someone. He paid well—and the village was a rich prize in itself."

"Who did he..." Her voice trailed off. "Ludella. He wanted you to kill Ludella. *That* was why you looked at the crucifix I wore, why you thought I was the children's mother. It is hard to believe, even of Kendric."

"You *do* believe me?"

"Yes, of course. But Adelar did not have to know, did he?"

"I would have told him about the traitor before he returned home. He will lead his people some day, and he must know there can be enemies anywhere."

Einar's prediction about Adelar would probably come to pass, Meradyce thought. He was a born leader, like Einar. "Must he learn *everything?*"

"Adelar is strong enough to know the truth, but that can wait," he said as he drew her closer. "Tonight I have no wish to talk of traitors."

She smiled at him, at the warmth in his voice, the tender regard in his eyes. He reached out for her hand and held it tightly.

"You are not ashamed, are you?" he asked suddenly.

"Ashamed?"

"Of being a Viking's wife?"

She frowned, and he felt dismayed until she spoke. "Adelar has a way, when he speaks so forcefully... For a moment, maybe I was." She gazed at him. "But I could never be anything but proud to be your wife."

He bent down and kissed her gently. "And I am proud to be your husband. Come, it is too cold out here."

As they began to walk toward the village hand in hand, Meradyce said, "Adelar was so angry..."

"Jealousy is a terrible feeling. But he is young. He will soon forget it."

"I hope you are right," Meradyce said doubtfully.

"Let us go home, wife. It is getting dark and I want to go to bed."

"Are you tired?"

Einar grinned wickedly. "No."

* * *

"I am not going to run outside naked," Meradyce warned as she watched Einar throw water on the heated rocks. "And I am certainly not going to jump in the river after this."

A cloud of steam rose in the already hot bathhouse.

"But that is the best part," Einar asserted, sitting beside her. "It is the shock of the cold water that really makes you feel alive."

"I have other ways of feeling alive, thank you," Meradyce said decisively as she leaned back against the walls. The hot air made every muscle in her body relax, and she thought she could easily go to sleep if she was alone.

With Einar sitting beside her totally nude, however, sleep was not quite what she had in her mind. She opened her eyes and glanced at him. "I see you are not cold."

His hand traveled slowly up her bare leg. "I am quite warm."

"I thought this was supposed to be restful," Meradyce chided with absolutely no sincerity as her breathing quickened.

"I do not want to rest," Einar said, his voice a low growl as he turned to her. "If you are not willing to run to the river, I will have to think of something else to do."

Meradyce sighed as Einar's hands moved leisurely over her body. "What if someone else comes to the bathhouse?"

"They will have to wait until we are . . . finished."

"Einar?"

"Yes?"

"How many women have you loved?"

"What?"

She withdrew slightly, her mouth curving into a wistful smile. "You have known so many women—"

"Not that many."

She gave him a skeptical look. "I wish I knew more about pleasing you."

"I will be glad to teach you."

She pushed him away gently and stood up, going toward the wall that had no bench along it, then turned slowly, giving him ample opportunity to gaze at her beautiful body.

"Come here, Einar," she said softly.

He needed no urging, but rose quickly. "What is it? You don't want to leave?"

She put her arms around him, lifting her face to kiss him. "I want to know what it is like, standing up."

"What?"

Her hands moved over his back and then his chest as she smiled at him coyly. "I have been wondering, since that night I saw—"

"You *were* watching! I knew it! That was not very honorable of you, wife."

She blushed charmingly and it was an effort to keep from kissing her, but he wanted to hear her reply.

"Naturally, if you are going to do such things in a public place," she said with a hint of displeasure, "you should expect to have an audience. I did not know what you were doing at first."

"And even when you did, you kept watching."

She pressed against him provocatively. "It was rather interesting."

With a low moan, he tugged her close, kissing her passionately. "It is so much more than interesting," he murmured as he pushed her against the wall for support.

Some time later, when Meradyce and Einar returned to the longhouse flushed and heated—for they never did make it to the river—they were surprised to find a blazing fire in the hearth, a pot filled with delicious-smelling stew and the chest of clothes Einar had given Meradyce in one corner.

Einar grinned like a little boy. "My mother has been here."

Meradyce removed her cloak.

Einar glanced at her, now properly dressed. "Let us go back to the bathhouse," he said with an evil grin.

"My fingers are wrinkled as it is," she answered, trying to sound severe. "And as for my back . . ." She rested her hand on it as if in great pain.

Einar smiled and said in an offhand manner, "You wanted to know."

Meradyce did not respond as she reached down to pick up the cloak her husband had let drop to the floor. "It was not necessary for your mother to do all this work. I would have done it—provided my husband gave me a chance. . . ."

"Oh, of course. Blame me. I think one of the reasons women marry is so they have someone to blame when they do not get their work done."

"That might be true, but once a woman has a husband, she has three times the work."

Einar shrugged and grinned. "Surely married life has some compensations."

Meradyce tried not to smile. "Well, Einar, I will have to be sure and thank Olva. This house was filthy!"

He gave her a sour look. "Because I do not have slaves to do my cleaning." He frowned a little less. "And until now, I have not had a wife to do it."

She sat beside him at the hearth. "Why did you not have slaves, Einar? I thought all Vikings who had any wealth at all—"

"Because my mother was once a Saxon slave," he said. "That is how she met my father. He raided her village, and instead of running in fear to get away from the barbarians, she ran *to* him and begged him to take her away. So he did."

Meradyce looked at him in surprise. "I had no idea."

Einar grinned. "Of course not. I am sure the idea that any Saxon would actually find a Viking attractive is rather shocking."

She flushed. "Obviously your mother and I have quite a bit in common."

"Yes, you do. Me."

"I suppose . . ."

"I can think of nothing better for women to have in common."

"Of all the conceited—"

He laughed and pulled her into his lap. "Men who wanted you," he finished for her, "I got you. And I will thank the gods for it every day of my life." With that he gave her a gentle kiss.

She frowned, trying to look severe. "I still think you are conceited. And arrogant. And altogether too sure of yourself."

"You are just annoyed that I would not chase after you like Ull and the others. I would call *that* conceited. And arrogant. And rather sure of yourself, too."

"It would appear that we are very well suited, then," she replied.

"*I* think so." Einar laughed again and lifted her from his lap. "You are not the only one a little sore," he explained ruefully.

He picked up a spoon and leaned toward the pot, tasting the stew. "This is wonderful! Of course, it could be that all our recent activity has sharpened my appetite."

"That probably means Endredi has been here, too."

"Are you saying my mother is not a good cook?"

Meradyce dished out some stew for them both. "No. I am saying that Endredi is an *excellent* one."

"I know very little about my daughter," he answered pensively.

She put down her bowl and took his face gently between her palms, seeing a wistful expression in his eyes.

"It is not too late to learn," she said softly.

"It was a tavern. That is all I know," Lars answered as he pushed through the crowded, narrow streets of Hedeby with Ingemar beside him.

"Was he not worried, going alone among the Saxons?"

"No." Lars spotted Nils' inn. "Here is the place we usually stay. We must eat."

"Was it far?"

"What?"

"The Saxons' tavern."

"I do not know. I did not ask."

Ingemar decided she had better not question Lars any more today about Einar and his Saxon friend. They were both tired and hungry, and she was beginning to wonder if Lars regretted coming with her.

After leaving their village, they had ridden to a neighboring one, where they sold their horses and bought passage on a merchant vessel leaving for Hedeby. It had been a long journey, and Lars had been strangely silent for most of the way.

Perhaps he was sorry to leave the men he had known all his life. Perhaps he felt he would never regain the respectful place he had as the steersman of Svend's finest vessel. And perhaps he was doubting she would ever let him . . .

Ingemar smiled to herself. Tonight she would let Lars do as he wished, and then surely he would have no regrets.

He should also remember that she had given up some status, as well, for her father, Bjorn, was the finest shipbuilder anyone had ever known.

She frowned as she recalled her final farewell with her father. He had been distracted, as usual, for he had had a new idea about the shape of the mast for Svend's newest vessel.

She had not listened very carefully to him, and he had not listened very carefully to her—such had always been their relationship.

She was happy to be gone. She had refused to stay and endure the women's sly looks, knowing they were comparing her to the Saxon.

"Lars!" a young woman called out as they entered the inn. "Are you alone? Where is Einar?"

Ingemar frowned as the pretty girl came closer.

"Good day, Sigrid. I came alone—" Lars began. Ingemar nudged him. "I came with Ingemar. My wife."

Ingemar suppressed a sour look. She could not deny that she might as well be Lars' wife, but there had been no formal exchange of gifts.

Sigrid eyed Ingemar, who stood haughtily by Lars' side. "We have a very nice room."

"Good," Ingemar said.

"Follow me."

Sigrid led them through a throng of men, many of whom watched Ingemar with greedy eyes, which pleased Ingemar greatly.

"It is a pity Einar is not with you," Sigrid said as they went to an adjoining building.

"Einar is married," Lars said.

"Oh, really?" Sigrid replied with some surprise.

As she opened the door, she glanced slyly at Lars. "When he comes in the spring, will he bring his wife?"

"Probably," Ingemar answered for Lars. She was glad to see the disappointed look on the girl's face. It helped to quell the jealousy raging in her, for she was sure this girl had been with Einar.

Her hatred of him grew even more, as did her determination to have her revenge.

She would persuade Lars to tell her where the Saxon tavern was. Then she would go there and tell them exactly where the Saxon children—and that woman—were to be found.

She waited until Sigrid left, closing the door behind her. Then she smiled sweetly at Lars and began to remove her gown.

Ull yanked Siurt out of bed.

Siurt cursed loudly, as did his wife, but Ull ignored them both. "Get dressed," he ordered.

Siurt was about to complain until he got a good look at his brother's face. Ull had been drinking, and there was no arguing with him when he was drunk. Not unless he wanted a fight. "All right," he muttered.

Siurt dressed quickly and followed Ull outside and down to the docks. It was a dark night, with no moon. The ships rocked gently at their moorings.

"Svend should not have given the woman to Einar," Ull began petulantly.

Siurt stifled a sigh. Obviously his brother was going to complain again—and the night was cold! "He could not give her to you. Ilsa would have divorced you!"

"I wanted to be rid of that bitch anyway."

"Her father would have been furious."

"We could have taken care of him and his men."

Siurt knew it was pointless to argue. "It does not matter now. It is done."

"It is time Svend was no longer chieftain."

"Einar does not want to be chieftain."

"I never said anything about Einar."

Siurt's eyes widened. "You want to be chieftain?"

A fierce look came into his brother's eyes. "Yes."

"But Einar—"

"Damn Einar and damn Svend and damn the rest of his spawn!"

"You do not have enough men to follow you," Siurt began, his tone placating. "It would be foolish. Better to start a new village elsewhere. I will go with you."

"I have a better plan than that—one that does not depend on the rest of the fools who live in this stinking village! One that will give us more power than you can imagine!"

Siurt took a step back. "What are you talking about?"

"If we take the Saxon children back to their father, he will be grateful."

"You want the ransom money?"

"I do not want money. I want men."

Siurt stared at Ull, appalled. "You would use Saxons against your own people?"

"Against Svend and his sons. Once I am chieftain, I would have no further need for the Saxons."

"What if they won't leave?"

"Then we will kill them," Ull said dismissively.

Ull was convinced his plan would work. The Saxon thane would surely give him men and weapons to use against the Vikings who had taken his children. Once

Svend and his sons were dead, the other villagers would not dare to rise against him. The Saxons would go back home or die.

"What about the woman?"

Ull smiled cruelly. "If the Saxon wants his children, she will be a part of the ransom payment to me."

"But Ilsa..."

Ull shrugged his shoulders. "Ilsa *nothing!* She can go back to her father." He rubbed his beard thoughtfully. "Or better yet, I will use the Saxons to attack her father's village, as well. Two villages to rule is better than one, eh?"

Siurt nodded. He wasn't pleased by the idea of using Saxons, but if Ull thought his scheme would work, it probably would. "When will you do this?"

Ull shivered in the cold winter wind. It would be better to wait for spring, although he was impatient to act. "We sail as soon as possible in the spring. Einar is always cautious. We will go while he is still waiting for perfect weather."

"We do not have a ship."

"We will steal one."

The fact that Ull was willing to risk death by stealing a ship convinced Siurt that his brother was absolutely determined. He had little choice but to help him. If he did not, Siurt had no doubt that his brother would kill him for knowing what he intended to do.

Meradyce sighed contentedly and snuggled up against Einar's warm, strong body. Who would have guessed a Viking could make her feel so happy?

He moved slightly and she reached up to brush the hair away from his face. He looked young and boyish in his sleep. She pressed a gentle kiss on his smooth cheek, then lay back down beside him.

Outside, the wind howled like a hungry wolf. Einar had said it would snow again soon.

She hoped he was right when he insisted that she not worry about Adelar. The boy still would not speak to her or even look at her. He treated her like a traitor, and perhaps, to him, she was. Einar was certain he would see that she was happy and become used to the marriage, but Meradyce was still uncertain. Reason had very little to do with feelings.

Einar stirred beside her, and his hand reached out to touch her. She smiled, certain that today would begin as most days had since Svend had declared them married, with lovemaking. She was also certain that tonight would be as nearly every night. Einar would take her in his arms and carry her to the enormous bed. They would not sleep for a long, long time. . . .

There was a sound at the door. Meradyce sat up, pulling the covers with her.

"What?" Einar mumbled, sitting up. His father, smiling broadly, stood in the doorway.

"I am sorry to wake you, my son, but Asa has need of your wife."

Einar turned to Meradyce with a grin.

"Asa?" Meradyce questioned.

"Yes. Her time has come."

His smile quickly disappeared as he saw a fleeting expression of concern cross Meradyce's face. "Is something wrong?"

Meradyce got out of bed and dressed quickly, trying to ignore Svend, who still stood in the doorway. "I am going. Will you fetch Endredi?"

"Endredi?"

"She wants to learn to help me. And I will need her."

Einar rose, unmindful of his nakedness as his father tapped his foot impatiently.

"What is it?" Einar asked quietly in Saxon.

"Asa is carrying twins. They are often difficult."

"Does Asa know?"

Meradyce shook her head as she swiftly filled a basket with herbs and other medicines. "No." She glanced at him and smiled slightly. "I will do the best I can. She has carried them longer than some, so all may yet be well."

Einar was certain that if anything could be done to help Asa, Meradyce would know what it was and how to do it.

Meradyce was ready. She hurried out the door, needing no guide to the bathhouse. Einar and Svend went together to fetch Endredi.

Olva smiled when she saw the men come inside. "Einar! We see so little of you now! And Svend! To what do we owe the honor?"

They both grinned at Olva's teasing tone. Betha came toward them from the back of the longhouse. "How do you like my new kitty?" she asked, holding up a black kitten.

"Very nice." Einar looked at his mother meaningfully. "Meradyce needs Endredi."

"Ah, it is Asa?"

They nodded.

"She is having the babies now?" Betha asked happily.

"Yes," Olva replied.

The men stared at Betha as she carried her kitten to her bed, surprised that she was so fluent in their language.

"Babies? What does she mean, babies?" Svend demanded.

Olva ignored him. "Adelar, Endredi has gone to milk the goats. Find her and tell her that Meradyce needs her."

Einar had not seen the boy in the shadows. As Adelar wordlessly went outside, Einar saw the smoldering hatred in the boy's eyes.

Einar wondered if he should have paid more attention to the boy, but surely it was only natural that a man would want to be with his new and wonderful wife. He had heard from Olva that Adelar was spending most of his time with Thorston, and then had thought no more about him.

"What did she mean, babies?" Svend asked again.

Einar turned to his father. "Meradyce thinks Asa is carrying twins."

"By Odin's eye! Really? Two, eh? I have never had twins before!"

"And *you* are not having them now," Olva pointed out. "Go and see if they need anything. Water, or food, or more blankets?"

"She did not tell me she was having twins," Svend said.

"She does not know," Einar said.

"In the name Freyja, why not?"

"Because Meradyce did not want to worry her."

"Oh." The notion that there might be more risk to such a birth seemed to dawn on Svend. "Oh."

"Meradyce said it is a good thing she did not begin her labor sooner."

Svend gave his son a thankful look and clamped his meaty hand on Einar's broad shoulder. "It seems it was a very good thing you did not kill her after all, my son. I was not so sure at first."

Einar smiled. "I will go to the bathhouse and find out if they want anything," he said, ducking out the door.

"What was that all about?" Olva demanded of her former husband. "Kill her? Kill Meradyce? What are you talking about?"

"That son of yours did not obey orders. He is too much like you sometimes, Olva." Svend sat down beside the hearth. Olva looked about to protest, but instead she joined him.

"He is *your* son, too. You told him to kill her?"

Svend sighed heavily. "A Saxon thane wanted his wife killed, and he was offering a lot of money, so I said we would do it."

Olva gave him a black look. "Since when do you kill women, Svend?"

"Obviously never. She is not dead, is she?"

"Thanks to Einar, no."

"All right—but as you said, he is my son. He knows a fine woman when he sees one, eh? Just as well, too, since she was the wrong woman!"

Olva's eyes lit up with understanding. "It was the children's *mother* that was supposed to..."

"Yes." They sat silently for a few minutes, then Svend gave her a sidelong glance. "Our son seems happily wed, does he not?"

Olva smiled broadly. "You do some things right, Svend."

His grin was the image of Einar's. "Lots of things, if your memory is good. You know, Olva, I have always been sorry you divorced me."

"I would not share my man with any other woman, thank you."

"Pity."

"You never change, do you? I am a happily married woman—and your youngest wife is about to give birth!"

"I hope Einar's wife will give him sons."

"I do, too. She is already giving him happiness."

Svend nodded, then stood up. "I should go see how my wife is."

"Yes. Tell her I wish her the best. And you, too."

Svend went out the door and Olva sat by the fire, dreaming happy dreams for her son.

For the moment she had forgotten Betha, who sat on the bed, unmindful of her kitten, her face filled with horror at the knowledge that her father had wanted her mother dead.

Chapter Thirteen

Meradyce smiled as Svend gently picked up his sons. He cradled one in each large arm and smiled at them. They were surprisingly big for twins, and Asa had had a difficult labor, but all had gone well.

Asa would live, and so would her babies. Endredi had proved capable and competent, helping without being told what to do. Even now, she was preparing the infants' beds.

"By Odin's eye, they are fine sons!" Svend exclaimed, giving his wife a grin that reminded Meradyce of her own husband as she went outside where Einar was waiting. He looked relieved when he saw her smile.

"They are well?" he asked softly, drawing her into his arms beneath his cloak. It was very dark, but she had no idea if it was late afternoon, evening or deepest night. The air was freezing, and snow was beginning to fall heavily.

"Yes, they are all fine. Svend, of course, is delighted with two more sons."

She huddled in Einar's warm embrace, turning her head to look at him. "How many children does your father have, exactly?"

Einar looked at her upturned face with a wry grin. "Well, there's Hamar, his firstborn by his first wife, then comes his finest son—"

"You?"

"Of course," Einar said with a deep chuckle. "Then he has three girls and two more sons by his third wife, who died. By his fourth wife, Vedis, who is still married to him, four daughters and three sons. His fourth wife died in childbirth, as did the baby. His fifth wife, Brynhild—"

"The heavy one?"

"Yes. She's had three sons—"

"She's with child again."

"Really? With Brynhild, it is hard to tell. She always looks as if she is with child."

"And his sixth wife?"

"Oh, she divorced him the minute she got here and found out about his other wives."

"Asa does not care about the other women?"

Einar shook his head. "No." His brow wrinkled with thought. "My father truly cares for her, you know. I have never seen him that way over a woman."

"Olva said something like that to me the other day. About you," she teased.

"Must be the winter air," he said offhandedly.

Meradyce pinched him.

"What is that for?"

"It must be the winter air," she replied.

She was delightfully happy. She had never felt so free to tease and play. It was as if, in becoming a woman, she had finally found the freedom of a child.

He laughed softly, then his arms tightened around her. "I am so glad you are here, Meradyce." He pressed a tender kiss to her forehead. "Not just for my sake—although that is plenty. If anything had happened to Asa, it would have broken my father's heart."

She returned his embrace, lifting her lips to his for a more passionate expression of her feelings. His hands slid up her arms.

"Meradyce!"

She moved away at the sound of Olva's voice. Einar's mother had come just after the babies were born and had offered to bring some food and wine.

But when Meradyce saw her now, hurrying through the blowing snow, the woman had nothing in her hands. "Meradyce!" she called urgently, panic in her voice.

"What is it?" Meradyce demanded, stepping out of Einar's arms.

"It is Adelar and Betha. They are gone!"

"Gone?" she replied blankly. How could they be gone?

Olva halted in front of them, panting heavily. "I left them sleeping. Thorston was in the hall with the other men, and I knew I would just be away for a short time. But when I got back, they were gone!"

Before Meradyce could say anything, Einar walked away with long, purposeful strides.

"They cannot have gotten far," he called over his shoulder. "We will find them."

Then he was gone, his body disappearing in the darkness and the drifting snow.

Betha clutched Adelar's cloak tightly, although her fingers were so cold she could hardly feel them. "I am getting tired," she said, her teeth chattering, her numb feet stumbling.

Adelar glanced at her, nearly tripping on the too-large cloak he wore. "We have not gone far enough." He saw the weariness and strain on his sister's face. "Do not worry. Thorston says there are huts the herdsmen use in the summer near here."

Betha nodded and began to walk again. It seemed a very long time since Adelar had shaken her awake and told her they were going home.

She had looked at him with wonder and surprise.

She had no wish to return home. She missed her mother, but not the anger and resentment between her parents. She had known they did not care for one another, but she had been shocked and horrified to learn that her father was willing to have her mother killed.

She could not tell Adelar what she had overheard. She would not give him the pain she had experienced with the knowledge. And she had seen the unmistakable look of determination in his dark brown eyes when he woke her. He had made up his mind to go, and go he would, with her or without her.

So she had agreed to leave with him. He had not told her much about how they were going to get home, but she trusted him. If he said he knew how, he knew how.

By this time, not only were her feet numb with cold and fatigue, but so were her legs. The snow had been falling lightly when they left the village. Now it was falling so heavily she could hardly see Adelar in front of her.

Just when she thought she could not go on any longer, he halted. She heard the scrape of wood on wood and realized he had found a hut and was pushing in the door.

She stumbled after him into the dark interior, which smelled of old wool.

"Sit here," Adelar said, and she obeyed.

He took off his cloak and wrapped it around her shoulders. She wanted to protest—he must need it—but she was so cold and the cloak felt so warm.

As her eyes grew used to the darkness, she saw Adelar reach into the bundle he was carrying and pull something out. He knelt beside the circle of stones in the center of the hut and pushed together some bits of wood and straw. Then he struck two objects he held in his hands, and a spark hit the straw.

He had made a fire! With relief, she went near it, but he gently pushed her away. "You are wet! You will drip on it. Wait until I find more wood somewhere."

She sat on the floor. There was no wood to be seen, but there was an old stool missing a leg. Adelar lifted it and smashed it on the floor, shattering it.

"We will need more," he muttered, and she heard the weariness in his voice. "But this will do for now."

He returned to his bundle and brought out a hunk of bread. "Eat this," he said, offering it to her.

Betha was too tired to eat, but there was something in Adelar's voice that made her try. As she chewed, some of the exhaustion left her, at least enough for her to give voice to her curiosity. "Where are we going?"

"I told you. Home."

"But how?"

"I have been listening to Thorston and asking questions. I know where there is another village. Someone there will help us."

"Why would they do that?"

"Because we have lots of money." Adelar reached down to a leather pouch on his belt, which had been hidden by his cloak. It jingled softly.

"Where did you get money?"

"It does not matter."

"You *stole* it!"

Adelar scowled at her. "So what if I did? They stole us."

"Not Thorston," Betha remarked softly.

"We need this money if we are to get home."

Betha looked around. "How long are we going to stay here?"

"Until it stops snowing."

"That might be a long time."

If Adelar thought so, too, his face did not betray it. His face also did not betray his sudden overwhelming guilt.

Had he been wrong to bring Betha with him? She was so little... And yet, he could not leave her with the Vikings.

But she was happy there, with Meradyce. Einar had said he would take them home in the spring.

Not Meradyce. He had stolen Meradyce from their village and from both of them.

He would hate Einar forever.

Betha yawned and he realized she was still shivering, although the fire had warmed him thoroughly.

"Lie down and rest," he told her softly.

Einar went at once to the stables, his two dogs with him. A quick look told him that none of the horses were missing. The children could not have gone far, but it also meant they were on foot, trying to make their way through the deepening snow.

He went directly to Svend's hall. The ground was hard and slippery with the wet snow, and he could not see his hand in front of his face. Fortunately, the raucous voices of the men led the way as surely as a beacon of fire.

Most of the men were gathered there, listening to the storyteller and getting drunk, anticipating Svend's pleasure at a new child.

"A son?" Thorston and some of the others called out, their smiles wide as he entered.

All the men fell silent as Einar strode to the middle of the building. "The Saxon children are missing," he said.

Ull jumped up quickly, the ale sloshing out of his drinking horn. "What?"

"The Saxon children are gone. We have to find them."

Siurt, nearly asleep, spoke loudly. "It is snowing too hard. We could not find our own bellies in this."

Hamar stood up. "I will help you."

Einar nodded.

"I will come, too," Ull called out.

Einar did not bother to hide his surprise. He would have thought Ull would be the last person to help him. Nonetheless, they would need every man they could get. More volunteered.

Einar strode to the door, almost colliding with Meradyce. "I am coming, too," she said.

"No. The snow is too thick. It is too dangerous for a woman." He pushed past her and into the storm.

As he entered the stable, someone tugged on his tunic. He turned to find Meradyce, her hair white with snow, at his elbow. "It is my fault this has happened. I am going to help."

Einar shook his head, her concern and fear stabbing him. This was as much his fault as anybody's, he knew, although her eyes held no blame. If he had left the children behind as he was supposed to, the boy and his sister would be safe at home—with a father who would coldbloodedly pay for the death of their mother, as well as betray his own people. A surge of anger filled him at the injustice of the gods giving such a man so fine a son.

"No," he said, his anger making his voice as cold as the snow swirling outside. "You cannot come."

"But—"

"No."

Meradyce looked into the eyes of the man she loved and knew it was pointless to argue. "Then find them quickly and bring them home safe to me."

He nodded, mounting his horse and whistling for his dogs. Then he rode into the cold darkness.

"I am to blame for this," Meradyce said, standing at the door of Olva's house, staring into the night, unmindful of the blowing snow and cold winds tugging at her gown. "I knew Adelar was upset, but I thought..."

Olva came to her and put a comforting arm around her shoulder. "We all thought he would come round. Who would have guessed he would do something like *this?*"

"I should have, if I had been thinking of *him,* and less of myself."

How many times during that long night had Meradyce cursed herself? She had forgotten her duty to the children, letting her own happiness overshadow everything else.

Olva gave her a motherly squeeze. "And I should never have left them alone. We can all blame ourselves. Thorston feels terrible for speaking of the nearby villages and for leaving his chest unlocked."

"For Adelar to steal, he must have been truly desperate to get away."

"Then I do not think you could have stopped him," Olva said softly.

As the snow swirled around her feet, another horrible image of Betha and Adelar, alone and shivering, invaded Meradyce's mind. "Will this storm never end?" she cried helplessly.

"The men have taken their horses. They can go faster and farther than the children."

"If there was only something we could do!"

"I will pray to Freyja. You pray to your god."

The storm had ceased shortly before the feeble dawn, but the bitterly raw wind did not slacken. Up near the edge of the summer pasture, Ull looked around at the nearby trees, their branches heavy with snow.

Many times in the night and early morning he had silently cursed the Saxon brats. They were fools, the pair of them, to set out anywhere in a snowstorm!

He hoped they would be found, and soon. If they died, his plans would be ruined. He needed the help of the Saxon thane if he was to have any chance of defeating Svend and his sons.

Soaked through from the snow, and hungry, Ull gave up in disgust. He would go home and eat, then begin searching again, if necessary.

He turned his horse and headed down the mountain, occasionally spotting another mounted man moving slowly through the trees.

After several more minutes, he stopped to relieve himself. That was when he noticed the hut, almost buried in the snow. He quickly finished and walked toward it.

Pushing open the door, he peered inside. Empty. He looked closely at the hearth, then went in farther.

Someone had been there recently. Very recently. He bent down and felt the ash. It was still warm.

A slow smile twisted his lips. If he found the children, surely Svend would reward him. Should the children be cold and hungry, they would welcome his rescue, and perhaps they would even come to trust him. That would make it easier to take them away in the spring.

He went outside, scanning the snow for tracks. Surprisingly, he could see nothing. Perhaps the lad and his sister had left the hut before the snow stopped, although he doubted the boy was smart enough to plan to have his tracks covered.

Ull went to his horse, contemplating which way they must have gone. They could not be far off.

Why not stay here for a few minutes, he thought suddenly. It was still warm inside the small building. He could use some wine, too.

He reached for the leather bag strapped to his horse and returned to the hut.

Adelar watched Ull from beneath some nearby pines. There were low bushes around the trees, and he and Betha had crawled under them. The ground was damp but not snowy, and he felt hiding was safer than trying to run.

When Ull went inside the hut, Adelar wondered if they should move on, but decided it was better to wait until Ull had mounted his horse and gone away.

Adelar looked at Betha, who lay on her side, all curled up like one of her kittens.

It had been a long time before she stopped shivering the night before. After that, he had slept fitfully, waking just before dawn as the snow was tapering off. He realized at once that the best thing would be to go before the snow stopped completely, so that their tracks would be hidden.

It had been difficult to wake Betha, but he knew she was very tired from the walking. Finally, she had moaned softly and when she sat up, her face had been flushed from sleep.

They had just stepped out of the door when he heard the sound of a horse. He spotted the bushes and urged Betha to hurry to them.

He pulled her cloak more tightly about her throat as he waited for the red-haired Viking to leave.

After what seemed a very long time, Ull came out of the hut, scratching himself and belching loudly. Adelar's lip curled in disgust, but he was pleased that the man was finally departing.

He had a moment of fear as Ull looked around and seemed to stare right at the clump of bushes, but at last he got on his horse and rode off slowly through the trees.

Several more minutes passed, then Adelar nudged Betha. "Come. We can go now."

Betha stirred fitfully but did not open her eyes.

"Come! We should go," Adelar whispered urgently.

Still she did not respond.

He pushed her again, noticing that her face was very red. He touched her cheek. It was burning.

"Betha!" he cried desperately, lifting her up so that her small head rested against his shoulder. "Betha! Wake up!"

Chapter Fourteen

Einar was cold, wet, tired and hungry, but he kept searching. He could not bear the thought of returning home without the children, to face the desperate look in Meradyce's eyes.

He scanned the sky and tasted the wind. It would snow again soon. It was nearly noon now. Night would come all too quickly, and he cursed the early evenings of winter. If they did not find the children before then...

He tried not to think about that as he kept riding slowly through the pine woods and the meadows.

Where did the children think they were going?

His dogs halted. Einar spotted another mounted man and called out. The man turned toward him.

It was Ull.

In the beginning, Einar had wondered why Ull had been one of the first to join the search. Now it no longer mattered.

Ull rode in Einar's direction. "They spent the night in a hut not far from here," he shouted above the wind.

"You are certain?"

"There was a fire there not long ago." Ull reined in his horse. "I do not think anyone else has used the hut."

"Show me where." A small moment of hope lightened the dread he had been feeling. At least the children had been warm for part of the night.

It took a few minutes to reach the hut. Einar was off his horse in an instant and went inside. Yes, someone had definitely taken shelter there recently.

He came out. "You saw no tracks going away from here?"

Ull shook his head and pointed. "I rode up there, but could not find a thing."

"Einar?" a voice called plaintively.

Both men turned and saw Adelar. He was holding a large bundle unsteadily. Einar began to run toward him.

"It is Betha," Adelar said, and Einar realized that it was Betha the boy held cradled in his arms. "She is sick. She will not wake up."

Einar reached down and quickly took Betha from her brother. Her face was flushed with fever, her breathing rapid and shallow, and her clothes were soaking wet.

"Oh, Freyja!" he whispered, at once a cry of despair and a prayer for help.

"Come!" he barked as he hurried to where Ull waited. He gave Betha to Ull while he mounted his horse. He held out his arms. "Now give her to me. You bring Adelar."

Without another word, Einar yanked on his reins and headed for the village.

* * *

Meradyce had not been able to eat or rest, but constantly paced between the hearth and the door. Wisely, Olva said nothing, sharing Meradyce's wordless agony of uncertainty.

Endredi had stayed with Svend to help Asa with the babies, but both women knew of her deep concern for Betha and Adelar. She would not rest, either, until they returned.

Thorston had joined the search. Several of his silver coins were missing, but both Meradyce and Olva knew he was much more concerned about the children's welfare.

Meradyce opened the door to look outside yet again, but this time, she gave a wild cry and darted out of Olva's longhouse.

Einar was coming, and he had Betha in his arms.

She ran to meet him, unmindful of the wet snow although she wore no cloak. She saw another rider behind him—Ull, with Adelar.

"Oh, Einar! You found them!" she cried joyously.

Then she saw her husband's face.

She looked at Betha. "Oh, dear God! Give her to me!"

He did, and Meradyce, clutching Betha's small body to her own, ran to Olva's house.

Meradyce could feel the fever raging in Betha and heard her delirious murmuring.

"Help me get these wet things off her," Meradyce said to Olva. "Then I need cool water."

Einar came to the door. She glanced at him. "Is Adelar sick, too?"

"No."

"Thank God!" she replied fervently. Quickly they removed Betha's wet clothes, put her in bed and pulled a blanket over her.

"I need my basket," Meradyce told Einar. "The one with all the medicines. Olva, please leave us—and do not let anyone else come here."

"Why—" Olva began.

"Her illness may be catching."

Einar stood as still as stone. "Catching?" he whispered. As much as he feared for the little girl, he began to fear for Meradyce.

"Yes. Now please go! Einar, I need my medicines. Olva, keep Endredi and Adelar away. They will try to come."

Einar went at once and got the basket, all the while telling himself that the illness would not be contagious. Meradyce would make Betha well. Everyone would—must—be well.

As he hurried back, he saw Adelar, still sitting on Ull's horse, although Ull was nowhere to be seen.

"Get down and wait for me," Einar said, his voice low and ominous.

First he would take the medicines to Meradyce. Then he would speak with Adelar.

"Where in Odin's name did you think you were going?" Einar demanded of the young Saxon. He had to know what had prompted the boy's foolish, dangerous act.

"I was going home," Adelar answered peevishly as he sat sullenly, his body wrapped in Einar's fur-lined cloak, his wet garments in a heap on the floor.

"Over land?" Einar asked scornfully.

Adelar shook his head. "No. I was going to buy passage on a ship."

"In the winter? Are you stupid?"

"No, I am not stupid! I am a Saxon being held against my will!"

"How were you planning to get home?"

"Thorston told me about Kaupang, on the other side of the coast. He said it was a big town. I thought someone there would take us home across the sea, if we had enough money."

"Huh," Einar grunted. He pulled off his wet tunic and put on a dry one. He had half suspected Ull had had a part in this ludicrous plan, perhaps hoping to take the children back to their father for the ransom money.

Apparently, he was mistaken. "You are telling me the truth?" he demanded, glaring at the boy.

Adelar did not quail. "Yes."

Einar believed him. He tossed more wood on the fire, making it hotter and brighter. "Where were you going to get money?"

"I had some."

Einar stopped pouring out two chalices of wine and slowly turned to look at the boy. "How did you get it, or should I say, where did you get it?"

The boy did not answer.

"Did you steal it?"

Adelar gazed steadily into Einar's eyes. "Yes."

Einar gave him a chalice half filled with good wine. "Drink this, or you will be falling sick, too."

Adelar's brave expression faded and he looked at the chalice. "What is wrong with Betha? Is she very sick?"

"I do not know," Einar answered honestly. He sat down beside Adelar. "Why did you take her with you?"

"She is my sister."

Einar nodded. "But why in the winter?"

"So it would be harder for you to follow us." Adelar sighed raggedly. "I did not think it would be so hard for Betha..."

"Meradyce will make her well."

Einar saw the tears on the boy's face and turned away. Like any warrior, Adelar would not want another man to witness his grief.

"Oh, dear God, help her!" Meradyce whispered, clutching Betha's warm little hand tightly. It had been two days since Einar had ridden home with the child, but the fever still possessed her tiny body. Now it was deepest night—the time when many souls made their final journey, as Meradyce knew full well.

Olva sat dozing near the hearth. Meradyce had tried to keep her out of the house, but the indomitable woman would have none of it, proving beyond a shadow of a doubt where Einar got his stubborn perseverance.

Endredi was still staying with Svend and Asa, but she came often to stand outside and enquire about Betha's health.

Thorston had gone on a journey to the nearest village. There was a woman there who made fur robes noted for their warmth and softness, and another who made dolls. He was determined to get both for Betha.

Betha stirred slightly. Meradyce leaned over her at once, wiping her perspiring brow with a damp cloth. Betha opened her deep brown eyes and tried to smile. "Meradyce," she whispered. Even that effort made her breathing more labored.

"Do not talk, dear," Meradyce whispered gently. "Drink this."

Betha, so hot, so small, so thin, swallowed some of the medicine that would lower her fever, but not much. "My mother is dead," she said softly.

"No, no, she is not," Meradyce protested.

But Betha seemed so certain.

Betha opened her eyes again. "Father did not really do it, did he?" she asked urgently. "He would not want her killed." She began to cough again.

Meradyce tried to mask her surprise. Had Betha somehow learned . . . ? But how?

Another spasm of coughing shook the child, and Meradyce blanched at the sight of blood in the phlegm. The hoarse sound of the girl's breathing filled the house. Betha was getting worse, and there was nothing more Meradyce could do to help her.

She took Betha's hand in her own. "Oh, God," she murmured, "oh, dear God . . ."

Once again, Betha opened her eyes. "Take care of Adelar," she whispered. "He . . . he still likes you. Very much."

"Do not talk, Betha," Meradyce urged.

"Be happy for me, Meradyce. I am going to be with my mother."

Then there was a gasp, followed by a silence as still as death—until Meradyce's agonized cry burst from her throat.

Olva woke up, took in everything with one glance and buried her face in her hands.

Einar, pacing in his longhouse, heard the anguished cry. At once he ran to Olva's house.

Meradyce knelt on the ground, her arms around the child in the bed, sobbing.

"Betha!" Adelar cried out from behind him.

Einar spun around at the mournful wail. Adelar rushed past him, throwing himself at the bed. "Betha!"

Meradyce lifted her tear-streaked face, her countenance full of anguish. "Take him away," she pleaded. "The fever..."

"No, I will not go!" Adelar screamed as Einar came closer. "No!"

It was not Adelar whom Einar touched gently on the shoulder.

"Meradyce," he said softly, "come with me. It is Adelar's place, to be with his sister now."

Meradyce looked at Einar, then at Adelar. Slowly she stood up. "I did everything I could," she said, her voice choking as she reached out to embrace Adelar.

"Do not touch me," the boy said, his voice low and cold, his body stiffening. "Never touch me."

Meradyce drew back, and the agony in her eyes tore at Einar's heart. "Adelar! I tried. I did everything I knew how."

"I know," he replied without looking at her. "Now go away and leave us alone."

Olva, her face streaked with tears, went quietly out. Einar put his arm around Meradyce and guided her to the door. "Come, we will go home," he said softly.

He led her to their longhouse and made her lie down on the bed. He did not leave, but sat silently nearby as she continued to weep.

At last, her sobbing subsided. He rose and bent over her. "I will get you something to eat," he said in a hushed voice. She had eaten almost nothing for two days, and his great fear was that she, too, would fall ill.

She gazed at him with tortured eyes. "I tried so hard...."

He stroked her cheek. "I know, beloved, I know."

"How will I tell her mother?" she whispered.

"You will not. I will."

Meradyce shook her head. "No."

"We will speak of this later." Einar fetched some bread and a chalice of wine.

"I am not hungry."

"You must eat, or you will get sick."

"Adelar...?"

"Olva will be with him now." He set down the food and sat on the bed, reaching out to touch her. "My place is here with you."

Meradyce yanked her hand away. "*My* place was with Betha."

"It was her time to die," he said, trying to find some way to comfort her.

Meradyce sat up abruptly, glaring at him. "It was *my* fault, Einar! If I had paid more attention to them, to how Adelar felt. If I had kept them with me, as I should have! If I had not—" She halted and looked at the floor.

"And if I had not taken you from your village, she would yet be alive."

Tears sprang anew to Meradyce's eyes, but she could not stop them. She did not want to. Betha was dead, and it was their fault.

"Do you think I have not thought of that?" he demanded quietly. "Do you think I have not cursed myself a hundred times for taking them from their home? The thane had wanted assurances that his children would not be harmed, but I defied both him and Svend because I thought you were their mother. I thought you would want them with you."

"I should have told you then they were not my own. I tried to protect them, but I have failed." She sighed heavily. "Please, Einar, go away. I cannot be with you right now. I need to be alone."

"No!" He pulled her up, holding her tightly by the shoulders and staring into her red-rimmed eyes. "Do not shut me out! I did not want a wife because I did not want to care. But you *are* my wife, and I do care about you, Meradyce!" His voice softened, and he loosened his grip. "Meradyce, I am truly sorry about Betha. But I cannot bring her back, not from death. Meradyce." His voice dropped to a whisper. "I have lost children, too."

She gazed at him, seeing truth and grief.

"Endredi was my first child, and the only one I ever acknowledged, but there have been other women, and other children. One came too early. One was born dead. The other, a son, did not live past six months."

She heard the pain in his voice and took his hand in hers. "And their mothers?"

"Not from this village. I did not care about any of them, beyond my own pleasure. To my shame." He sighed raggedly. "Who knows why such things happen? I wish with my whole heart that I had never set eyes on Betha and Adelar."

He reached out to brush back Meradyce's tear-dampened curls. "But if I had not, I would not have found you, either."

"Oh, Einar." Meradyce said nothing more, but buried her face against Einar's chest. "Will Adelar ever forgive us?"

"Surely, in time, he will."

In time, Adelar did forgive them, but it took much longer than anyone would have supposed. As the winter progressed, he kept to himself and never spoke to Einar again. Gradually, he softened a little toward Meradyce, but only a little. The only person he ever said more than a few words to was Endredi, and even then he was guarded and aloof.

A part of the boy had died with his sister, leaving a bitter young man who hated himself for taking a little child into the dark, snowy night.

Chapter Fifteen

After Betha's death, Einar suggested a proper Viking funeral, for Betha was a favorite among the village women.

Both Meradyce and Olva disagreed. She was a Christian, and they should bury her as a Christian. Einar and Svend conceded. Adelar said nothing to anyone.

On the day of the burial, it began to pour with a chill, driving rain. Einar wanted Meradyce to stay inside, for she looked ill and pale, but she insisted on going—and he knew he could not stop her.

Many people gathered around the small grave. Most of the women were crying, and even the hard-hearted Ilsa's eyes were moist.

No one spoke except Olva and Meradyce, who said prayers in Saxon and Latin. Adelar attended, standing as silent as a spirit. When it was over, he turned and walked away.

For days afterward, Meradyce busied herself with anything and everything during the day. At night, she made frenzied, passionate love with Einar, as if she was trying to forget what had happened and could only sleep when she was completely and utterly exhausted.

Then, one morning, Einar heard her coughing beside him in the bed. He realized she was shivering, although he was warm beneath the furs.

"Meradyce," he called softly.

She rolled toward him. "Einar," she whispered.

He gasped. Her eyes were sunken in dark circles, her face white. She coughed before speaking, and this time he saw blood on her lips.

She was going to die! That was the first thought that crashed into his mind. *She must not!* was the second.

He hurried out of the bed, pulling on his clothes. "I am getting Endredi," he said.

She reached out to him. "No. No one. Just bring the medicines and leave me."

"No."

"You might . . . get sick."

"No, I will not get sick."

She tried to smile at his arrogant assumption, but her chest hurt too much. She could only hope that he was right. She wanted to tell him to leave again, but another spasm of coughing racked her body and she knew she was too weak to tend herself.

"Tell me what to do," he demanded urgently.

She did, whispering the method for making some medicine, wondering how long she could manage to speak.

She had barely enough time before she was too weak to continue. He listened intently, his brow furrowed in concentration.

He began to go to the hearth, but turned back, taking her hand in his own. "You will *not* die, Meradyce." Suddenly, he blinked rapidly, his eyes glistening. "You *must* not."

Meradyce grew weaker as the day passed. He tried to get her to eat, to drink to some wine, some water, but she was soon too ill to respond.

Toward nightfall, Endredi came to the house.

Einar met her at the door. "Meradyce is sick. You should not come inside."

Endredi pushed past him.

He yanked her back. "I said, you cannot come in. She is ill."

Endredi gave him a determined look, and when she spoke her voice was coolly logical. "I can take care of her. I know what to do."

"But if you become sick . . ."

"Then I get sick. Now let me pass." It was not a request. It was a demand, an order.

Einar hesitated. He did not know what to do. Meradyce's instructions had been brief and unclear.

But would Endredi be able to help any better? She was so young. Did she have the wisdom and knowledge to heal Meradyce, or was he only putting Endredi at risk, the way he had the Saxon children when he stole them from their home?

He looked at his daughter, so calm and so sure of herself.

He would trust her judgment.

He nodded and she quickly went to Meradyce. She felt Meradyce's forehead, then listened to her chest.

She smelled the liquid that Meradyce had told him to make and looked at the untouched bowl of stew beside the bed. "Has she eaten anything?"

"She would only take a little water."

"Tell Olva to bring some broth, clear and hot." She pulled the fur coverings away from Meradyce. "First, help me get her shift off."

"But she is sick—"

"She is burning with fever. We must get her cool. Help me!"

Einar moved to obey.

"Where is there water?"

He nodded at a bucket.

"Is she with child?"

He shook his head. "No."

"Good. Being with child would take away her strength. Now go to Olva. Keep everyone else away. And you stay away, too."

"But—"

Endredi stood up and smiled grimly. "If you fall ill, who will keep Ull in his place?"

Einar looked at her. His heart filled with pride—and for the first time, it did not matter whether she was the daughter of his body or not. She was his child in ways beyond the bond of blood. He nodded slowly. "As you wish."

A quick, sudden look of pride flashed across Endredi's face—until Meradyce coughed again.

"Make her well!" Einar said as he went to the door, his words a plea and a demand.

"I will try," Endredi said, bending to her patient.

* * *

Ingemar crept quietly through the snow-covered streets. It had taken her days to get Lars to tell her where the Saxon tavern was, and even longer to persuade him to tell her the name of the man Einar dealt with.

At least she knew enough of the Saxon tongue to make herself understood. She had persuaded Olva to teach her, hoping that would help Einar see that she should be his wife. Now, the knowledge would help Ingemar betray him.

She pulled her cloak more tightly about her face and looked around. It was dark and cold, and few people were outside, but it was never safe for a woman alone—especially one as young and pretty as she was.

She went along a narrow street and heard the sound of boisterous laughter. A tavern, certainly.

Ingemar hesitated. It was a risky thing, going to speak to this Saxon she had never met, but she must not stop now. She frowned, a small twinge of remorse pulling at her. Naturally, Einar and the other men would fight. Some might even die.

She straightened her shoulders. She would never forget the insult Einar and the Saxon wench offered her!

She stepped into the filthy, snowy street, making her way around a small, steaming pile of dung.

After pushing open the door to the tavern, she waited on the threshold while her eyes grew accustomed to the unfamiliar brightness.

Suddenly a hand reached out and pulled her inside. "What is this, then? Lonely?"

She glared at the bearded, smelly man before her. "Where is Selwyn?" she demanded, insulted rather than afraid. To think any Saxon would dare lay a hand on her!

The man grinned. "Might have known, eh, boys? He always picks the pretty ones!" He pointed at a dark corner. "Over there."

She began to walk away, but the man stepped in front of her, a lustful leer on his face. "If he does not want you, I am willing!"

She ignored him and the jeers of the others in the crowded, stinking tavern.

There was a man seated at the corner table, draining a mug of ale. It was so dim she could barely see. "Are you Selwyn?"

The man set down his mug with a bang. "Who wants to know?" He glanced up, saw her and smiled toothlessly. "Not that it matters much. Sit down here, my lovely, and join me." He patted the bench beside him.

She sat. "You know the Viking Einar?"

"Maybe I do and maybe I don't. Give me a kiss and I'll tell you."

Ingemar gave the man her most charming smile, although inwardly she felt nauseous from the smell of the room and the odor of the man beside her. "Answer me first and perhaps I will."

Selwyn threw back his head and barked a laugh. "Fair enough. I do know him. Where's my kiss?"

Ingemar would rather have kissed a pig, but she bussed him on the cheek. The man's hand snaked around her waist.

"I want to go to the Saxon village, the one Einar raided last," she said quietly.

"I don't know what you're talking about. How about some ale?"

"I do not want any Saxon ale!" Ingemar twisted out of the man's grip. "I want to go to that village! I have information for the thane."

Selwyn leaned back. "Information? What kind of information?"

"I can help him get his children and the woman back."

"He will, anyway. All he has to do is pay the ransom."

"I can tell him exactly where to go. He will not have to pay the ransom."

Selwyn's eyes narrowed. "Why would you do that?"

"Because I would."

Selwyn surveyed her with a meditative expression. Kendric would certainly welcome the opportunity to get his children back without having to give a ransom. Surely he would pay for this woman's information.

On the other hand, that meant a lower payment for him.

The woman shifted on the seat beside him.

But this woman would fetch a fine price, from Kendric or some other Saxon lord.

"When were you planning to make this journey—*if* I agree to take you?"

"Now."

"It is not yet spring."

"It is close enough. We must get to the Saxon village before the Vikings return."

"Very true. And how would you pay me for *my* trouble?"

Ingemar merely smiled.

Selwyn grinned lasciviously. "Surely there's no need to rush away right this moment."

"If you value your life, we should go at once. I did not come to Hedeby alone, and he will soon discover that I am gone."

It would be so easy to let go.

To stop coughing. To quit struggling for breath. To sleep beyond the painful dreams. To be with Betha.

She was burning all the time, with no rest. And the thirst! Her throat was hot and dry.

She was tired, so tired. And weak. She could not even open her eyes.

Vaguely aware that hands were touching her, that liquid occasionally passed her cracked and dry lips, Meradyce lost all sense of time or life or hope.

What did it matter, after all, if she lived or died? She had not saved Betha. Adelar had no need of her.

She was too weak to cry and too parched to have any tears to shed. Better, yes, better if she let go and slipped so quietly, so gently into everlasting sleep....

"Beloved!"

She knew that man's voice. It was Einar—but not Einar. Never had she heard him whisper anything so gently, so desperately, not even in the midst of their passion.

"Beloved!"

Surely it was a dream. A hope.

"Oh, my beloved!" She felt his kiss on her cheek, his lean, strong hand clutching hers. "Do not leave me."

His lips were so close to her ear that she heard the catch in his breath. "Meradyce, please do not leave me. I need you so much!"

She stirred weakly and forced her eyes open. Yes, it was Einar, kneeling beside her.

"Meradyce!"

She tried to lift her hand to touch his face. *He* needed her. *He* cared for her.

She would not give up. She would find the strength to fight her illness, for Einar.

She tried to take a deep breath. It made her cough, but not as painfully as before.

She should rest. She knew it. She had often told others that when they were getting better.

And she was so tired! She would sleep. A pleasant sleep, knowing that Einar cared for her so very much.

Before she did, she struggled to say something that would let him know she had heard him. With a great effort she managed to whisper, "Beloved!" before dropping into unconsciousness.

Einar stared at Meradyce, almost afraid to believe that she had spoken. For him, the past few days had been a vision of the land of the dead, Niflheim, a place of eternal darkness and cold and ice. That would be how his days would seem without Meradyce. She was his light, his warmth.

"Endredi!" he called out, and in a moment his daughter was at his side. "She spoke!"

Endredi reached down and touched Meradyce's forehead.

She turned to her father with a smile. "The worst is past."

"She will live?"

"She will live."

With a ragged sigh, Einar crossed his arms and laid down his head.

Endredi busied herself with cooking, wondering if she should leave but knowing Meradyce would need food now.

She grew aware of the silence.

"Endredi?"

She turned to see her father rise and walk toward her, a warmth and love in his gray eyes that surprised her, then filled her with joy. "Thank you," he said softly. "Daughter."

With a strangled sob, Endredi flung herself into her father's open arms.

"Ingemar?" Lars called softly.

He looked around the room they shared and frowned. He had been gone the whole day and well into the night. Ingemar had sent him to sell some of her jewelry, and he had met some old friends. They had gone to another inn for some ale.

He wondered if Ingemar was not answering because she was angry. The woman had a fierce temper.

"Ingemar?" He went toward the bed.

Sigrid heard him calling and entered the room. She liked the dark-haired friendly man, although she had no use for his woman, who was always demanding and rude. "She is not here."

"Where did she go?"

Sigrid shrugged. "She certainly did not tell me, or anyone else, that I know of."

"When did she leave?" The big man stood in the small room looking like a lost little boy.

"Oh, just after you did."

"Where would she go? She does not know anyone here."

"I am sure I have no idea."

Sigrid was about to leave when she remembered something. It had struck her as odd at the time, but she hadn't thought too much about it. "She had a bundle with her."

Lars felt as if a sword of ice had pierced his body. He began searching the room for Ingemar's things. Sigrid shrugged and went out.

Nothing. There was nothing. Ingemar had taken all her goods, and gone.

For a moment Lars stood motionless in the room. She had betrayed him.

Another thought came into his mind like a hammer thrown at his head. She was a shipbuilder's daughter—she had knowledge that could be invaluable to their enemies.

She had asked so many questions about the Saxons and how Einar had contacted them. Suddenly, he knew that she was a traitor, knew it for a certainty.

Lars reached for his sword and ax. She had a day's start, but he would find her. Somehow, even if it meant journeying alone into the heart of the Saxon lands, he would find her.

Chapter Sixteen

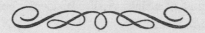

Meradyce watched her husband and his daughter from beneath lowered lids. Yes, she had not dreamed it. They were speaking softly together, and there could be no mistaking the devoted look Einar gave Endredi. Somehow, during her illness, the gap between father and daughter had been bridged.

She had no recollection of anyone around her while she lay ill, but Einar—Einar had always been there.

Meradyce had been gaining strength for some time. She wasn't sure how long she had been ill, but she was sure she was well enough to say all she had to say and do what she very much desired to do. For that, though, she needed to be alone with her husband.

She waited silently until Endredi bid her father farewell and went out.

"Einar," Meradyce called softly, lifting herself to a sitting position. He turned with such a joyful smile on his face that for a moment she had trouble drawing breath, and it had nothing to do with her illness.

He was beside the bed in an instant. "Yes?"

"Einar, have I been sleeping alone?"

He looked away and a flush stole across his face. "You were so sick, I thought you would not like to be . . . disturbed."

"How do I look?"

His brow wrinkled with puzzlement. "What do you mean?"

She pointed at a silver chalice beside the bed. "Give that to me."

He did, and she examined her face as well as she could in the polished silver. She looked so thin and pale, except for the dark skin beneath her eyes.

"I am ugly!" As she said it, she realized that, despite her wish to be unattractive, she had been very proud of her physical beauty.

Einar took her face between his palms and looked at her intently. "These are the eyes of my beloved wife. These are her lips." He kissed her gently. "*Nothing* has changed, Meradyce, except that I cherish you even more."

She smiled at him, then twisted her head to kiss his palm. "I am better now, Einar."

"I know." He grinned, and that made him look wondrously young and boyish and shy.

She felt rather shy, too, knowing how much he cared for her. She was not sure she deserved to be so happy, or if any mortal did. "How is everyone? Endredi? Adelar?"

"It was Endredi who nursed you back to health. She is well, I am glad to say. It seems it was more exhaustion than contagion that brought on your illness."

"You sound proud of her."

He smiled warmly. "I am." His smile disappeared in a serious, tender expression. "I have told her everything about her mother and me."

Meradyce nodded, pleased. "And Adelar?"

"He still will not talk to me, but he asked Endredi how you were." He sighed softly. "I think he blames himself for Betha's death."

Meradyce reached out and took Einar's strong, callused hand in her own. "You are well?"

"Yes," he replied, but she saw his weariness. Then he smiled slowly, enticingly. "Now that you are getting better, I feel wonderful."

She shifted forward, running her hand up his arm. "Einar, it was not Endredi who made me well." She paused, gazing steadily at his face. "It was *you.*" She saw that he did not understand. "I could have died so easily," she explained. "I felt myself slipping away— and part of me wanted to go. There would be no more fighting, no more choices... But you called me back."

She leaned forward, pressing her face against his strong chest. "You called me beloved. And I knew then that I did not want to die. I wanted to be with *you.*"

She kissed him, letting her lips show him what she could not trust mere words to express. He pulled her closer as their kiss deepened.

Desire flared in her, and she drew him down, welcoming the weight of his body on her own. With quick, impatient movements she tore at his clothes. She wanted—needed—to touch his naked skin.

She wanted him inside her.

Einar pulled back, his expression something between hope and worry. "You have been very ill."

"I am feeling much better. Completely cured."

"I am not sure—"

"*I* am."

One look at her face, at her eyes, and he knew she was certain. Ready for him.

Rejoicing, he tugged at the drawstring of her shift, then lowered it so that her lovely, soft flesh was within his touch. He hesitated for a moment, until she began to kiss him. Whimpers of desire escaped her throat as she pressed her lips along his neck, down his chest, capturing a nipple.

He stood to shed his clothes and, gloriously naked in the flickering light of the fire, he looked at her with a smoldering gaze that sent fresh flames of need coursing through her veins.

When he was with her again, there was no time for gentleness.

With a wild cry, she arched to meet his ready flesh, wrapping her legs around him, pulling him deeper. Her hands clutched at his shoulders as he thrust, his own need urgent and undeniable.

Then, together, the tension shattered. Einar, panting, rolled so that she lay upon his body, still joined with him. Slowly he smiled, his eyes full of tenderness.

"Beloved," she whispered.

"Excuse me, my lord?"

Kendric got off the servant girl and out of his bed. "What in God's name is it?" he demanded, angry at having his pleasure interrupted. The air was cold on his half-naked body, and he grabbed a robe. The serving girl covered herself.

As Kendric came around the screen, he glared at the two people standing near the entrance to his hall. "Well, what do you want? It had better be important."

The man stepped inside, where Kendric could see his face. "Selwyn?"

The man nodded.

Kendric stuck his head behind the screen and barked, "Leave us."

The wench hastily put on her gown and fled out of the hall as Kendric sauntered to a large chair and sat.

He gestured for Selwyn to come closer. "Who is with you?"

A young woman stepped out of the shadows. She was pretty, with long blond hair and fine features. Kendric smiled appreciatively. "Selwyn, so kind of you to visit! Who is your charming companion?"

"Her name is Ingemar and—"

"Ingemar!" He gave the woman his most appealing smile. "Come closer. Take off your cloak and sit!"

When she did, Kendric stared at her shapely body hungrily. If Selwyn had brought her to be sold, she would be worth a high price.

Still, it would not be wise to seem too eager. "What brings you to my village, Selwyn?"

"A matter of business, my lord."

"Naturally." His gaze strayed to the woman. "What kind of business?"

Selwyn scanned the empty hall and cleared his throat. "First let me express my condolences about your wife, my lord."

"Thank you. It was a most unfortunate accident."

Selwyn suspected that Kendric's wife's "accident" was anything but. The story went that she had been thrown from her horse while riding with her husband, and had struck her head upon a rock. But he had it from a relative of one of the villagers that, if the tale was true, she must have landed on a pile of rocks—all exactly the same size and shape.

But Selwyn knew better than to indicate his disbelief in any way. "A great pity."

"Yes," Kendric said, not even attempting to sound sincere.

Suddenly the woman spoke. "Your children," she said in the halting manner of a person speaking a foreign language, "I can take you to them."

Kendric raised his eyebrows as he looked at Selwyn. "Is this true?"

Selwyn nodded. "She comes from the same village as the Vikings who took them, my lord. She is willing to lead you there."

Kendric leaned back in his chair thoughtfully. He had no doubt that Selwyn knew exactly where the Viking village lay, and he had been planning to send for him when the weather grew warmer.

But now here was Selwyn, with a most interesting guide. "I see. Why would she lead us there?"

Selwyn shrugged. "She won't tell me her reasons."

"We cannot sail before spring."

"She knows that."

When Kendric smiled at her again, Ingemar smiled back coyly. It was a long time until spring. This man was rich and handsome and, apparently, wifeless. She was sure he would be most amusing. At any rate he would be better than the Saxon pig Selwyn. His love-making had all the finesse of a rutting ram.

Nor would the Saxon be as tentative as Lars. Her blood surged at the thought of this Kendric taking her, fiercely, strongly... like Einar.

Kendric stood up and poured himself a goblet of wine. Ingemar's pulse began to quicken as she noticed the thane's long, lean, muscular legs. "How are my children?" he asked coolly.

"They are well," Ingemar said.

"And Meradyce?"

Ingemar sneered. "I suppose she was beautiful once, but now that all the men have used her..."

Kendric's eyes widened. "A pity," he said lightly.

Clearly, Ingemar thought, he has no special interest in the wench, and that pleased her greatly.

"Selwyn, you may go," the thane said.

"But my lord—" Selwyn protested.

"What is it?"

"There have been ... expenses. We had to pay a lot of money to get here—"

Kendric eyed him coldly. "We will discuss it in the morning."

"But, my lord—!" Selwyn's gaze shifted from Kendric to Ingemar and back again. He knew what was happening. But this woman was his! He had no intention of giving her...

Then he saw Kendric's expression.

After all, she was only a woman.

Without another word, Selwyn left the hall.

Several weeks later, Meradyce sat in Olva's house. She had recovered completely from her illness. Indeed, she had never felt better in her life.

Olva worked at her loom near the door, her body shifting as she moved the shuttle quickly through the warp. She paused for a moment to beat the weft threads upward so that the finished weaving was close and tight.

Endredi sat nearby, preparing the fish for one of her fine stews. Einar had gone out hunting, for the day was remarkably warm. The sun shone on the remains of the snow with all the promise of spring.

Meradyce's life had never been sweeter or happier—except for one thing. Adelar still kept too much to himself, rarely speaking and never smiling.

But today, Meradyce's thoughts were not on the impending journey to take Adelar home or the boy's brooding silence.

"Olva," Meradyce said nonchalantly, "next winter Endredi might not be able to help you quite so much."

Olva's fingers slowed. "Oh? Why not?"

Endredi also stopped working.

"Einar is not thinking of marrying her to somebody, is he? Without asking me?" Olva demanded.

"Or me?" Endredi added softly.

"Oh, no. It's just that . . . I might need her help."

Olva turned to her, her face full of concern. "Are you ill again?"

Meradyce smiled broadly as she shook her head. "I think I am with child."

Olva screeched happily and hurried to embrace her. Endredi smiled warmly and gave Meradyce a hug when Olva finally stopped squeezing her.

"When?" Olva demanded.

"I am not yet sure," Meradyce said, trying to be calm, as reason demanded. "It is too early to be certain, so do not say anything to Einar. I do not want him to be disappointed."

Olva put her hands on her hips. "Well, if *you* do not know when someone is pregnant . . ."

Meradyce had to laugh. She was fairly certain, for several of the signs were there, and yet it was also true that it was too early to be absolutely sure. She had wanted to tell Einar for days and came perilously close to revealing her thoughts. But she knew that if she was wrong, he would be very disappointed. Rather than risk that, she decided to divulge her secret to Olva and Endredi.

"I am going to be a grandmother again," Olva said gleefully. Then she tried to sound serious. "Of course, I am rather young yet for such a thing."

The women laughed, giggling like girls.

"What is so funny?"

They all turned to the door as Einar strode in, then tried to look as if nothing very important had happened. Unfortunately, that proved to be impossible, because Olva began to sputter helplessly. Then Meradyce started to laugh. Endredi began to giggle.

"Have you all gone mad?" Einar put down the three rabbits he had caught and skinned. "Or have you been into the wine?"

"One of us has been *into* something, but not the wine!" Olva said with a knowing wink at Meradyce.

Meradyce was scandalized—but she could not help smiling, especially at Einar's confused expression. He crossed his arms over his chest. "What are you talking about?"

"It is a *small* thing."

"What?"

"You will find out soon enough," Olva said lightly.

"You are not going to tell me, are you?"

Olva grinned wickedly. "No, my son."

"Very well. I shall go away and leave you to your laughing."

As he stalked out petulantly, Meradyce whispered, "Sometimes I feel like I already *have* a child."

They looked at one another and burst into a gale of laughter.

Einar threw himself down on his chair in Svend's hall. Meradyce had returned from Olva's and still refused to say what they had all found so humorous, so he was not in one of his finer moods.

"What is it, my son?" Svend asked, passing him a drinking horn filled with ale. "You look as if you've sat on your sword."

"Women! I do not understand them sometimes."

"Who does? Who wants to?"

"I took Olva three fine rabbits—and not one word of thanks do I get. They all just stood there and...and *giggled.*"

"Giggled?"

"Giggled."

"What about?"

"They would not tell me. As if they had some very important secret."

Svend turned to his son, a smile growing on his face. "Women. Giggling. A secret?"

"Yes."

Svend began to laugh heartily. Einar frowned.

"Oh, my son! It is obvious you do not know women as well as I thought you did. When a bunch of women giggle and have a secret, it is usually one of two things. Either one of them desires a man and the man does not know it yet, or one of them is with child. It could be that Endredi has her eye on some warrior or that your beautiful wife is pregnant."

Einar could not quite catch his breath.

"And it is about time, too. Of course, I should not dismiss Olva. She might be—"

Einar was already out the door, running through the village. Meradyce with child! Of course! Of course! He had been so stupid, so blind!

Meradyce—bearing *his* child! The sheer joy was almost too much to bear.

He burst into their house. Meradyce was sitting by the fire, sewing on one of his tunics. He pulled her up and kissed her fiercely. Then he drew back, holding her at arm's length. "Is it true? Is it?"

"Who told you? Was it Olva?" Meradyce tried to look stern, but it was no use.

"Then it *is* true?"

Meradyce had to frown. "I *think* so. I cannot be sure for a few more days—"

He held her tightly. "I am so happy!"

Then he stopped and moved away slightly.

"What is the matter?" Meradyce asked.

"I am not—I did not hurt anything, did I?"

She smiled. "No."

She moved forward to embrace him, but he drew back warily. "Is this what you were laughing about today?"

She nodded sheepishly. "I had to tell someone, Einar, and I did not want you to be disappointed if I am wrong."

He frowned, but there was a sparkle in his gray eyes. "Next time I want you to tell me *first.*"

"Yes, husband." She kissed him lightly on the cheek, then she drew back. "I hope the next time does not take so long."

He picked her up in his strong arms and spun her around. "Next time, we will just have to try harder...."

Chapter Seventeen

Kendric smiled with satisfaction as he looked at the ship laying ready in the river. It was beautiful, with the low, sleek lines of a Viking longship—only better, of course. He had hired the finest shipbuilder from London to construct it. He had bought the best wood and employed the best tradesmen, paying great sums to ensure that they built his ship swiftly.

The Viking woman Ingemar had proved to be invaluable in showing the workers the methods the Vikings used. The result was a ship as fine as any vessel on the seas.

And his reconstructed town was better than any other so close to the coast. The villagers had not protested when he had told them he wanted a bigger, stronger wall and a stone keep. Indeed, they had worked all the harder since the Viking raid.

Kendric looked up at the cloudy sky. Ingemar said it was too soon to try to sail across the open sea, but surprise was important. He would risk an early voyage.

He turned and caught a glimpse of a lone rider approaching from the south. A big man, but not familiar. No doubt he had heard that Kendric was offering a good wage to any man who cared to fight for him.

Kendric smiled and began to saunter to his hall, where Ingemar was waiting.

In his bed.

Seething, roiling anger built in Lars as he stared at the ship. Someone had shown the Saxons a few things about building a vessel like that of the Vikings. Someone like Ingemar, a shipbuilder's daughter.

What seemed a large crowd of men were employed on the various tasks necessary to complete the vessel. Lars had never seen so many skilled laborers in one place, but that would explain the speed with which the Saxons had constructed the ship now rocking gently at its moorings.

Nonetheless, he thought as he smiled grimly, the proportions were not quite right. Like most Viking shipbuilders, Bjorn often worked only by instinct, with no formal plan. No one could duplicate such a method—although clearly someone had tried. If Ingemar was here, she could not deny that she was a traitor. He would find her, the same way he had found this place.

He had discovered that she had been seen in the company of the Saxon, Selwyn, and learned where they had gone.

Following them to Saxon land had been a dangerous journey for a lone Viking. Many times he had hidden to avoid enemies, adding days to his travel. The weather and his lack of knowledge of the land, as well as his prey's exact destination, had also made his journey difficult.

He looked at the land around him and had no doubt that this was the village they had raided. The Saxons had rebuilt it. And with better fortifications.

He had surmised that Ingemar was planning to find the Saxon whose children Einar had taken, although he had convinced himself that she only wanted money for what she knew of them—and nothing else.

Now, as he stood staring at the ship, he knew the whole truth.

Ingemar was a traitor to her people. She had to have helped the Saxons build this ship, for it had too many of her father's touches. He could even believe, as he remembered her hatred for Einar, that she would lead them to their home village herself.

"Here, now, you. What do you want, eh?"

Lars spun around, lifting his ax. The laborer stared in disbelief, eye to eye with a Viking warrior. His shock did not last long. In the next moment he was dead.

Fueled with raging and burning fury, Lars ran to the village and through the open gate. He knew where the thane's hall had been and headed in that direction. Who else would Ingemar sell her people to, but a wealthy thane?

Sure enough, another, even larger hall stood in the same spot. Some soldiers idled outside, and they turned to stare at the huge man bearing down on them, his ax raised.

The nearby villagers fled as the Viking quickly slaughtered the two soldiers as easily as a man swats a fly.

"Ingemar!" Lars shouted as he burst into the hall.

A woman screamed. A screen at the other end of the room fell over as a man scrambled to get his sword. Ingemar crouched naked on the bed, her eyes wide with fright.

Lars charged forward, but before he could reach her, several soldiers clambered into the hall.

Lars turned to face them.

The Saxons had never seen anything like this Viking. His eyes were wild, his teeth bared like a cornered wolf.

The soldiers began to back away.

"Take him, you fools!" the thane shouted.

Lars spun around and stared at him. Two soldiers tried to grab his arms, but he shook them off as if they were children. Another lunged at him with his sword, only to find himself staring dumbfounded at his hand, or rather, the place where his hand had been.

Ingemar began to scream, high, piercing cries.

The thane struck at Lars with his sword. The blade pierced the Viking's side, but he did not stop his swinging. Another soldier lashed out at his back, also drawing blood.

Still Lars kept fighting.

He came straight at Ingemar, his eyes filled with hatred. "Spawn of Loki!" he cried. "Daughter of Hel! I curse the day you were born. I curse the day I met you. I curse the day I left my home with you!"

He was bleeding from several wounds, but he kept advancing. Ingemar kept screaming. The soldiers slashed at him. He was nearly there. Although he was weak from loss of blood, with one great effort Lars lifted his ax and brought it down.

Ingemar, the traitor, lay dead. She could not lead the Saxons to his village now.

He left the ax imbedded in her chest and turned, unsheathing his sword as he prepared to enter Valhalla.

Kendric curled his lip with disgust as he stared at the body of the dead Viking. Around him, he could hear the panting breaths of the soldiers and the moans of those who were wounded.

"Get that lump of dung out of here," he ordered a soldier who was standing nearby. "I want him skinned. Nail his pelt to the church door as a warning to other barbarians who dare to attack me."

He glanced at Ingemar's body as he reached down and picked up the Viking's bloody sword. "Get her out of here, too. And the bed. Burn them both." His hand wrapped around the grip of the fine weapon. "Then find me Selwyn."

Selwyn's eyes widened as he looked around the thane's hall. There were still puddles of blood on the floor, and Kendric had not bothered to remove his bloodstained tunic. "Yes, my lord?" he asked softly, trying not to gag.

"You will lead us to the Viking village," the thane ordered, seating himself in his large chair, his sheathed sword striking the arm.

"Me, my lord?"

"You."

"But I do not know where it is."

"Yes, you do."

"No, my lord, I swear it."

In an instant, Kendric was out of his chair, his sword pressed against the merchant's throat. "Are you sure?"

"My lord, please!" Selwyn gasped. "I . . . I am not sure, but I have a good idea. . . ."

Kendric lowered his sword. "I thought you might. We sail tomorrow."

Selwyn took a deep breath. If the Vikings saw him on the Saxon ship, his life would be over within the year.

On the other hand, if he did not lead Kendric and his men there, his life would be over this day. "Very well, my lord."

"Do you really have to go?" Meradyce asked softly as she lay beside Einar, her head pillowed on his shoulder.

He kissed the top of her head. "I do not have to, but Thorston is convinced there will not be any of his wine left to sell later in the spring if he does not leave now. Svend has taken quite a liking to it."

Meradyce twisted so she could smile at Einar. "And naturally you have to go with him?"

"Woman, I make my own decisions," he said. His mouth frowned, but his eyes sparkled with laughter. He did not really *want* to go with Thorston, but his stepfather had told him that he could find a maker of fine cradles in the village where he wanted to sell his wine. Einar had decided to go, but to say nothing of the cradle. It would be a surprise.

"Of course you do. It is just that I will miss this—" She kissed his chin. "And this—" She kissed his cheek. "And this—" She reached underneath the furs.

Einar's hand clasped hers. "I see I have married a wanton woman after all," he said, grinning. Then he let go of her hand. Undeterred and undaunted, Meradyce continued what she had started. Einar's grin disappeared as he closed his eyes and moaned softly. "Maybe I do not have to go. . . ."

She stopped. "You have already decided, have you not?" she asked mischievously, moving away from him.

"Oh, no, wife." Einar reached out and pulled her back so that she lay on top of his naked body. "You cannot leave now."

"*You* are leaving."

"That is different."

She was about to argue, but the smoldering passion in her husband's eyes suddenly made any argument, however playful, completely unimportant.

Sometime later, Meradyce watched as Einar pulled on his breeches. "How many days will you be gone, exactly?"

"Exactly, I do not know. We have got good horses, but there still may be snow in the valleys. It should not be more than a week."

"Einar?"

"Yes?"

"How long before Adelar must go home?"

He turned to look at her, saddened by her expression. "We should be able to sail very soon now."

"I hope I will not be quite so sick this time."

"You are not going."

She sat up abruptly, her dark hair curling about her rapidly flushing cheeks. "Of course I am. I have to."

"You are with child. The voyage would be dangerous."

"*I* must tell Ludella about Betha. It is my duty."

"It is your *duty* to do what I tell you—and to make sure our baby is healthy!"

At his last words, her growing anger dissipated. She knew how much he wanted her to have a safe childbirth and a healthy infant. He had insisted that she teach Endredi everything she knew, just in case, and he had even suggested she teach Olva, too. Meradyce thought he was far too worried. She felt fine.

She got out of bed, pulling a covering around herself as she went to him and gently touched his hand. "I should go, Einar. And I *want* to go. Not just for duty, but for Adelar, too. As long as we do not encounter any storms, I should be well."

Einar looked at her, recognizing her stubborn determination to do what she believed was right. "Oh, very well. It is clear you can make me do whatever you wish." He brushed his hand along her cheek. "But then I will not set sail until I am certain we will have good weather."

She nodded, lifting his hand to her lips.

"Stop that, woman! I have to make sure the horses and goods are packed properly for the journey."

"Right this moment?"

Einar groaned as he pulled her into his arms. "I knew you would cause me trouble the moment I first laid eyes on you...."

Chapter Eighteen

"I tell you, it has to be now!" Ull glared at Siurt's doubtful face. "There could not be a better time. The weather is good enough to sail, half the village is up in the hills gathering flowers for the ceremonial cart, Einar is gone and others are prepared to join us."

"But Einar's due back anytime—what if he arrives today? He will give chase and we will die for sure."

"The weather has been terrible for the past three days. Even if they traveled through the wet, the road would be pure mud! They could not get here today. Even supposing they get home tomorrow, we will still be a whole day's sail ahead of them. Besides, we will have the best ship. All the others wallow like sows compared to Einar's craft. There is no way he can catch us before we reach the Saxon village. Come on— the others are ready and waiting!"

"I do not know, Ull. Maybe the Saxon will blame us for his daughter's death. Maybe we should not try this—"

"Do not be a fool. We will have the boy, that is the important thing. He will be what the father wants.

What he will pay for." Ull stared at his brother, one hand on his sword. If Siurt refused to come, Ull knew he would have to kill him. "Are you with me in this, or not?"

"I have been thinking, Ull, that is all. I mean, letting any Saxon know where the village is—it is taking a risk."

"You are the only one who pesters me with such nonsense, Siurt! I told you—if you are worried about the Saxons, all we have to do is kill them once we control the village. With Svend and his sons out of the way, the villagers will accept our leadership."

"And what if the Saxons will not come?"

"Then the boy will die. I do not think his father will refuse."

"Suppose he *does?* We could not come back here. Our lives would not be worth the tenth part of a silver coin."

"So? We will have enough men to start our own village, maybe in the Danelaw."

"But our wives..."

"By Thor's thunder, we can get other women!"

Siurt began to smile. "I suppose we could, at that. Young ones, eh?"

"I see you are finally understanding something," Ull said sourly. "Let us get the boy."

Meradyce frowned as she tried to imitate Endredi's movements and tie the stems of the wildflowers into a garland. The day was warm, with the promise of spring in the sunshine. A soft breeze wafted the scent of new grass over the hillside and the sounds of the other women and children gathering flowers.

"I cannot seem to get this right," she said ruefully, holding up a rather pathetic example of a garland. It looked like it would fall apart any moment.

Endredi returned her smile. "You have done it. It just takes practice."

"Very well, I will keep trying!"

Meradyce smiled at her companion. She and Endredi were fast friends, and knowing that all was well between Einar and his daughter added to her feeling of well-being. "How many do we need?"

Endredi nodded at the ceremonial cart, which had been brought to the hillside by the women and children. There was a wooden statue of the god Freyr standing inside. "We fill the cart with the garlands. It is an honor for our village to prepare it this year, and we want to do a good job."

"So it looks nice?"

"So that Freyr is pleased—and the other villages impressed."

"It does not stay here?"

"Oh, no. It goes to all the neighboring villages. Hamar will lead it this year—a very great honor, I assure you."

Meradyce looked at the flowers in her hand and frowned. This garland was not turning out any better. And she was also wondering about the propriety of helping prepare for this Viking ritual. To be sure, the Saxon villagers had their own rites of spring to ensure a good harvest, but the Lord was always invoked—not one Viking god among many.

Still, Einar would be pleased, and she wanted to make him happy, as well as fit into her new life.

Endredi looked up at the clear sky. "I hope this weather holds. Svend is anxious to plow the first furrow. If my father and Thorston do not return soon, he may do it without them."

"Is that so bad?"

"Well, they will both be sorry to miss the feast." Endredi gave Meradyce a sidelong glance. "Adelar has not spoken to anyone for three days," she said softly. "I have not seen him at all since yesterday."

Meradyce paused in her tying. "I wish I knew what to do," she said. "He has always acted this way when something has hurt or disturbed him. He lets no one get near."

"He is strong," Endredi said firmly.

Meradyce looked at the girl as she worked, her head bent so that her thick red-gold hair hid her face. Endredi would not want sympathy and comfort, either, she thought. She would lick her wounds in silent privacy.

"A ship!"

All the women and children stopped their preparations and looked at the fjord. Hamar, Einar and Thorston had gone by horseback, and there were no ships expected.

Everyone watched silently as the large ship moved down the fjord. There was no breeze, so oars propelled the vessel through the smooth water.

"That is not a Viking ship," Endredi said almost immediately.

"No," Meradyce replied, a feeling of dread stealing over her. The vessel was of a design similar to the Viking longships, but it was too narrow.

A figure moved toward the prow of the ship. "Endredi..." she began.

"What is it?" Endredi asked anxiously.

Meradyce stared, telling herself she could not believe her eyes. She must be wrong. She must be.

It could not be Kendric in the prow of the ship. Then the man moved, and there was a glint of sunlight on metal.

She threw down her garland and began running to the village.

Adelar, sitting on a rock on a low rise outside the village, saw the ship. He had not gone with the women and children up into the hills. He would have nothing to do with Vikings or their religion.

He did not hate most of them. He simply felt... nothing. It was as if the cold of winter had entered his heart, freezing it in ice.

Once, he had cared for Meradyce with all the passion a boy could feel, but that had died, too, first with her marriage to a Viking warrior, and then, finally, with Betha. Meradyce was merely a woman to him now.

But Einar... Adelar hated Einar. If it had not been for Einar, Adelar would never had been taken from his home. He would never have gone out into the storm. His sister would be alive.

As the boy watched the ship, he compared it dispassionately with Einar's, which rocked gently at the pier. It was not as sleek as Einar's longship, and there was something not quite right about the bow....

Suddenly he heard someone shouting. Meradyce. He watched as she ran into the village, her skirts flying. Endredi was running right behind her.

He stood up, wondering what had happened.

"Saxons!"

Adelar heard the panicked cry from the village and turned to stare at the ship.

With joy filling him, he started forward. "It is my father," he whispered. "He has come for me!"

Svend and the men who had not gone with Einar swarmed out of the longhouses, their weapons ready.

But Kendric had brought as many men as his huge vessel could carry. Even before the ropes were tied to anchor the ship, soldiers had lined up on the shore.

The enemy did not move forward, however. Svend halted outside the village gate. "Wait!" he called to his men, who continued to run ahead. *"Wait!"* he bellowed, and they finally stopped, shifting nervously as they looked at the Saxon soldiers.

Meradyce, with Olva and Endredi behind her, stood at the gate. They watched Svend walk toward Kendric, who sauntered arrogantly toward the Viking chieftain.

Meradyce wondered where Adelar was. If he appeared now, perhaps there would be no need for fighting. Surely Kendric had come only for his son. He would not know that Einar and the others were away.

She moved forward. She could help Svend talk to Kendric, and she had another duty to perform.

"What are you doing?" Olva cried softly, reaching for Meradyce.

"I can help them talk to one other. And I should be the one to tell Kendric about Betha," she said.

"*That* is the children's father?"

"Yes."

Meradyce pushed through the waiting warriors. Kendric's eyes widened when he saw her, and his gaze raked over her body, lingering for a moment on her rounded belly.

Then he smiled. A cold, empty smile. "Meradyce," he said politely. "How good to see you. I see you have managed to find a way to appease your captors."

Before she could answer, Kendric continued, his voice no longer courteous. "Tell this barbarian pig I want my children."

Meradyce fought the urge to denounce Kendric in front of his soldiers, for both his words and the way he looked at her, but Adelar might be listening nearby.

She turned to Svend. "This is Kendric, Adelar's father," she said quietly. "He has come for his children."

Svend looked surprised. "The traitor?" he asked scornfully.

"Yes." She faced Kendric and took a deep breath. "I am sorry to have to tell you this, but Betha is dead."

Kendric's eyes narrowed with suspicion but no sorrow. "Where is Adelar?"

"He is well. Betha fell ill. I did my best to heal her—"

"I am sure you did." Kendric's mocking gaze filled her with anger and dismay. "When you had a moment to spare from the men's attentions."

"Father! Father!" Adelar pushed through the ranks of Vikings.

"My son!"

Adelar ran to his father's side. "I knew you would come for us! I knew it! Take me home!"

Kendric looked at the Vikings, his face triumphant, Betha obviously unimportant. "So, no thanks to you, I have my son back. Go to the ship, Adelar," he ordered.

Adelar hurried toward the pier. He hesitated and glanced at Meradyce. And Endredi.

"You will go now?" Meradyce asked.

"Oh, yes." Kendric nodded, and suddenly his men moved forward, drawing their swords.

All around Meradyce, weapon clashed upon weapon as the Vikings rushed to fight. The women began to scream.

Adelar appeared at the side of the ship. Running forward, Meradyce called out, "Stay there! Stay there!"

A man shouted in pain. Someone else cried for Odin. Meradyce spun around. Several of the Saxon soldiers had circled the Vikings, outnumbering them nearly three to one.

But the Viking warriors fought like men possessed by demons. Again and again Saxon soldiers fell before their terrible strokes.

Meradyce stood motionless with horror. She had never seen a battle, never witnessed death and blood like this.

Then she saw Svend, crouched like an animal before Kendric. Kendric circled him, and there was such a frightening look of excitement on the thane's face that she could scarcely believe this man was Adelar's father.

She looked at Svend. She had never thought to see Einar's father afraid, but Svend was terrified.

At once she realized why. He had no weapon. If Kendric captured him alive, his fate would be death by hanging or something equally shameful, and he would be denied Valhalla.

At that moment, Meradyce did not think. She did not decide with her mind, but with her heart.

She belonged with Einar—and his people.

A Saxon soldier lay dead not far off. Meradyce pried his sword from his bloody fingers.

But before she could get to Svend, Olva suddenly appeared. She threw herself at Kendric, pushing him back. The Saxon lifted his sword and struck Olva. She cried out as she fell to the ground, her hand at her side, where a huge red stain grew.

"Svend!" Meradyce shouted, tossing the sword to the chieftain.

With a fierce glow of triumph in his eyes, Svend snatched the weapon from the air and turned on Kendric. He lunged at Kendric, but missed his aim. Kendric did not, and Meradyce watched in horror as

Svend slipped slowly down into the dirt, the sword knocked from his hand by the blow that sliced the vein in his neck.

Then Ull emerged from the battle and bore down on Kendric, his ax whirling. The Viking drove the Saxon into the thick of the fighting.

Meradyce ran to Olva and knelt beside her as the older woman crawled to where Svend's sword lay on the ground. Olva gripped it with savage intensity, then, ignoring Meradyce, she slowly turned toward Svend and pushed the weapon into his empty hand.

"Olva!" Svend whispered as Einar's mother died before their eyes.

Meradyce moved closer to Svend, lifting his head as his life drained from his body with his blood. "Asa... Vedis... My children..."

"I will take care of them," she vowed.

He nodded and gripped the sword. He smiled. "The Valkyries are coming for me."

Then he, too, was dead.

Meradyce, her eyes blinded by tears, stood up. And saw that she was too late. The battle was over. All the Viking warriors were dead or wounded.

No one was watching her. She could run away. Adelar was safe. She could hide. Wait for Einar to come back. Einar.

She began to run, glancing over her shoulder.

Then she halted abruptly. Kendric had found Endredi. He pushed her roughly toward the ship. Behind them, Meradyce could see other women and children being driven like cattle toward the vessel as the Saxon soldiers killed their wounded enemies.

Meradyce took the sword from Svend's hand. He didn't need it now, and she did.

She stared at it, cold and wet with blood. What good would a sword do? Kendric or one of his men would kill her without giving it a thought.

She put the sword beside Svend's body.

Kendric saw Meradyce walking toward him and smiled coldly as she drew close. She had a barbarian brat in her belly, her long, luxurious hair was gone, and she was thin and pale.

But she was still the most beautiful woman he had ever seen.

Nevertheless, she had helped that Viking chieftain, and he had no doubt she had given herself freely to him or one of his men. He knew no man could take her without her consent. A woman like Meradyce would kill herself first.

Yet she had refused *him*.

"Kendric, take me with you," she said.

"Gladly," he replied.

Yes, he would take her. One day.

He saw her concern for the girl he held onto. What was this Viking wench to Meradyce? He would enjoy finding out, after he was finished with the girl.

"You are as beautiful as ever," Kendric said, a pitying smile on his face as he pushed Endredi to join the group of women being herded on the ship.

Meradyce said nothing, but she saw the contempt in his eyes. She did not care what he thought of her, as long as she was able to help Endredi and the others.

"Being with child becomes you, although I am sorry we could not get here sooner to... help you."

"You are here now," she said quietly. "You have your son back. You have had your vengeance. Surely there is no need to take all the women and children."

He frowned, and she spoke quickly. "They will make the voyage troublesome."

"Perhaps, but that is not any of your concern. When they are sold as slaves, they will repay some of the cost of the vessel and the rebuilding of our village."

"How did you find us?"

"It does not matter." His gaze raked her body. "Is the brute who did this to you among the dead?"

"Yes," Meradyce lied.

"Good. Come." Kendric took her hand.

Meradyce let him lead her onto the ship.

Einar slouched in his saddle. Usually they stopped at one of the smaller villages for a night's rest on the way home from trading, but he had been anxious to return.

The steady rain had delayed their departure and made the roads nearly impassable with mud, even though they were using sleds and not carts for just such a reason. Thorston had suggested that they linger another day or two, but once he saw Einar's expression, he said nothing more about that.

Einar glanced over his shoulder and saw that Thorston was almost asleep on his horse. "Not long now," he called out.

"Huh? What did you say?" Thorston said with a start. He looked around. "Oh, nearly home. Good. My back feels like a giant stepped on it. I am not used to this much riding all at once. I understand your impatience, Einar, but you should have had pity on an old man."

"You admit you are getting too old to go on trading journeys?"

Thorston's eyes widened. "Never—but you cannot expect a man my age to ride all day. It is too hard on the insides."

Einar gave him a sly look. "My mother will be very upset that we were so long delayed."

"Am I to be held responsible for the weather? I did not ask Odin to make it rain. Or Freyja, or any of them. You just want to make sure you do not miss the feast."

"Speaking of feasts," Hamar called out from farther down the line of packhorses, "Svend will be unhappy you sold all your wine."

Thorston twisted around. "He has only himself to blame for that. I would have saved him some, if I thought he would give me a fair price. We all know he gives his money to his women!"

The men in the cortege began to laugh. Like Einar, they were anticipating being at the village soon, and they were ready for a hot meal and the company of their families. It had not been a long journey, but the delay had been most unwelcome. Most of them had made a profit trading, however, so there had not been many complaints.

"Svend will not be happy if he is kept waiting," Hamar remarked.

"I have never understood his delight in plowing," Thorston replied.

"It is only one furrow," Einar pointed out. "I think he likes to show everyone he can do more than fight."

"From the way he boasts about it, I think you are right," Thorston said with a chuckle. "'See how straight I made it, how long, how wonderful.' The only thing I care to have long and straight has nothing to do with dirt."

Einar grinned but did not reply. Thorston's joke had turned his thoughts to other, more personal things.

"That is a fine cradle," Thorston said after a moment. "I think you paid too much for it, though."

"You always say I pay too much for anything and everything."

"True."

"But I suppose you could have gotten it for a few coins less."

"Perhaps, but I must say you were not too badly cheated, Einar. Something about the size of you—and your sword—seems to bring out the honesty in merchants."

The light was fading fast, but soon they were at the hill overlooking the fjord. Einar pulled his horse to a stop and looked at the village. His dogs went motionless, then began to whine.

Something was wrong.

Thorston also stopped. "What is it?"

Hamar nudged his horse forward.

"There is no smoke," Einar said slowly. "No one moving about."

Hamar nodded as the men crowded forward to see.

"Thorston, you pick five men and stay here with the packhorses. All the rest, with me."

Einar spurred his horse to a gallop and pulled out his sword.

Too late. Einar dismounted and looked around at the bodies of his fellow warriors, his sword in his hand. His mother and father lay dead. And Bjorn. And too many others. They had returned home too late.

Hamar ran past him like a madman, crashing into his house only to run out moments later. "They are gone!"

Einar's blood went cold in his veins. "Meradyce! Endredi!" he shouted, but their names echoed off the empty houses.

He hurried through the village, looking at the bodies. Most of the warriors' corpses were outside the gates, but inside there were some bodies of women who had obviously died fighting.

There was no sign of Meradyce, or Endredi, or Adelar. The rest of the women and children had disappeared, too.

Einar's hand gripped his sword convulsively as he strode to the gates. *He would make whoever had done this thing wish he had never been born,* he vowed silently.

The men had gathered, and he looked at their stricken faces. "Whoever has taken them, wherever they have gone, we will find them."

"Who would do this?" Hamar demanded incredulously.

"Saxons!"

Einar turned to see a barely recognizable Ull staggering around the corner of the building where Bjorn worked. His face was swollen and bruised, and his right hand clutched his bloody left shoulder. His left arm dangled limply at his side. "Saxons. I heard them. The Saxon boy called their leader father and I saw *her*—your wife—with them."

Einar stared at him. "What do you mean, with them?"

He asked the question softly, but those nearest him moved away. No man wanted to be close to Einar when he was enraged.

Ull came closer, his bloodshot eyes staring at Einar. "I saw her myself. She walked up to their leader, went with him willingly, called him by name—"

"What name?"

"Kendric."

"And Endredi?"

"The Saxon had her." Ull swayed and almost fell, but he grabbed Einar with his right hand. "Get her back, Einar. Endredi is my daughter."

Einar reached out to support Ull as the wounded man slipped to his knees.

"Forgive me!" the wounded man whispered.

Einar nodded, then beckoned to one of the men standing nearby. "Take him inside and tend to his wound as best you can."

He watched them go, knowing there was a time when he would have killed Ull for his admission.

But now all he could think about was Meradyce and Endredi among the Saxons, at the mercy of a traitor.

"You know of this Kendric?" Hamar asked. He had seen the look that crossed Einar's face when Ull spoke the man's name.

"He is the father of the Saxon children."

"Then we know where his village lies."

Einar smiled. A cold, cruel, ruthless smile. "Yes."

Hamar looked at the fjord eagerly, then gasped. All the ships were damaged: masts broken, holes in the timbers, sails missing. Some were half-submerged in the cold, still water.

Einar's gaze followed his brother's. "First we bury the dead. Then we repair a ship. After that, we attack the Saxons."

Hamar put his hand on his brother's arm. "Your wife—you do not think she..."

"Betrayed me?" Einar stared at the ground for a long moment. Then he lifted his face and shook his head slowly. "She went because of Endredi and the others, just as she would not abandon Betha and Adelar. I know it as if I had been here myself, Hamar."

His mouth became a grim line of determination. "I will kill the Saxon for this. If he has harmed Meradyce or Endredi or any of the others, his will be a slow and painful death. I promise this by the blood of our father."

Chapter Nineteen

Meradyce sat huddled with Endredi and the other captives in the stern of the Saxon ship. Once again, she had watched a village as it disappeared from sight. This time it had been day, not night. There had been no flames of destruction. Just an awful silence. And this time, she truly felt she was leaving her home behind, because she was leaving Einar.

Somehow, Meradyce vowed silently as she looked at the women and children clinging together, they would return. Somehow, she would find a way to get them all back safely.

During the voyage she had been very glad that Endredi was with her. The girl stayed calm and was a great help with the younger children.

Mercifully, the weather stayed fair, for the ship leaked like a cracked jug. It also lacked the speed of Einar's longship, and seemed to wallow through the waves like a pig through mud. It would have been an easy matter for Einar's ship to catch them, but she had watched Kendric's men wreck the longship.

Her gaze went to the bow where Kendric stood talking with Adelar. Her breath caught in her throat.

Adelar looked so like Einar standing at the bow of the ship, his legs planted apart, his body shifting easily with the motion of the vessel.

For the first time, she noticed the bloodstains on Adelar's clothing and the sword hanging from a belt at his side. Had he fought, too, for the Saxons?

She hoped Adelar would ask his father for mercy. He knew many of these women and children. Perhaps he would find a way to convince Kendric that they should not be sold into slavery.

There was another man watching them, a short, dirty man missing most of his teeth. He had the eyes of a rat and the calculating gaze of a slave dealer. She looked away to see Adelar's shoulders suddenly slump.

What had happened? What had Kendric told him? What did that posture of defeat mean as he came toward the back of the ship?

She stood up and, unmindful of Endredi's detaining hand, went toward him.

He looked at her with sorrowful, dry eyes. "My mother is dead," he said in a flat voice. "She died weeks ago." Meradyce remembered what Einar had told her about Kendric's bargain. She glanced at him, wondering if he had caused Ludella's death, but Kendric was arguing with the short man and pointing toward the land that had appeared on the horizon.

"I am sorry, Adelar," she whispered, feeling his grief.

"Why should you be sorry?" he demanded.

She did not answer. How could she tell him what she knew about Kendric and Ludella? He already carried a heavy enough burden, and it was just as likely that

Ludella had died a natural death. "Adelar, you must help us," she said after a long moment.

He simply stared at her.

"Adelar, these women and children have done nothing to harm you. Ask your father for mercy. Do not let them be sold into slavery."

"My father told me what the Vikings said. They were going to sell *me,* if the ransom was not paid."

"Do you believe that?" she asked urgently. "Do you believe that Einar would sell you?"

The boy was confused and puzzled, and her heart bled for his troubles, but there were too many lives at stake to spare him. "Einar cared for you like his own son. He knew your father could pay—would pay."

"How could he be so sure?" Adelar asked, his gaze intense.

She could not lie. He would know it. "Because your father had already paid a lot of money."

His brow wrinkled. "What for? He would not have anything to do with Vikings."

Kendric came down the center of the ship. "Get back with the other women," he ordered. "Get back with the barbarians, as you deserve."

Meradyce wanted to disobey, to tell Kendric to his face that she knew he was a traitor. That she knew he had paid to have his wife murdered and that she suspected he had somehow found a way to kill her himself.

But not now, when she was a captive on his ship. And maybe not ever, if they could find a way to escape soon.

* * *

As they entered the river that would lead them to Kendric's village, Meradyce realized that the men were constantly looking at their human cargo and talking amongst themselves. With cold dread, she knew they were picking their prizes.

Endredi seemed to be more and more preoccupied. Meradyce put her arm around the girl's slender shoulders. "Try not to be afraid," she said softly. "Your father..."

Endredi looked at her with an expression of surprise. "I am not afraid." Her brow wrinkled. "I do not think we can count on my father rescuing us before we are sold. It will be up to us, I think, Meradyce." Her gaze went to the surrounding countryside. "I am going to have to remember that fork in the river we just passed, for when we escape."

Her voice was so calm and confident that Meradyce suddenly felt that, together, they might succeed. "We must try to stay together," she whispered, "all of us."

Endredi nodded. "All we have to do is get a ship."

"And sail it home," Meradyce reminded her, trying not to sound dismayed by that notion.

Endredi smiled. "We are all Viking women here. The sea is in our blood, and surely Thor will be on our side. The hard part will be stealing a ship."

One of Asa's babies began to cry. Meradyce went to see if she could be of any help. She felt more hopeful than she had since the voyage began. In her heart she knew that although it would not be easy, they would escape, and they would not leave anyone behind.

* * *

Einar and the remaining men dragged two of the half-submerged ships out of the water and onto the shore. The vessel with only one hole in its side would be repaired and used to follow the Saxons. The other would be the ship that would carry the dead to Valhalla.

Thorston, speechless with grief, prepared a grave for Olva while Einar helped fix the ship. He laid her body in the ground, together with her loom and her finest jewelry. Then he went to find Einar.

Together they stood by the grave, each lost in his memories of the woman before them. Tears fell down Thorston's cheeks, and he made no move to wipe them away.

"She was a good woman," he said softly. "A good wife. The best a man could have. Never really complained, although I gave her good cause." He sighed raggedly. "Oh, Einar, I'm going to miss her so much!"

Einar shook his head in disbelief. His mother was dead. His wife and his daughter gone. A huge wave of grief rolled over him, but he pushed it back. "They will pay, Thorston," he said quietly.

"Yes, they will." Thorston's voice was full of sorrow, but also determination. "I will see to it."

"You are not a warrior, Thorston. Some of you should stay here to begin the repairs—"

"Not me!" Thorston looked at his tall, strong stepson. "Sometimes a man has a cause to fight—and *must*. If I never lift a sword again, I will lift one when we find the Saxons who did this. And so will the others. We will not be left behind.''

Einar nodded, seeing the resolution in his stepfather's face. Then he turned and walked to the shore, where he would say a final farewell to his father.

The warriors had prepared their dead quickly. The bodies of the slain warriors were placed on board, and each man's weapons were laid at his side. Bjorn and his laborers were also given the honor of lying on the deck, their tools beside them. Large logs were laid around the outside of the damaged vessel.

Lastly, Einar put Svend's sword in his father's cold, stiff hand as Hamar placed his ax in the other.

After a moment of silence, Hamar went to the bow of the ship and spoke to the grim men gathered around. ''Friends, comrades in battle, we know that our fellows will be feasting in Valhalla, beloved of Odin. They died as a Viking wants to die, fighting, weapon in hand. And for them, an added glory—they were fighting for their home.

''Now only we remain to rebuild our village, and save our families. I vow by Odin that I will not rest until I have my family back. I know you all join me in this vow. Let us work swiftly to prepare our ship. Let us pray to Odin for success in our battle. Let us ask Njord for good seas and good wind to take us quickly on our journey. Let us ask Thor to give us strength and Balder to give us wisdom!'' His voice dropped. ''Let us ask Freyja to watch over our wives and our children until we can be with them again.

"Now, let us send our friends on their final journey, to glorious Valhalla, where we hope to meet them again."

He took a burning torch from a man nearby and kindled the pile of wood.

Soon the logs were burning with a fierce heat. The ship shuddered, and they heard the hiss of wet wood as it dried, then cracked, then caught on fire.

Slowly they turned away and went back to work.

The women and children were led off the ship, prodded and poked by jeering, laughing Saxon soldiers. Some prodded more than necessary, enjoying having Vikings of any kind at their mercy.

Meradyce looked around for Kendric and Adelar but could not see them. Perhaps they were already off the ship.

She wondered where they would be taken, but soon found out. They were herded into a long, low barn outside the village.

Before the huge door was closed, Kendric entered, accompanied by two brawny soldiers. He pointed at Endredi.

Meradyce's heart began to pound, and her mouth went dry as she quickly stepped forward. "Kendric!"

"What do *you* want?"

"I would speak with you."

"I am busy," he said coolly before nodding to the guards. They grabbed Endredi roughly.

Meradyce ran to her, but they knocked her to the ground. As she wiped the blood from her lip, she saw Endredi being led away.

The door banged shut, plunging the building into darkness. The women gasped and children began to cry with fear.

Meradyce rose slowly. There could be no waiting now. She must help Endredi, and soon. But how?

"Gunnhild? Asa? Reinhild?" she called out.

"Here!" the answer came three times.

"I am here, too, Saxon," Ilsa said.

"Good," Meradyce said. The women were not crying, and for once, she even welcomed Ilsa's presence. They would need everyone if they were to succeed. Her knowledge of the Viking language was not good, but she struggled to make herself understood. "Can anyone see a way out?" she said quietly. "Feel the walls. Look for loose timber or wattle and daub."

After several long minutes during which Meradyce forced herself to concentrate on the walls and not on what might be happening to Endredi, she heard Ilsa give a little cry of triumph. "Here!" she called softly. "At the bottom."

Meradyce hurried to join her. Yes, the material making the wall was old and crumbling here. If they pulled hard together, a large part of it would give way.

But that might make too much noise. "We must tug on it gently, and move it just enough so that we can slip out," she said. "I will go first. I must go to the thane's hall and get Endredi."

Ilsa laughed scornfully in the darkness. "Do you think we are fools? You will go to the thane's hall, all right—"

Ilsa never finished what she was going to say, because Meradyce grabbed her by the throat. "I threatened to kill you once, Ilsa. Do not tempt me again. I will get us all away from here. And *I* will go out first!''

She let go, and Ilsa moved off in the darkness. ''You are too fat.'' It seemed even a threat of death would not silence Ilsa.

''The board will have to move enough for *everyone* to get out. And I'm not that big yet.''

''Always the proud one, Saxon,'' Ilsa chided, but Meradyce heard what sounded like respect in the woman's voice. ''Get out of the way so that I can help you.''

''Gunnhild?'' Meradyce called.

''Yes, I'm here.''

''Help me with this.''

''I will dig at the bottom. I have a spoon,'' Reinhild whispered loudly.

''A spoon?''

''I was stirring stew when the Saxons came and did not let go of it. Then I hid it in my dress. I have a knife, too.''

''A *knife?*''

''Not a large one.''

It was better than no weapon at all, Meradyce thought grimly.

It took several minutes, but at last they had broken away a big enough space for Meradyce to crawl through. ''Give me the knife,'' she whispered.

She felt it on the palm of her hand. It *was* a small one.

''Gunnhild,'' she said quietly, ''you all go out after me. There is a small wood nearby. It reaches down to the river. Go there and get as close to the water as you can. I will get Endredi and meet you there.''

"But what will we do then?'' Reinhild's voice was full of worry.

"We will get a ship and sail home.''

"What?" Ilsa cried softly.

"The soldiers will not be expecting a group of women and children to do anything. They may not even have a guard on the ship.''

"Meradyce,'' Gunnhild said in a hushed voice, "it's too dangerous to go for Endredi. What if you are seen? Then none of us will get away.''

"I know the village well. No one will see me. Or if they do, I will run away from the river. You will know if I have failed. Forget us, then, and take the ship.''

"We cannot sail—''

"I can,'' Ilsa said firmly.

"There's no more time to waste,'' Meradyce commanded. "I will not leave without Endredi. If we do not join you soon, take the ship and go.''

Meradyce gripped the knife in her right hand and crawled under the board. She stood up and looked around. As she had expected, Kendric had seen fit to post guards only by the door to the barn. It was also clear that the guards were not expecting the women to try to escape, for they leaned against their spears and talked quietly to each other.

Creeping around the far side of the building, Meradyce kept in the shadows. Then she dashed toward the wall. It was not completely rebuilt, and she began to climb. Because she was with child, it was more difficult than she had expected, but the stones were rough and she was able to get over it.

She climbed down carefully and headed for the back of the closest house, keeping to the shadows and moving as swiftly as she dared.

Her biggest fear, apart from discovery, was that she would not be able to find Endredi. Before Einar and his men had burned the village to the ground, she had known every street and house. But Kendric had obviously taken the opportunity to change the position of buildings as well as increase the fortifications. As she cautiously moved forward, she thanked God they had been put in the barn outside the walls, or they might never have been able to get away.

She peered around a corner and saw a large hall. She smiled grimly. Of course Kendric would build himself a fine new house. And of course it would be the first thing finished, even before the walls.

She surveyed the open space in front of it. No guards. If she moved quickly, she could be inside in a moment, and she had no doubt that Endredi would be there.

She began to run toward the hall. The door opened. A beam of dim light illuminated Meradyce as she halted, confused, alone in the road.

The light vanished almost instantly as the door closed. "Meradyce?" a voice called softly.

Suppressing a cry of relief and happiness, Meradyce ran forward and pulled Endredi into the shadows. Although she would dearly like to have known how Endredi had gotten away, she put her finger to her lips. This was not the time or the place for explanations. They had to join the others at once.

She led Endredi over the wall, pausing near the barn. The guards were still talking.

She took Endredi by the hand and ran to the forest, heading for the river. There was some light from the moon, but the sky was cloudy.

As they drew near the shore, someone grabbed Meradyce.

"It is me, Gunnhild. You have Endredi!"

"Yes. Now, has anyone seen if there are guards on the ship?"

"Two, one fore, one aft," Reinhild said softly.

"We only have one weapon." Meradyce thought for a moment. There was little they could do with only one weapon and two guards.

"I will take one, you the other," Endredi said softly. Her voice was low but determined.

"But how?"

Endredi held up a stout piece of wood. "With this. I have already bashed one Saxon on the head with it."

Meradyce smiled as she nodded. "We will have to climb aboard when their backs are turned, if ever that happens."

"I will go over there," said Ilsa, pointing along the shore. "I will distract them."

She saw Meradyce's doubt. "Trust me. I want to get away from this stinking Saxon village more than you do. But do not sail until I get there."

Meradyce nodded. She believed Ilsa would do what she said.

The women moved off—Meradyce and Endredi toward the ship, Ilsa downriver.

When Meradyce and Endredi were near the ship, they heard a bush rattle. The guards also heard the sound and turned to look, walking toward the bow. Quickly Meradyce and Endredi crept to the gangplank, keeping their bodies low, as Ilsa continued to shake first one bush, then another.

"What do you think that is, eh?" one of the Saxons asked.

"I do not like it," the other replied.

At that moment, Meradyce and Endredi crept up behind them. Endredi swung her piece of wood as if it was an ax, striking the soldier on the head. Meradyce thrust the small knife into the other soldier's side.

With a gasp, he turned to face her, grabbing her with his strong hands. Before the guard could cry out, a bowstring twanged and an arrow struck the soldier through the throat. He fell to the deck, dead.

Meradyce spun around. Endredi stared.

Adelar stood on the shore, his bow in his hand.

Chapter Twenty

Adelar slowly lowered his bow. Then he turned and walked toward the village without saying a word.

Meradyce looked sorrowfully at his retreating back before beckoning the women and children onto the ship. They boarded quickly and quietly, even the youngest sensing the need for silence.

Ilsa came last. She saw the two watchmen lying on the deck. "We should get these Saxons off the ship," she whispered hoarsely.

Meradyce nodded, but before she could move, Reinhild came forward. Together, she and Ilsa picked up one by the arms and legs, carried him to the gangplank and rolled him down to the pier. Endredi and Meradyce took the other man and did the same.

Meradyce gasped as she felt a sharp pain below her stomach.

"Sit down and rest," Endredi said.

"No, I am all right. I can help—"

"Sit down."

Meradyce wanted to protest again, but Endredi's calm, confident voice told Meradyce she would brook no argument.

She sounded just like Einar when he gave his orders.

"Undo the bow lines," Ilsa called out. "We must let the ship swing around so that it is pointing upriver toward the sea. We will have to row. There is not enough wind for the sail."

Endredi and Reinhild untied the ropes as Ilsa moved to the stern of the ship, telling the women where to sit. Then she took her place at the steering board. "Gunnhild! Help me hold this."

The ship did what Ilsa expected, moving slowly in the current. The stern rubbed against the dock, creaking loudly, which made some of the children begin to cry.

A shout went up from the shore. The women glanced at the village nervously, knowing that they had been seen.

A group of soldiers were running toward the river.

"Out oars!" Endredi shouted, not waiting for Ilsa to give the order and no longer taking care to be quiet. The women lifted the huge oars and shoved them through the leather locks.

While Ilsa and Gunnhild kept hold of the rudder, Endredi and Reinhild quickly undid the ropes that held the stern. They fell with a splash into the river.

"Pull!" Endredi yelled, and the women moved in unison, bending and pulling their oars through the water as Endredi called out the pace.

Suddenly, Ilsa cried out and clutched at her arm as she fell into the bottom of the ship.

"Down, everyone down!" Meradyce shouted, crawling back to look at Ilsa's wound. There were more splashes, and Meradyce realized that arrows were hitting the water.

Meradyce checked Ilsa's arm. An arrow had grazed her, but the wound was minor. It could wait for tending. "Stay down," she ordered. Ignoring the pain in her stomach, she took Ilsa's place at the steering board beside Gunnhild.

The women rowed with all the strength they possessed, and the ship began moving swiftly into the river.

Back on the shore, Adelar watched the ship sail away. Above the din, he could hear his father shouting orders and curses.

"Farewell," he whispered.

The Vikings sailed their vessel close to the Saxon village.

Einar led his men as they climbed over the side of the ship and made their way to shore. This time he hoped the Saxon traitor had sentinels posted. He wanted a warning cry that would send the villagers running for the safety of their sanctuary. Only this time, the Vikings knew about the caves, and the Saxons would find no safety there.

Near the village, a terrified voice shouted out an alarm. Einar turned to Hamar with such a cold-blooded grin of triumph that even Hamar pitied the Saxons.

Then Einar began to run, leading his men to the gate at the back of the surrounding wall.

It was easy, very easy, to capture the Saxon villagers as they tried to flee.

Meradyce and Endredi were not among them. None of the Viking women and children were there.

Einar suppressed a surge of rage and hoped they were not too late this time, too.

Leaving some men to guard the women, children and old people, Einar and the rest of his warriors entered the gate.

Kendric and his men stood facing the main entrance—until they heard the Vikings behind them.

Einar walked toward them, his ax in his left hand, his sword in the right.

Kendric stared at his enemy. Although this fellow seemed calm, one look at his eyes convinced Kendric that nothing this side of death would stop him. Kendric knew he could fight and die or he could try to surrender and live.

Kendric threw down his sword. "We yield!"

Einar halted, his blood hot with wrath. He wanted to kill this man, but not this way.

All the Saxon soldiers followed suit.

Einar looked at the sword lying on the ground. Lars' sword.

He approached Kendric. "Where is my wife and my daughter?" he demanded, his hands gripping his weapons, hoping the Saxon would lunge for the sword so that he could strike. "And the man who owned that sword."

"Gone—and dead," Kendric replied, his voice shaky.

"Who is gone and who is dead?"

"The man...the man is dead. The women are gone, two days ago."

"Sold?"

"No! No, they escaped. They were all well when they left this place—"

"You are lying."

"He is telling the truth, Einar." Adelar stepped from behind the line of men. "Look at the river. My father's ship is gone. They took it two days ago."

Einar gazed steadily at Adelar, certain he could believe the boy. The women and children had escaped.

"Meradyce and Endredi and the others. Were they hurt?"

Adelar shook his head. "No."

Einar felt relief flooding through him.

The alleviation was short-lived. How could it be that their ships had not passed each other? It might be possible, if the Saxon vessel had reached the sea before they had arrived at the river. "They had no help at all?"

"No," Adelar said, but Einar saw the hint of a smile on the boy's face. He nodded, hoping Adelar would know his gratefulness.

"Where is Lars?"

"I do not know who you mean."

"Why are you speaking to my son?" Kendric demanded.

"Because he will tell me the truth," Einar said scornfully. He looked at Adelar. "Your father had a Viking sword."

"That man is dead. He attacked my father, and his soldiers had to kill him."

"Did he have a woman with him?"

"Shut your mouth, boy," Kendric said harshly. "Say nothing to them."

"Selwyn brought her. The Viking came later, and killed her."

Einar closed his eyes for a brief moment, thankful that Lars, at least, had not betrayed them. He faced the Saxon thane. "Because I respect your son, I will not kill you. And my men will leave your village unharmed . . . this time."

He walked closer, and Kendric could see the naked, primitive hatred in the Viking's gray eyes. "But you do not deserve such a son, *traitor.* Tell him how we knew where your village was and that it would be unprotected. Tell him how much you paid to have his mother killed."

He heard the gasps of the Saxon soldiers at his words and saw Adelar's face go pale.

The boy had to know what kind of father he had.

He turned to Adelar. "Adelar, someday you will be a leader among the Saxons, and men will flock to follow you. Be a better man than your father."

With that, Einar marched away, signaling to his men to follow. He knew that they would go back to the longship reluctantly, preferring vengeance.

But for now, it was more important to find the Saxon ship.

Einar and his men searched the coast for days. Believing that the women would never dare set out across the open sea for home, they sailed up every river that might hide a vessel as far as they could, but it was as ⸍ Odin had snatched the women away.

By now, some thought that the women and children must have been recaptured by Saxons, or gone down with the ship, and that it was hopeless to continue the search.

Hamar looked at Einar, noting the weariness and strain on his brother's face. This voyage had taken a toll on them all. "Our food is running out," he said quietly. "We must either sail for home now, or plan to raid one of the Saxon villages."

"I know," Einar replied.

"What do you want to do?"

Einar sighed deeply. "I want to kill every Saxon on this cursed island. But I think we should make for home."

"Abandon the search completely?" Hamar asked incredulously.

Einar nodded. "There is a chance they went home."

"Women? And children?"

"If the women set their minds to do a thing, do you doubt they would try it?"

"But it is not possible..."

Einar gave his brother the glimmer of a smile. "Perhaps it is, brother. The weather has been mild and the wind fair. After all, the women are the wives and daughters of Vikings. Once they reach the islands, surely they can find our fjord. Who is to say they might not succeed?"

For the first time in days, Hamar looked hopeful. "Gunnhild has been on many short voyages."

"We should go home first, then try the other villages and towns near our own."

So it was decided. Einar explained his belief to the men, who, like Hamar, were skeptical at first. Then hope, long dwindling, began to revive. After all, who would have guessed women and children would be able to steal a ship, either?

But as they set out across the open sea, it seemed Njord had had enough of mild spring weather and calm waters. A day's sail from the Saxon shore, he sent a tremendous storm.

Meradyce looked out at the pouring rain and the trees lashed by the high winds. She glanced at Endredi and saw her own fears mirrored in the girl's face.

"Surely they will be all right," Meradyce said fervently, but the words sounded hollow, even to herself.

Endredi reached past her and pulled the door of the longhouse closed. "We were fortunate that we did not meet the storm," she said quietly. "It was a difficult journey as it was."

Meradyce nodded, remembering the uncertainty she felt as they sailed across the sea. Many of the women had been frightened, believing that they would get lost or drown. There had been no food except the fish that they managed to catch, and little water.

Endredi had never lost confidence, especially after she found the strange instrument on board the ship. She had listened, she said, to the men telling of their voyages, and knew how they used the instrument to plot their course using the sun. She knew where they were and was sure, as long as the weather stayed good, hat she could pilot the ship home. Meradyce believed her. And so, surprisingly, had Ilsa, who chastised anyone who voiced any fears.

Nonetheless, they had all cheered with joy and relief when they entered the calmer waters behind the guardian islands of the coast.

But when they arrived home, they found the village deserted, except for the men's dogs, who had been left to guard the houses. The women saw the damaged vessels and quickly realized two were missing. The burnt remains of one lay on the shore. Those women who had lost their husbands and sons to the Saxons cried out and wept, for they all knew that such a thing could only mean that it had been a funeral pyre.

They found no sign of the other longship. They supposed that the men had repaired it and set sail after them.

Whatever their fears, the women set about fixing their houses, finding food for their children and rounding up the scattered livestock. Often they would pause and glance at the fjord, searching for a Viking ship.

Then the storm had started, and many had begun to worry that the vessel, and its crew, lay at the bottom of the sea.

Inside her house, in a dark corner, Meradyce had found the packs Einar had brought home from his journey, and among them a baby's cradle.

"Dear God, bring Einar home!" she whispered.

Three days later, Meradyce heard a loud cry. She recognized Endredi's voice and hurried out of the house.

There was a ship coming slowly up the fjord. A Viking ship—or what was left of one. The mast was gone, and several timbers were missing. The prow had been snapped off as if it had been a twig.

The men inside were rowing, but the oars stopped moving as the crew stood up and began to shout.

And then Meradyce saw Einar moving quickly forward until he was at the prow.

She ran to the pier like a madwoman, so overjoyed that she was laughing and crying at the same time.

Before the vessel was even tied to the pier, Einar jumped over the side and ran to embrace Meradyce.

"Meradyce, Meradyce!" he whispered over and over, kissing her cheeks, her hair, her lips. She held on to him tightly, all the emotions of the past several days washing over her.

It was over. Einar had come home to her.

The men swarmed out of the ship, finding wives and children. Those women who no longer had husbands smiled at the others' happiness as they brushed away their tears.

Later that night, Meradyce snuggled up to her husband under the fur coverings of their bed. "I am glad Hamar is chieftain," she said quietly. "He will be a wise leader."

Einar smiled at her as he wrapped his arms around her. "I should think you would want your own husband to be a chieftain," he said, feigning dismay.

"Oh, no," she said, reaching up to kiss his cheek. "I do not want to share you with anyone, and especially not the whole village."

"So I suppose I should not take another wife?"

"Definitely not."

"But I will have to share you with our children."

"Yes."

Einar looked at her, his brow suddenly furrowed with concern. "The voyage... Do you think the baby will be all right?"

"The baby will be fine. He kicked me several times today, so I am sure that he is healthy and strong. Besides, Endredi made me rest—and there was no disobeying her. If it had not been for Endredi, perhaps none of us would have gotten home." She gave Einar a sidelong glance. "She is too much like you, in some ways."

"Ull told me he was her father before he died."

"Did you believe him?"

"Yes—but it does not matter. Endredi is my daughter."

She knew Einar meant what he said, and that made her very happy.

"You said he," Einar said suddenly. "He? The child is a boy?"

"Well, no one ever knows for sure. It could very well be a girl."

"But you believe it to be a boy?"

She raised herself on her elbows. "Would a girl be so terrible?"

"If it is a girl like her mother, she will be anything *but* terrible."

"I think some of the younger men are *very* interested in Endredi, you know," Meradyce said thoughtfully. "Maybe it is time you thought about her marriage."

"Perhaps. But right now, I would rather think about you. And kiss you. And touch you..." His hand began to caress her naked back.

Meradyce sighed with contentment and bent down to kiss him gently. "If we have a son, what shall we name him?"

"Svend."

She smiled as much at Einar's confident tone as at the name. "And if it should be a girl?"

"Her name will be Betha."

He reached up to brush the tear that fell on Meradyce's cheek. "Do you have any regrets, Meradyce?" he asked her softly.

"None," she whispered, nestling against him, safe and content in the Viking's arms.

*   *   *   *   *

though they were using sleds and not carts for just
such a reason. Thurston had suggested that they lin-